THE LASER FROM ABOVE

Xavier Paulson

Copyright © 2023 Xavier Paulson. All rights reserved.

ISBN 979-8-9890091-1-4

Website: www.xavierpaulson.com

Youtube: https://www.youtube.com/@xavierpaulson/featured

E-mail (for fan messages): xavierpaulson.fans@gmail.com

E-mail (for business and media inquiries only): xavierpaulson.official@gmail.com

More coming soon!

This book is a work of fiction. Names, characters, places, and incidents are the product of the author's imagination or are used fictitiously. Any resemblance to actual persons, living or dead, is purely coincidental.

Author's Note:

This book contains explicit language, violence, drug addiction, and themes of sexual assault.

Prologue

Less than a year ago, and getting an internship at the International Space Hotel had been the biggest thing on Skye Calvert's mind.

Early October 2047, and she found herself sitting in an office. The only sound was the clicking of an old out-of-place grandfather clock that starkly contrasted with the modern, gray room of the HR office of the International Space Hotel's business headquarters. Well, it wasn't the *only* sound. There was also the shallow breathing of the five individuals waiting in the room, among them the antsy Skye Calvert.

Skye, of course, wasn't in space, but in an office near the launch pad in Florida Island. All of the expenses of traveling to interview had been covered by the International Space Hotel, and when she'd received the notification from her phone that she'd been selected as one of five finalists for a position as a communications intern, she'd been ecstatic. To get to this point, she'd passed through two rounds of remote interviews already. She'd originally seen the listing on a job board at her school, and decided to take a flyer on it. Even with a near-perfect collegiate GPA and a laundry list of different clubs and volunteer activities she actively participated in, actually landing the job seemed like such a far-fetched possibility that Skye never would have guessed that she'd find herself here. Yet here she was.

There were four other interns waiting in this room. All of them were in a similar position to her: all of them were undergraduates, all of them were ambitious students, and she would have to beat out the three other women and the one other man if she wanted a chance to secure an internship. She'd heard about these space internships. It sounded like they set you up for life if you landed one. Skye *had* to do this. It was the best shot she'd ever gotten at being something. The other interns must've felt the same way, because they all dressed to impress. All of the women wore formal dresses, and the man, a new-looking suit with a shiny tie.

"Julie!"

The interviewer called out the first name after opening up the door a crack. There was more, and while others stared at their phone, likely flipping between tabs and apps endlessly and trying to distract themselves from the ever-growing anxiety that threatened their mental health; Skye didn't do the same. She just stared at the ticking grandfather clock, wondering if one of those old-fashioned birds was going to shoot out, yelling "coo-coo!" or whatever it was that they did.

"Heath!"

The man was called only five minutes after, the same interviewer (or whatever you would call her) calling his name. Around five minutes later, another name was called. That left her and one last intern, and this time, when the attending woman opened the door, Skye felt that she might scream if it wasn't her name being called.

"Skye!"

It was her turn, finally, and Skye stood up, relieved, as the woman shook hands with her, guiding her down the hallway.

"You ready?" The woman asked. Skye was getting a feel for the woman, as she figured she was the one who was going to be interviewing her.

"Yes," Skye lied, her heart thumping so hard she thought it was going to escape her chest.

Skye found herself led into another office, the interviewer beckoning her through, and she paused when she saw the inside.

"Uhhh…" Skye started, her voice trailing off.

"Please, sit down!"

Skye found herself in a small office, with a suited man who looked to be in his fifties, and another intern, Heath had been his name, sitting down already, his hands fiddling with his shiny tie before resting back down on the table when the man looked at him.

"My name is Jared," the man said, as Skye took a seat, the woman closing the door to the room. "I am an HR representative for the International Space Hotel. We're going to be playing a game."

"What game?" Heath asked. His face was all sweaty, and Skye prayed she didn't look as nervous as him.

"Tell me," Jared said, standing in between both of them and making a dramatic sweeping motion with his hands. "Do you know of the prisoner's dilemma?"

Heath frowned. "I've heard of it."

"You?"

Skye shook her head, but it was a lie. She'd taken a couple Economics courses in high school, and an Introduction to Economics class in her freshman year of college. She was going to keep her competitive advantage while she had it.

"I don't quite remember," she lied. "I've heard of it, but I don't remember any details."

"Heath, what about you?"

"It's something about prisoner's snitching on each other," Heath said. "That's about the extent of my knowledge."

"That's good to know," Jared said, setting a couple of blank pieces of paper onto the table in between them. "I've studied your transcripts, both of you, so I know that only one of you has taken an Economics class, but I don't think your background knowledge will be an advantage, if your class materials are any indication and if you are being honest."

Skye felt the beads of sweat forming on her forehead now. It had to be a bluff. Right?

"We're going to be playing one game, and then I'll be conducting another interview," Jared explained.

He paced around the room for a couple of seconds, before stopping right in between them again.

"You will be presented with two possible options. Please write your answer down in a secretive manner."

Jared handed each of them a pen, and they took it.

"Both of you are prisoners. Now here's the following scenario, you can write it down if you want: you are both arrested in a bank robbery, but there's a lack of evidence, because your faces were covered with a mask, so no one knows for sure if you're responsible. Now, you're both guilty. And you know it. But you know this: if neither of you talk, then you only will each get two years of prison. Now if one of you snitches, and the other says nothing, then the one who snitches will only get twelve months of prison, and the other one will get ten years. There's a third scenario, of course. Both of you snitch on each other, and get three years each. Now please write down either *cooperate*, or *defect*, on your piece of paper, depending on what you want your decision to be. This is assuming that you don't know the other person's choice, of course. You have sixty seconds to decide. Flip over your page when you're done."

Skye pulled the piece of paper to the edge of the table, covering it out of view from Heath, and Heath did the same.

Skye thought deeply for a few seconds, jotting down a couple of notes. She knew from her experience what the supposed "rational" thing to do was to defect, to confess to their role in the crime. She felt bad for the guy that she had her previous advantage of having studied the same dilemma in college. According to Economics, the dominant strategy was to defect: even though both would be worse off than if they'd kept silent, it guaranteed that she wouldn't be going to prison for more than three years.

But maybe that was the twist of this entire test. Perhaps, she was meant to cooperate. Maybe the test of the puzzle wasn't doing what was the most rational thing to do, but working together, as a team. From what she'd gathered preparing for this stage of the interview, teamwork was greatly emphasized, putting the company and the International Space Hotel before yourself.

But this is a crime, Skye thought, *so there's no reason to not defect in this scenario. Admitting wrongdoings and coming clean is better than lying about a crime. Maybe that's the twist.*

Skye wrote down her answer, flipping the page over, and within ten seconds, Heath did the same.

"Please flip over your paper," Jared said.

Jared looked down, and frowned. Heath's piece of paper read *Cooperate*, and Skye's, *Defect*.

"Now, Heath's going to be sentenced to ten years of prison," Jared announced. "And Skye, only a year."

Heath glared at Skye, and Skye had to avoid his gaze by looking at Jared.

"Why did you choose the answers you did?" Jared asked. "Heath?"

"I wanted to be cooperative," Heath said, still glaring at Skye. "She was my teammate, so I trusted her. It was misplaced trust."

"Skye?"

"Defecting meant I was guaranteed a relatively short sentence," Skye replied, staring at Jared. "Besides, it was a crime. I wasn't going to lie about doing something wrong. I would've taken responsibility for myself, and rebuilt my life."

Jared scrawled down some notes, and Skye swore she could she could see a sliver of a smile on his face. Skye felt satisfied knowing that she'd come up with a more creative answer than her opponent.

"Good," he said. "Time for the question portion of this interview."

The rest of the interview was strange. Whereas the questions of the first two interviews (which had been held remotely) had consisted of primarily generic personality questions, these ones were very specific, and, in some cases, quite stupid, at least in Skye's mind. Each question cycled between her answering first, making the playing field a lot more level between them. Skye was asked about how she'd handle an unruly customer, to which she explained how she would remain calm, exude empathy, and align herself with the ship's objective. She also tapped into her personal experience as a waitress, and that answer seemed to please Jared.

They were also asked what single item they would bring if they were stranded onto a desert island, to which Heath answered his multi-tool, while Skye provided the smart-aleck answer of a functioning boat.

Then there was the craziest of them all.

"Why are manhole covers round?"

"I think they're round for production costs," Heath answered first. "Helping the bottom line."

"I…" Skye said, her brain flying a million miles a minute. "Who doesn't like a circle? Circles are practical, round, smooth, strong, and easy."

When the interview had concluded, Jared thanked Heath, shook his hand, and the same woman who'd ushered them both into the room escorted Heath out. That left Skye alone with Jared for a brief minute, who shook her hand and leaned into her ear to whisper.

"Good job," he said. "You win."

The man had been telling the truth. Within a week of the final interview, she'd secured one of the most competitive internship slots in the country.

On the way out of the office, Skye passed a new batch of interns waiting for their interviews. One of them she recognized as another candidate from her school who she had met through the interviewing process at the employment center.

"Good luck, Graham," she said, waving goodbye to Graham as she took her purse out the door, ready to return to her hotel and fly back to Michigan.

Graham smiled, waving back.

"Thanks," Graham replied. "I know it's just an internship, but it feels like it's the most important thing in the world. Who knows, maybe it will be the difference between life and death someday. Probably not, though."

Chapter 1

Following the eventful night in which Skye and Graham had overthrown Lusky's leadership and prevented him from evicting a great portion of the population, including Skye and Madison, back to Earth, Skye slept like a rock. She ended up sleeping in for eleven hours, at which time there was a knocking on the door. Given she hadn't fallen asleep until almost 5:30 in the morning, it was around 4:30 in the afternoon, space-time, when she finally stirred.

Skye looked over at the clock, and exhaled. When she saw how much time had elapsed, she leapt from underneath her covers and scrambled over to the door, wearing nothing but her onesie.

"Hello?" she called through the door. "Who is it?"

"It's me!" Graham replied.

Skye opened up the door. Graham was donning a button-up shirt and pants, and the hallways behind him were illuminated to its full capacity, indicating that it was, for all intents and purposes, daytime in the International Space Hotel.

"What's up?"

"Sleep well?" Graham asked.

"Y'betcha," Skye replied. "Like a baby. And not the kind that wakes up every hour and screams at the top of their lungs."

How strange, Skye thought after making the comment. *I killed a man yesterday, and somehow, I slept soundly, even though after I saw Kyra I could hardly sleep. Am I a sociopath?*

"That's good," Graham responded. "I got six hours of sleep, and then I got up. I'm tired, but I figured we have a lot of work to do… So, we probably need to do that instead of delaying the inevitable."

"Where are Marcell and Maddie?"

"Maddie's sleeping, still," Graham responded. "She was up later than either of us. Marcell, he's in the infirmary, still recovering. Doc says he's got to stay in bed for now, and take it easy for weeks. He was lucky. According to Dr. Silva, the bullet missed any major organs and it looks like he's going to make a full recovery."

"I somehow forgot about that," Skye admitted, surprised that such an important fact had slipped her mind. "What a night. I'm glad he's okay."

"You can say that again," Graham agreed. "It's going to take a long time, probably. And of course, then there's the so-called issue of the painkillers."

"Issue?"

"He's in agony," Graham said. "But he also says the supply of painkillers is too slim to be wasting on him. I'm worried for him. He's got the sweats and I'm worried the pain's going to kill him."

"Aw Jesus," Skye moaned. "And Maddie's hoarded some of the pills for herself. We should go and take them from her."

Graham waved it off. "Yes, she's taken a little bit off the inventory. I talked to some woman called Sarah who works at the pharmacy. She says some of the inventory's missing, and we should investigate."

"We?" Skye asked. "You mean to say… that they don't know?"

"Not as far as I know," Graham replied. "Right now, everyone thinks that Fritz is in charge now, and has been asking questions. Well, I think most people have probably heard about what happened from the survivors. But right now, people are demanding a lot of answers. We set up some security gates around the prison wing, just to stop some people retaliating you know, lynching them, or something."

"Wow," Skye responded. "And to think... I was asleep during this entire time, and I had no clue."

"It's okay," Graham replied. "How about you get dressed, and then we go out. First things first, I think everyone on board deserves an explanation as to what happened last night. Go and make the announcement. Breakfast has already been served, but I think we also need to seriously consider cutting our meals down from two a day to once a day. It will allow our reserves to stretch out another week."

"Is the situation really that bad though?" Skye asked. "I've just heard a lot, but I've never seen any proof at all."

"I'll show you the reserves after you make the announcement," Graham promised. "But yes, it is really that bad."

"Okay," Skye replied. She moved to close the door, but Graham stuck his hand in and cleared his throat.

"One other thing."

"Huh?"

"We've... finally got an official death toll from last night."

"Death toll?"

"Yes, Skye, death toll. I think you deserve to know. Unless, of course, you want to, you know... not... know."

"No," she replied. "Tell me."

"There were two in Lusky's quarters... Not to mention the two guards in the Oxygen center. Someone else in their room died. The gas did spread out a little bit, you know? And you know Lucas?"

"What? What about him?"

"Lucas ran around, and he... he ran around and got knocked down, split his head open on some metal railing. Someone discovered his body a couple of hours ago. He's dead."

"Fuck."

"Six people died last night. But I think, all things considered... It was better than a hundred of us."

***

Madison was coming off the tail end of getting high yet again.

Following the extreme stress of the previous night, remembering once again what a burden she had been to her friends, and how she had almost cost her friends, and herself, their lives, Madison had given into the cravings. Despite her relapse, however, she found herself oddly reinvigorated and determined now that she had a chance to reflect on things.

Madison knew she might have to detox a bit, but she didn't care. It was time for this old habit to die hard before it emerged into something worse.

"I'm done," she stated loudly. She might not have been in a completely lucid state of mind, but she was sober enough to know what was best for herself and to know how to go about doing so.

"Huh? Wha...?"

The voice came from her own bed, which she had, somehow, been kicked out of. Madison hadn't the heart to tell the two guests about how only a day before, she'd wet herself in that same bed, and how she hadn't the time to even clean the covers, not with the eviction process having been underway.

But Minnie and Drake were high, much higher than her. Only Minnie was awake, while Drake was now snoring soundly. They didn't seem to notice, or care, about the wretched state of the bed. They were, at the very least, not stripping down and trying anything on her bed. For now. If that happened, Madison was determined she'd kick their ass so hard they'd be propelled back down to Earth, no thrusters needed.

Now that she thought back to earlier, Madison remembered how this had even happened. In the middle of the night, she'd run into Minnie and Drake when helping clear some of the bodies and bring them over to the morgue. She'd overheard their desire to get high on something, and one thing had led to another and she'd invited them back to her room to get high with her on painkillers.

I'm done, Madison thought. *Done. Never again. Of course, I thought last time I would never do this again, but this time I mean it.*

It felt good, getting high, although nothing could come close to what she'd felt a couple of days before with the morphine. But her willpower was unbreakable, for now. Madison ended up getting a bag she had lying around in her room and stowing away everything in it.

"W-what are you doing?" Minnie asked, looking up at her, confused.

"Picking up trash," she answered. She had to bite her tongue in order to conceal a grin from blossoming on her face.

"Ah, okay," Minnie said, and then she fell back down on the bed like a rock.

Madison then rushed out to the pharmacy, bringing her bag and praying the place was open. Sure enough, the gate must've been opened several hours ago, the lights of the business on, and she could see Sarah standing there at the front desk. Almost like everything was normal again.

"Madison," Sarah greeted her. "I'm so glad to hear you're okay. I heard-"

Madison slammed the bag on the counter, and Sarah's jaw dropped.

"What is this?" Sarah asked. "What are you doing?"

"Drugs," Madison answered, and she broke out into a slight giggle. Her hand still gripped the bag tightly, and for a few seconds, riding the wave of pleasure, Madison couldn't let go, as if her hand was like a magnet attracted to a bag of opposite polarity.

I could still take it, Madison thought. *I don't need to let this woman have this. It'll go to waste otherwise.*

"Maddie... What...?" Sarah asked. "What do you mean?"

"You're missing drugs, right?"

"Yes. Maddie. How... How did you get this?"

Madison finally let go of the bag. Then she flipped around on her heels without another word, and she didn't turn back. If she did, she worried that she'd regret what she'd done, and then she'd be back to square one.

***

Skye first prepared herself to log the deaths in the system. She felt that she needed to, or she would shirk her duty. She was, fortunately, provided all the names and relevant information, meaning she didn't have to go through all the work of asking around. Fritz, who now was in one of the front offices, gave her the names of the dead, written out on a piece of 3D-printed paper. He also handed them a paper copy of the so-called "List" that Lusky had compiled of those to be removed or kept on board. Graham tagged along all the while.

"Keep this in mind when you make your decision," Fritz pressed.

"What do you mean?" Skye asked.

"You're the one in charge now," Fritz explained. "It's up to you to decide who stays and goes. If someone's on the list and in league with Lusky, well… That's something important to keep in mind."

"I thought the plan was that the council was in charge. It's not like I'm the sole leader or something."

"I don't see any damn council," Fritz said. "If you can assemble one, fine. But right now, I'm just sitting on my ass and pretending I'm important. Which is exactly what I'm okay with."

Graham raised his eyebrows. Fritz was never one for subtlety, it seemed.

Graham and Skye next walked over to the comms room. When they arrived, they found someone waiting who they hadn't expected.

"Lex," Skye said, and she was beaming as she wrapped Lex in a hug.

"Skye…" Lex said.

"I'm glad you're okay," Skye said. "I didn't ever see you last night."

"Only just," Lex replied. "You stopped them before they could get to my room, I think. I never heard anything about this plan, they never approached me. I would take a guess and say that they were going to kick me off."

After a few seconds of Skye shrugging, Lex's face fell as she evidently remembered something.

"Franco. He's gone, isn't he? I haven't seen him in a couple of days, and he never responded when I knocked on his door."

"Yes," Skye replied, nodding. "But I'm here to set things straight. Well, the best I can. I need to make an announcement."

"Okay," Lex said. "You can take the comms. You deserve to let them know."

"I've never done that before."

"All you do is press a button, and then speak," Lex said. "I'll be here to help."

Skye nodded. She stepped forward, mentally preparing herself before realizing she didn't know exactly what to say.

"Fuck..." She mumbled. "I think I'm going to need a pencil and paper."

"I got you," Lex said, and she opened up a drawer in which there were plenty of papers and pens for Skye to choose from. She pulled out a piece of paper and pencil, and then she began writing. Skye scrawled on the paper for a few minutes, until she figured that she had a sufficient skeleton of a speech. When she was finished, she held up the paper.

"Good enough," Skye said. "Can you look this over, Graham? What do you think?"

Graham scanned the paper for a few moments.

"Well put," he said. "It's very presidential. Better than I ever could put into words."

Skye nodded. "All right. I'm ready."

Lex pushed the button, and Skye deeply exhaled. Then she started to speak.

Chapter 2

"Hello, everyone on board the ISH. My name is Skye. I... Well, never mind what I used to be. I'm here because yesterday, as most of you know, something horrible happened. Alan Lusky and his management attempted to follow through on their executive decision to forcibly remove most individuals off of this ship. They wanted to return you down to Earth in escape pods, because we were running out food and they wanted to thin the herd. I want to make this very clear. In the past couple of weeks, we received a transmission from Earth, telling us that the Earth is not safe, and that we should wait weeks, if not potentially a couple of months, before returning to the surface. Unfortunately, we might run out of resources, specifically food, and be unable to survive for that long. But it is *not* safe to go down right now.

"It's difficult to believe, but management wanted to get rid of us. Send us to our untimely demise. We're not going to be revengeful. What we are going to be is just. We are going to survive here, together. But it isn't going to be easy. We're going to need cooperation. A capable leadership. We're all working on that. I don't want to, but we're likely going to have to limit rations significantly. If we run out food in the next couple of weeks, because it looks like we're heading in that direction no matter what we do, then we'll make the decision, not in the shadows, and not against everyone, but as a group, on how we move forward with our population. In the meantime, everything resumes as normal. Everyone works their essential jobs. If you have any questions, please direct them towards Fritz Nussbaum. Thank you all for your understanding."

The announcement clicked off, and Madison and Marcell were impressed from in the infirmary.

"Wow," Madison, who was pacing around in the infirmary, said. "At least now she's up again and about."

"Skye is something, isn't she?" Marcell asked from over on his bed. "That woman never fails to impress me."

"Yes, she is," Madison responded. "I knew she was a good person when I first met her, but I had no idea that she was… well, gifted like this."

"Yes," Marcell said. "Is there any reason you came to see me, other than wishing me well with my recovery?"

"What are you, telepathic?" Madison asked, eyes widening.

"No," Marcell responded. "Call it emotionally intelligent. Although, the way you're pacing around, it's not exactly subtle."

"I just… I didn't know how I was going to tell you. I was beating up myself, you know?"

"Tell me what?"

"That I'm a piece of shit," Madison replied. "A junkie."

"You're not a junkie," Marcell said, rolling his eyes.

"What if I told you," Madison responded, "what if I told you that, after you told me about their plans to remove us from the ship, instead of telling Graham and Skye, I shot up myself with morphine, and almost overdosed? That I wasn't able to get my shit together until ten minutes before the curfew yesterday? What if I told you, still, the effect of the various opiates from the past couple weeks are wearing out, and I may or may not go into withdrawal?"

"Then I would be concerned for you," Marcell replied. He winced a little bit while he spoke, the wounds still clearly crushing his mood. "I would be very concerned."

"I wish I could tell you that I was joking. But I'm not."

"Do Graham and Skye know?"

"Yes," Madison said. "I was too guilty. I told them last night, when we made our plan."

"What do you want me to do?"

"I don't know. Curse at me? Place me under arrest? Give me a whoop upside the head?"

"I'm bedridden," Marcell replied. "If you get close to me, then I can slap you. Otherwise, you're out of luck."

Madison huffed out, frustrated.

"You don't get forgiveness from me," Marcell continued. "What you did was shit. Selfish. I've known people like you back on Earth. They always lied to others, and to themselves. They were chronic liars. I've learned a new side of you today, and I can't say I'm happy. I'm pissed off, actually, after putting myself on the line for you."

Madison could feel tears building up in her eyes. The words stung.

"But you don't need forgiveness from me," Marcell declared. "You need to find out how to move on and get your shit together."

Madison remembered having the same conversation with Skye not too long before, and she felt a whole lot better.

***

Logging the deaths was completely meaningless. There was no job for Skye to complete, and she wasn't even being paid anymore. Despite that, Skye was on the task instantly after completing her speech, and Lex and Graham didn't try to convince her to stop at all.

"It's a piece of history," she explained. "I *have* to do it."

"No one's saying no," Lex replied. "I did hire you for that job."

"Oswald Bertrand. Date of Birth, September 24th, 2039. Time of death, July 6th, 2048, 12:30 a.m. UST," Skye started. "Place of death, Penthouse 1. Cause of death, Noxium."

He was just a kid. A fucking kid.

"Tanya Egorova. Date of Birth, February 11th, 1997. Time of death, July 6th, 2049, 12:30 a.m. UST. Place of death, Room 256. Cause of death, Noxium."

A bystander minding her own business in one of the hotel rooms, until the gas diffused through the cracks of her door and had stopped her heart. A victim who Skye never saw herself, but was yet another one added to her personal body count. She hoped it was worth it.

"Benjamin Mosi. Date of Birth, May 27th, 2005. Time of death, July 6th, 2048, 12:30 a.m. UST. Place of death, Penthouse 1. Cause of death, Noxium."

How did he even die? Why did it kill only five percent of people? Skye knew that the gas had killed the husband of one of the managers, and then there was Lusky's earlier claim that he, as well as the child, wouldn't have even known anything about the plan. Skye wished that the Alan Lusky could've died instead. At this point, Skye also doubted her reporting method (it seemed like she was technically reporting on the manner of death, rather than the cause of death), but she figured she was splitting hairs and continued. Skye hadn't even personally gotten into contact with McFarland and the forensics lab, so it's not like she could make the causes of death official.

"Audrey Campbell. Date of Birth, November 1st, 2015. Time of death, July 6th, 2048, 12:15 a.m. UST. Place of death, Oxygen Center. Cause of death, gunshot wound."

Audrey had held doubts about taking her and Graham into custody. She wanted to spare them. But she was dead now.

"Lucas Zielinski. Date of Birth, May 14th, 2028. Time of death, July 6th, 2048, 12:15 a.m. UST. Place of death, Hallway 8. Cause of death, skull fracture."

That idiot… All he had to do was listen. All he had to do was not panic and run out.

The last one was the toughest of them all. Or so she thought it would have been going into it.

"Joshua Somogyi. Date of Birth, March 15th, 2021. Time of death, July 6th, 2048, 12:15 a.m. UST. Place of death, Oxygen Center. Cause of death, stabbed in throat."

Indeed, Skye had plunged the needle through that man's throat. The worst part of it all was that Skye didn't even feel bad about it. No, if anything, she felt guilty for not feeling guilty. If given the chance, she would absolutely do it again.

The next step of everything was to evaluate the food reserves. They were in as bad of condition as Graham had foretold.

***

It was in the freezer that something magical happened.

The reserves were depleted. That much was clear when Graham and Skye stepped in to see around ten crates sitting in the corner of a mainly vacant large freezer section of the storage warehouse.

"So, this isn't a lot of food, huh?" Skye asked.

"Yes," Graham agreed. "This might be great... If you were feeding ten people. Could probably easily sustain us for the entire duration we needed to stay here, and then some."

"I see," Skye said. She lifted off one of the lids to see compact units of food in sealed bags lined up neatly. The labels of this particular section read *au gratin potatoes*, and there were maybe ten bags total scrunched together in this particular layer. It looked like there were numerous layers underneath it, comprising a stack of several types of foods.

"Eleven bags of au gratin," Graham said without missing a beat when he saw Skye reading off the label.

"We have inventory?" Skye asked, surprised.

"Yes," Graham said. "They keep it in the records division, stored electronically in the mainframe of the ship. Last night we checked out the records and were able to see the updated inventory. I just remembered that. Plenty of other stuff I learned, too."

"I'm sorry," Skye replied, shaking her head. "I really was irresponsible sleeping in for twelve hours. Like I was a teen again."

"No," Graham responded. "You were exhausted. I bet I'll sleep like that tonight, too."

"Still."

"Still, you saved my life last night. I'd say that counts for something."

"I didn't save anyone," Skye replied, managing a slight laugh. She turned to make eye contact with Graham, who was staring at her, a blank expression on his face. Slowly his face warmed up into a smile.

"Nonsense," he insisted. "Guns were pointed in my face. And what did I do? I stood there, a complete coward."

"That's not your fault," Skye replied. "You were afraid."

"Fight or flight," Graham answered. "That's what it's supposed to be, you know? Either fight or flight. I didn't even do that. I just froze. I *fricken froze*, and what does that make me? A deer in headlights. Maybe not even. You, on the other hand. You didn't hesitate. You're a hero."

"I'm not a hero," Skye said, averting eye contact and blushing.

"Yes, you are," Graham replied.

Skye rubbed her arms, wanting to warm up, and yet, somehow, oddly entrenched in the conversation. She decided to bear the cold for a couple of more minutes, despite her teeth starting to chatter.

"Crazy how cold it feels," Skye responded as they continued looking through storage. "Reminds me of Michigan, or back home in Minnesota. Nostalgic."

"Yes," Graham replied. "I almost forgot. Winters in Michigan are a lot different from back home, plus with climate change, we almost never, ever get freezes at all in the winter."

"I bet," Skye replied. "I almost forgot what it was like."

"Skye."

"Hm?"

"How have you been handling it all?"

"Handling what?" Skye asked, returning her gaze to meet his once again.

"You know…"

"I don't," Skye admitted, shaking her head in confusion.

"You stabbed the guy… And all those other people. Six people, who are either directly or indirectly killed by us. How have you been living that down?"

"I was trying to live," Skye replied. "I didn't really lose much sleep over it. I'm surprised by how unaffected I feel."

"Yes, me too," Graham responded. "We had to make a quick decision at a moment's notice. And I stand by my decision."

"We did make the right call," Skye said. "We were trying to survive; the same way Lusky was looking after himself. Only we won, and they lost."

"No," Graham replied. "I wasn't trying to survive, myself. I was protecting the people I care for."

Graham inhaled deeply.

"I'm talking about you."

The entire room was completely silent apart from the quiet buzz of the freezer cooling the air. Graham wondered whether he'd overstepped his boundaries. He knew, regardless, that there would never be any going back in their relationship from here on out. But he was tired of waiting for something to happen. He was either going to commit himself to something more or stop pretending that he could live out a fantasy. The feelings had been nagging him for a couple of weeks, and they were eating him inside out.

"I don't need protection," Skye said, blushing. She turned to walk away, but remembered the lid was off, and she lifted the lid. Graham grabbed the other end and helped heave it up over the proper corner and set it down.

"I know," Graham replied, and then he was blushing. "You've done more of that than I have, and I'm ashamed."

Skye looked back at him when the lid was back in place.

"Graham," she said, shivering in the cold.

"I know. I know. We can't. It would be distracting, and we have responsibilities now. We got to secure our future, and living a lie isn't going to help us."

"That's not what I was going to say," she answered. "Not at all."

"Oh?"

Skye stepped forward, and leaned in. And then, they were kissing. Graham didn't know what the hell he was doing and simply held his lips forward and hoped to make contact, and, judging by the texture of her soft lips against his (as opposed to her nose or the cold edge of a blade), he thought he did adequately enough. After a couple of seconds, he realized he'd been holding his breath for a while, and he pulled away.

"Skye!" Graham gawked, gasping for breath after a couple of seconds, his face reflecting pure shock.

"I'm sorry," Skye said meekly, almost an apologetic squeal. Now she was so red that her skin glistened like an apple. "I'm sorry, Graham!"

"No... No... I... No. I liked it." And then Graham pushed himself back forward, and this time, he was less clumsy when he angled his head in, resulting in an audible smooch that was a lot louder than Graham expected. He thought his heart was melting.

Chapter 3

After the incident in the freezer, Graham struggled to contain his excitement. He was giddy inside, but knew he had to compose himself. After all, there was a time and place for romance. Right now was not the time. As much as Graham wanted to fast forward to tonight to see what could happen, there were more important and pressing matters right now. The first two things on the agenda were assembling the organization of leadership as well as figuring out what to deal with their new captives, who had, according to Graham, been sitting in their cells for over twelve hours, no food or water to speak of.

They first decided to seek the advice of Fritz. A line of around dozen people had formed outside his office, but it looked like some of them recognized Skye, because they parted out of her way quickly when they saw her.

"I promise this won't take long," Skye told those waiting outside in the line, although Graham frowned, because he wasn't so sure.

Fritz, meanwhile, opened the door almost instantaneously, ushering an older woman out of the office, who left, swinging her own purse as she waved back at Fritz.

"Have a good day!" Fritz replied, grinning, before he turned his attention to his two new guests.

"Oh…" His smile dropped, replaced with a frown.

"Can we come in?" Graham asked.

Fritz nodded, and Skye closed the door behind him. Fritz stood up behind his desk, looking down at him.

"What can I do for my two little proletarians?"

"My two *what*?" Skye asked.

"You don't know what proletarians are? Wow, our education system has truly gone down the drain."

"We know what they are," Graham replied, annoyed. "We didn't come here to joke around."

"I know, I know," Fritz replied abrasively. "I don't want to get my head chopped off, believe me. I value my life."

"We came for advice," Skye explained.

"Do I look like I have sage advice to give? Because I sure don't," Fritz replied. "And I don't mean that to be mean. I mean that to be honest."

"We wanted to officially assemble a council," Skye continued. "Are you interested?"

"Really?" Fritz asked, visibly shocked. "You want me in a position of leadership. With you?"

"Yes," Skye replied.

"Seriously?" Fritz chortled. "Because I'm different from your generation, and most of my generation. I'm a little bit more, how should I put it... traditional."

Skye had to stop herself from throwing her arms in the air in frustration. "So?"

"So, nothing. I accept. Is that all?"

"No," Graham replied. "Right now, we've got you, Marcell, and Skye slated for a position. We need two more to round up the group. Do you have any recommendations?"

"So, she'll be on it, but not you, huh?"

"No," Graham answered. "I think that's too much of a conflict of interest. Or I guess a stacking of the court. I'm okay staying out of it, but do you have any suggestions?"

"I dunno," Fritz shrugged. "I'd consider asking the head doctor. Dr. Chetana. Very principled woman, she is. We might not see eye to eye, but she's got a brain, a heart, and a mean stethoscope."

"Good idea," Skye replied. "Anyone else?"

Fritz shrugged. "No. Management's all gone, so I'm assuming they're off the board?"

"That's a topic for our meeting tonight," Skye answered. "Our first topic, actually. What to do with everyone responsible for the plan."

"We'll think of someone else to make it five," Graham promised. "They're going to meet in the meeting Room 01, tonight at 5:30. Be there."

"Okay," Fritz said, nodding. He checked the clock. "That's only in an hour, but I will."

Graham and Skye exited the room, and Skye slipped her hand into Graham's.

"Meeting Room 01, huh?" Skye acknowledged. "That's where Elliott got poisoned. Feels like a year ago, but it was only a month ago."

"Oh, that's bad," Graham mumbled. "I had no idea. Want me to change the plans? Or, I guess, you'd have to, since you're the announcer."

"No," Skye replied, "It's just a room. It means nothing to me now."

***

Graham and Skye went back to the infirmary, where they came across Marcell and Madison. Madison was under the covers on an adjacent bed to Marcell, not looking all that well. When she saw Graham and Skye entering the room, her eyes averted them.

"Maddie," Skye said, running over to her and hugging her again. "What are you doing here?"

"I'm fine," she said, averting her eyes. "I'm fine."

"Are you?" Marcell asked, and Madison groaned.

"I'm here to detox," Madison admitted. "That's it."

"Oh..." Skye mumbled.

"Don't worry about me," Madison replied. "You can have your talk with Marcell, and pretend like I'm not here."

"Maddie, did you..." Graham started.

"Return the drugs?" Madison asked. "Yes, I did."

"I'm rooting for you," Skye replied, and Madison grinned.

"Thank you, Skye. I'm going to get clean if it kills me," Madison responded.

At this point a nurse walked in to check on the lot of them, but she stopped in her tracks.

"Oh, hello," the nurse said, greeting the audience that had formed for Madison and Marcell.

"This is Nurse Steward," Marcell said, pointing at the woman, who waved awkwardly at the lot of them.

"Who's that over there?" Skye asked, jamming her finger towards an unconscious figure in the other room, whose back was turned away from them.

"Someone from the hotel," Marcell explained. "They were unconscious and couldn't respond. We're waiting for them to wake up. My guess, they're in a coma from the Noxium."

"That's horrible," Skye said, before looking back at Marcell. "Marcell, I hope you're feeling okay."

"I'm fine," Marcell replied. "Doctor's orders that I can't leave this bed yet, though. Not even in a wheelchair."

"Well, you have your spot on the council when you're healthy. Do you know where Dr. Chetana is?"

Nurse Steward called from the other side of the room. "Why?"

"We need to talk to her," Skye said.

"A council?" Madison asked, rising from behind her sheets. "What?"

"Well, we need to rule the group somehow," Skye replied. "I think it's better to rule by committee rather than by a single leader, and a true democracy isn't practical."

"Makes sense," Madison replied. "Man, to think this is actually happening. It's unreal."

"It is, isn't it?" Skye replied. "Right now, we're trying to organize things."

"We've already taken some steps," Graham added. "Do you know who can make the fifth member? It's Skye, you Marcell, Fritz, Dr. Chetana. We're looking for one more."

"I don't know," Marcell responded. "There are a lot of capable people. Of course, I don't know who was or wasn't involved with Operation Exodus. Their leadership is probably out of the question if they played any role."

"Let me rephrase my question. What type of person would you recommend?" Skye inquired.

"Well, someone with experience," Marcell said. "Not in security, and not a doctor. Someone not quite in management, but someone with specialized knowledge. Engineering, maybe."

Skye turned to Graham.

"Sound like someone?" She asked.

Graham nodded. "Yeah. I think I know just who to call up."

Chapter 4

Skye and Graham went to the holding cells together before even getting a chance to talk to Dr. Chetana to ask her about admission to the council. Fortunately, Graham had the keys necessary to get past the gate and then they were on their way to the main holding cell.

Graham's idea had been met with skepticism, but he was set on his goal: Mr. Xiong. It made sense. He was an expert in the field, and, while he may have had a partial role of some kind in the failed force eviction of many, his talents were undeniable.

When Skye and Graham opened the door, it seemed like people inside were more desperate, bolder, because once they entered through the door this time, they pushed close to them, including Alan Lusky himself, who bombarded them with questions.

"We're starving, and thirsty," Lusky said, standing close to them. "How long are you going to keep us in here? What do you want us to do?"

"Let us out!"

"Please have mercy on us!"

"My wife is starving! Look at her!"

"I know, I know," Skye replied, more sympathetic now to these people than she ever had been in the last 24 hours.

It was weird now seeing them like this, begging for mercy. They weren't all mad and fighting her, like she had thought; they weren't just sad and defeated, either. They were on their knees pleading for their life, because they were scared. It made the situation all the more real for Skye, who had been far more detached from the ramifications of their imprisonment when she had overseen the transportation of their unconscious bodies to the prison cell.

To think, hours ago they were in the opposite position.

"Listen up!" Skye continued. "We'll have a meal for you brought within the next several hours. Wait patiently. We will also bring water."

As soon as the words escaped her mouth, Skye found herself perplexed that those words had left her mouth.

Food? Why would we give them food, after everything they did to us? Skye questioned herself internally. The truth was, she didn't know why. Perhaps it was because she felt everyone was owed dignity in defeat, like the prisoners of old getting their last meal, or the condemned Catholics given one last opportunity for spiritual redemption in their Last Rites before being executed centuries ago. Or maybe it was something else: guilt, and this was her own way of penance.

But Skye's thoughts were interrupted by the loud question asked nearby.

"My son," a person who by now Skye had figured out was the father of Oswald Bertrand said from the fringes of the cell. "Where is my son?"

But Skye couldn't answer the question, because she had nothing to say. His son was dead, and they had moved his corpse out of the room for eventual disposal. The questioning man's eyes were wild, and he looked charged with a lightning bolt of energy as he stomped towards the door, towards Skye, only seconds away.

"Mr. Xiong!" Graham shouted, ignoring the miserable father's cries. From the back of the room, Mr. Xiong stood up hesitantly. "Come with us!"

"Huh?" He asked. "Graham, my intern?"

"Come with us," Graham repeated.

Mr. Xiong slowly walked over, but before he could even reach the door, there was someone else there in the path.

"I asked you a question," Mr. Bertrand said, lunging forward.

The man wasn't anything remarkable, physically speaking. He was your average father in his thirties, with an ever-growing bald spot and a potbelly. But what he did have was an injection of rage, and a primal instinct that had been activated. He knew something foul had happened to his son, and it was putting him at his wit's end. Graham didn't even fault him for it, but he knew that there was going to be a disaster.

Just calm down. Breathe. Don't do anything rash. I don't want to hurt anyone, Graham thought.

"Where is my fucking *son*!?" the man screamed, spittle flying from his mouth.

Mr. Bertrand got up into Skye's face, grabbing her by the collar and holding back his right fist like he was getting ready to pummel her. Skye could only look up at him, her eyes widening in fear and surprise.

This is it, Graham thought. *This is my moment.*

Then, without another second of waiting, Graham squeezed the trigger, and the man tumbled to the ground, the room erupting into screams and sobs as Mr. Bertrand's wife rushed over to her fallen husband, whose life appeared to be quickly fading, a red hole in his chest. Mr. Xiong and Skye rushed out of the room as Graham locked the door behind them. As they walked through the hallway, Lusky stared out through the window to the hallway outside, shaking his head.

I killed him, Graham said, lowering his gun and hurriedly making his exit into the hallways. He didn't know whether to cry, to grin, to scream. He had been anticipating this moment, ever since Madison had first been taken from Skye's room, the time he would have to take someone else's life. And it had happened. Graham thought he was going to burst into tears.

But then he thought of Skye, and knew it was worth it. His breathing slowed down to a more normal pace, and he thought about the reasoning, and hoped she knew it too.

I did it for you.

***

After re-setting up the gate to block off the hallway, Graham and Skye headed straight to the Meeting Room 01. Skye told him to sit and wait with Mr. Xiong while she fetched Dr. Chetana, and Graham sat there in silence for the next twenty minutes until Skye returned with Dr. Chetana as well as a clipboard with some papers on it.

Given Marcell's absence, the council of five was currently only a council of four consisting of Dr. Anjali Chetana, Nathan Xiong, Skye Calvert, and Fritz Nussbaum. Because of the possibility of a tie, they agreed to, for the duration of the meeting, have Graham sit in on his stead. The entire time at the start of the meeting, he was thinking about what had just transpired, and not about the luxurious surroundings within the meeting room.

I killed a man, Graham though again and again. *I killed a man. He isn't making it. Not with a hole in his chest.*

Yet despite that, he wasn't even considering crying anymore. He had defended Skye and proven what he had said in the freezer earlier. He was grateful he hadn't missed… If he had missed, or worse yet, hit Skye, he would've never been able to live with himself.

"Thank you all for being here," Skye said, in a tone more passive-aggressive than anything as Fritz came into the meeting around five minutes late. Graham was certain that if they hadn't had to have gone and retrieved Mr. Xiong themselves, but rather invited him out of the cell earlier to go to the meeting, that he'd have been at least ten minutes late.

"My legs aren't what they used to be," Mr. Xiong replied apologetically. "You don't need to dig into this old man."

"I am honored to be here," Dr. Chetana replied. "But is it true? What people have been saying, about you using a gas attack to knock people out?"

"Yes," Skye said. "We had no other options. You were on the list. You weren't there."

Skye tossed the clipboard into the center of the table, while Dr. Chetana's eyes narrowed into a frown.

"I can't support this," Dr. Chetana said. It looked like she was going to stand up and leave.

"Look at it if you don't believe it."

Mr. Xiong didn't even take a look. Only Dr. Chetana snagged the clipboard and flipped through the pages, as Skye figured that her reading the pages would be more compelling than any anecdotes she could provide.

"I want to apologize," Mr. Xiong said. "I was aware of the plan. I never supported it. But I didn't have a voice, and I couldn't think of any other solutions."

"It's okay, Mr. X," Graham said, nodding. "I picked you because you were a good boss, and I thought we could hear from your input."

"Thank you," he responded. "Please, call me Nathan. I'm your colleague now, Graham, so you may as well treat me like one."

"Okay," Dr. Chetana said from her seat after a couple of moments flipping through the pages. "It looks like what you've said is true, about them kicking people off the ship. But what you did, it was drastic. I have to lead with that."

"We're not here to debate over the ethics of what happened," Skye replied. "Because right now, the perpetrators who were going to eject us from the ship are all sitting in a prison cell."

The room fell silent, until Fritz spoke up.

"What the hell are we waiting for?"

"I need your opinions," Skye responded.

"You're the boss," Fritz replied. "This is on you."

"Hold on," Dr. Chetana said, shaking her head. "What does he mean? Just how old are you?"

"Does it matter?"

"I think it does matter," Dr. Chetana replied.

"I'm twenty."

"Twenty. Twenty years old. You couldn't even legally drink in the States, and you're in charge now?"

She has a point, Skye thought. *I didn't even get my college degree yet.*

"She's plenty capable," Graham countered. "More capable than almost anyone on board."

But Dr. Chetana wasn't convinced.

"We need to release them right now," Dr. Chetana replied. "Lusky and others have years of experience. They know how to run this. Let's stop these games."

"And have them send hundreds of people back down to their death? You selfish *bitch!*" Graham seethed. Skye put her hand on his shoulder, eyes wide in shock at the outburst, and Graham felt himself calming down.

"Well, this isn't clearly going anywhere," Dr. Chetana said, standing up. "Because you clearly want to just call me names."

"You sit right down, doc," Fritz replied, shaking his head. "I don't think it's that difficult. They tried to kill everyone on board, and keep their own families. You can't honestly support that, can you, doctor? That seems to violate the Hippocratic order in more ways than one."

"Well I... No," Dr. Chetana said, exhaling before plopping herself back down on her gold-threaded seat. She sighed in frustration. "Fine. I'll hear you all out."

"Nathan, you know as well as me who's most responsible for this, right?"

"Huh? Yes," Mr. Xiong answered.

"Lusky and his board of executives. I say we kick their asses off the ship and give them a taste of their own medicine," Fritz proposed. The willingness to go out on a limb and eject his former managers was very surprising to Skye: for Fritz this all seemed very personal, like he had something to get back at them for.

"No," Nathan Xiong protested. "They're my friends. We can't do that!"

"We vote," Dr. Chetana insisted. "There's five of us. It's only fair."

"Yes," Skye replied. "I support that. Yea or Nay... Let's vote on whether we kick the people responsible off this ship. Any objections?"

"We could do anonymous voting," Dr. Chetana suggested. "That's the most impartial voting system we could implement."

"Eh, let's just do this shit," Fritz replied. "I don't think any of our feelings are going to be hurt one way or the other, and it's not like the public knows what we're voting for."

"Yes. But before we vote, I have to ask," Dr. Chetana said.

"Oh great," Fritz interjected, rolling his eyes.

"Is the vote for us to send down the perpetrators to Earth, or the perpetrators and their family as well?"

"It's a good question," Graham stated. They all turned to Skye.

"Yes," Skye answered. "The vote is to either kick all of them off, or none at all."

"But the children!" Dr. Chetana protested.

They could be vengeful, Skye thought. *I'd kick them all of if I could. But the children are innocent.*

Skye thought deeply for a few moments, and then she nodded.

"Right. How about this as a compromise? If those who we deem uninvolved, partners, children, they have a choice to stay on the ship without those responsible, who are going down no matter what. If they want, then they can go down to Earth. Otherwise, they stay, but if they misbehave, do even anything questionable against the ship, then they are kicked out, no warnings, no exceptions."

"Well," Dr. Chetana replied, "when would we execute this plan?"

"I don't know. We'll make arrangements after this. I say as soon as possible."

Dr. Chetana didn't push for any anonymous voting or clarifications any further, so that one by one, they each voted. Mr. Xiong voted first, and then the order following was Fritz, Dr. Chetana, Skye, and then Graham.

"Nay."

"Yea."

"Nay."

"Yea," Skye said. Skye had to vote to kick them out. Because she knew that if she let any of the management stay, then they would plan their undoing. Especially because of Graham killing Mr. Bertrand. His body was still lying there in the cell, dead. She couldn't even begin to wrap her mind around how traumatizing that would be for the spoiled wealthy executives. And the poor kids.

"I... Uh..." Graham sat there for a few moments, indecisive. "I think..."

"Wait," Dr. Chetana replied. "This isn't fair that he votes."

"She has a point," Fritz offered.

"How?" Graham asked, flabbergasted.

"You were here for Marcell, correct?" Dr. Chetana asked, and Graham nodded.

"Well, as much as I am sure you are trying your best to vote on behalf of him, I think I don't speak for myself when I say I want to hear what he says."

"Okay," Skye responded. "You want to hear what he says himself, right? Then come on. Let's go ask him."

***

After explaining the current situation to Marcell, Skye folded her arms and waited for Marcell to cast her votes. She stood next to Dr. Chetana and Mr. Xiong, who wanted to hear the words from Marcell himself. Graham and Fritz still lounged back in the meeting room, too tired to want to walk across the entire ship.

The Laser from Above

"My vote is the tiebreaker," Marcell said. "Depending on what I say, people will either be sent off this ship, or stay here. Is that true?"

"Yes," Dr. Chetana responded. "The power is in your hands."

"Okay," Marcell said. "What do I say then? No and yes, or…"

"Yea or Nay," Nathan answered.

Marcell exhaled, looking down at his own hands for a moment before looking up to make eye contact with Skye and the others.

"Yea," Marcell replied. "My vote is yea."

"Bold move, cotton," Madison whispered from her bed. After everything they'd done, Madison knew they could never go back if they even wanted to.

"Okay," Dr. Chetana conceded, flustered. "Now it's a matter of logistics."

Marcell nodded. "If you need me to cast a vote again, come back. Otherwise, I trust you."

One by one, Skye and the others filed out of the room. When they were gone, Madison turned to Marcell.

"Damn, you didn't hesitate at all. That was cutthroat."

Marcell shrugged. "I know these people. Some of them are good people. Fritz, for example, he never was a fan of the whole thing. But those managers… They were scared, but they were dangerous. I don't feel safe with them on board."

Madison looked at the bandage on his side. "Yeah, I don't blame you. You got shot because of them. I wouldn't have the heart to do that, but that's why I'm not in charge."

Marcell nodded. He touched his wound gingerly and winced. "There is that. And where the hell is Nurse Steward? I need another shot of tequila right now."

Madison raised her eyebrows. "Careful, Marcell. Next thing you know and I won't be the only addict on board."

Chapter 5

There were a few issues to address with kicking everyone responsible off, and that wasn't even mentioning the ethics of it all.

"There's the issue of moving them off," Skye said. "If they run at us, they could overwhelm us. It could be a bloodbath."

"I'll help," Fritz said. "I'm sure I can get them in line. All we need is a few security guards with guns, and I'm sure I can also get a few able-bodied men from the ship to help if needed. We start with the people closest to the door, take them one by one. We should have enough spools of rope in storage to tie them up."

"Yeah, of course... But then there's the problem of the body in the way," Graham muttered.

"Body?" Fritz asked, confused.

"What have you done now?" Dr. Chetana questioned, a hint of disgust showing through in her voice.

"He tried killing us," Skye replied. "Someone in the hold. Graham saved me. He had to shoot him."

"I'll take care of that," Fritz said with a sigh. "Pain in the ass."

"Are you sure there's nothing else?" Nathan asked. "I... I can't imagine living here without them."

"That's over," Fritz said, shaking his head. "Sorry, Nathan."

Skye then offered to bring food and water as well, much to their confusion. Dr. Chetana appeared deeply confused as to why Skye would possibly vote to kick them off the ship and yet simultaneously drain the ship's resources while they were at it.

"If you're going one direction, may as well commit to it," Dr. Chetana replied. "That makes no sense."

Skye turned red in embarrassment.

"I promised them," Skye said. "This is one last gift to them. Before they leave."

"There's no honor among thieves," Fritz said. "You don't owe them shit. I don't think freeze-dried spaghetti is going to make them feel any better about their predicament."

"We can afford one last meal," Graham said.

That's right, Skye thought, *we can afford it. And more importantly, I promised it.*

"Why are you even here?" Fritz asked, turning to Graham. "We overrode your vote."

Graham sat up in his chair, feeling oddly hurt by the remark, but Skye stepped in.

"He speaks for Marcell this meeting, even if he didn't vote. End of discussion."

"It is… fair," Mr. Xiong agreed. "And yes, I agree it's worth the meal."

There was some further discussion about how they would handle removing management from the ship. Even if they sent everyone down to Earth in the escape pods, it might not have been the most conducive for success for the ship. Nathan made an argument that some of the individuals who had been arrested were too essential to be removed. He also hinted that there were a few people living in other hotel rooms who needed to be detained for their role in planning for this. He even name-dropped a couple of electricians and other employees who had not been in Lusky's quarters, who had held an active role in Operation Exodus.

"So how do we handle this?" Dr. Chetana asked.

Fritz wanted to kick them all out straightaway, but it was Skye who came up with a compromise: tentatively, they would remove anyone they held responsible in Lusky's quarters, as well as anyone who Marcell, Fritz, or Mr. Xiong strongly advised. If there was anyone who they thought should stay, then they would cast a vote, and, should the majority prevail one way or the other, then they would go with them.

"Most of the security force, they're decent people," Fritz said. "I can vouch for them. All of them. And we'll probably need them to keep order in the hotel."

After finalizing their plans for completing the removal of management from the ship, deciding to do so that very night at ten thirty, they moved on to the next topic, cutting rations to one meal for the next couple of weeks (of which they voted to do so in three days' time). The council then agreed to adjourn and meet every other day at the same time (seven o' clock at night) to discuss their plans. Graham would sit in on meetings until Marcell was good enough to attend the meetings, but Marcell would ultimately hold the power when it came to major votes.

The meeting ended with Dr. Chetana waiting around after Nathan and Fritz had left. Graham stood outside the door, waiting for Skye to leave.

"I have my eyes on you," she told Skye. "Everyone seems to have appointed you as the leader, but I'm not so convinced that you're cut out to lead."

"I want everyone to live," Skye responded, with as kind of a tone as she could muster. "I didn't exactly ask to lead. I was kind of thrust into the role."

Dr. Chetana shook her head. "I'm a doctor first and foremost. But I think in a time like this, we need a principled leader. If you feel forced into leadership, then, well, don't lead. I can take over."

Skye thought about it for a few moments. Dr. Chetana was clearly an incredibly intelligent woman. You didn't become a licensed head doctor of such an institution if you didn't have some sort of special intelligence. Not only that, but she'd shown morality and a willingness to run the group. There was probably no one more qualified in the entire hotel than her.

With all of these things in mind, Skye surprised herself with what she said next.

"Forgive me for being disillusioned with everyone who'd been kept on the bankroll by the International Space Hotel," Skye managed. "I'm happy with where I am, for now."

Dr. Chetana nodded understandingly before walking away. Skye couldn't help but feel like she'd made a mistake as soon as she disappeared down the hallway and Graham stepped inside to ask her what that whole conversation was about. Skye lied and said that Dr. Chetana was just checking in about the medical situation on the ship.

I'm doing this, running this ship, out of my desire to make everyone better... right?

Skye wasn't so sure anymore.

***

Skye did follow through with her promise for dinner.

Skye headed to the cafeteria with Fritz and Graham, where she talked to the head chef of the International Space Hotel. She ordered a great deal of chicken tenders and fries prepared on paper plates, bringing them into the cart before covering it all with a sheet. Skye wasn't about to supply the captives with glass

The Laser from Above

plates or metal utensils. Even plastic trays and utensils, she figured, could be turned into weapons to be used against them. During the whole encounter and conversation, it was readily apparent how no one recognized her as the leader. It didn't bother her, but everyone now acted like Fritz was the man in charge, which was an oddly sobering experience for Skye.

Because I look like a college kid. Because I am—no, I was—one.

Skye helped push a cart with all of the food and water bottles stacked together, while Graham and Fritz stopped to pick up a couple of assault rifles from the armory. Despite the general absence of an active security force, things had been oddly calm among the International Space Hotel. It seemed like the release of people the previous night, as well as the announcement Skye had made, had instilled a certain confidence among the population. Still, Skye didn't want to tarry around and wait for any unrest, because she knew that people would be furious once they learned that two meals would become one. But that was a problem to deal with tomorrow.

A few people did notice Fritz and asked him some questions, and followed the group as they moved through the hallway. Graham figured they were also probably instinctually drawn by the scent of food wafting from under the sheet, but Fritz dodged their questions adeptly before they managed to shake off most of them through an area accessible only via keycard.

Graham and Fritz went with her, armed with guns; and before they knew it, they were in the holding cells, and people ran up eagerly to earn food, so much so that people almost forgot about the dead body in the front of the room. Well, almost everyone.

The dead man's wife was mourning next to him, curled in a ball, and, as Fritz dragged out the body of the now-deceased man, she stood up and screamed like a banshee. Fritz tugged at the woman to get her away from the dead body; Graham helped pry her off. During the process, she scratched at Graham with his nails, and her emotions were palpable so that he almost choked up. It was a reminder of what he had done, and now it felt so much more real and impactful.

"You killed him! You killed him!" she screamed, getting close to him. "Haven't I lost enough!?"

Skye motioned for him to leave, and he did so before she could run at him. Fritz and Skye were enough to control the crowd, as the woman was more preoccupied with shouting at Graham through the window than dealing with them. Almost everyone scrambled to get their portions of food, and Skye handed each of them a plate and a water bottle. There were a few notable exceptions of people holding out from eating, likely not trusting the safety of their food, or perhaps standing up in principle against the opposition for killing one of their own ranks. Among the abstainers was Alan Lusky.

"You must be pretty dense if you think you can appease me with chicken tenders," Lusky told her, his butt still planted down on a nearby metal bench.

Skye stared at him and shook her head.

"I'm not trying to appease you," Skye replied. "I would've eaten those chicken tenders if I were you, though."

"Why should I?" Lusky asked. "Even if they aren't spiked with some sort of anesthetic, then I'm not going to accept this little gesture from you. Not after what you've done to us. Let me guess, this is our final meal?"

"That's up to you," Skye replied darkly, and at that remark Lusky fell quiet, absorbed in thought. He wasn't an idiot, and if his silence was any indication, he knew what fate awaited him.

Skye was relieved that they got in and out of there within a couple of minutes. But a couple of security guards were talking to Fritz now, asking him questions of why he was giving them food, what was happening.

"You five," Fritz replied. "Come with me."

"Yes," Skye replied, motioning for them to exit. "Come on."

Despite the pleading of some of the others, Skye and Fritz ensured that only the former security guards, almost all of them the ones who Marcell had lured into the lobby to be knocked out the previous night, were let through. Yet many of the other staff and their families accosted Fritz, asking why he was being left behind, why he was betraying them and freeing the guards but not them. It was a harrowing sight. That was the second to last time Skye would ever check on Alan Lusky. The final time was within a few hours later.

***

Fritz did, in fact, find a handful of people to help assist in extracting people from the cells and moving them to the escape pod. They came in the form of the security guards who he had taken out of the hold. Skye learned this information from the conversation she had with Fritz in his office.

"I'll whip them all into shape," Fritz promised. "Make them see the error of their ways, and see why that other man has to go."

Fritz also coordinated to have a few people arrested as quietly as possible, and had them brought into the holding cell, although Skye wasn't in the area to witness any of the fallout. As a matter of fact, Skye didn't have to help with the final stage of the removal process, and neither did Graham. Fritz advised them that he had this covered, and that the process would probably be better if security handled it. But despite that, she and Graham watched the whole eviction process transpire in the hallways, Madison joining them as well.

The three friends watched as the security guards extracted the captives, one by one, from the holding cell; then they tied their hands with rope. It looked like they were tying them up to prevent them from escaping or fighting back, rather than keeping their arms securely fastened, which was good. Skye imagined they would be able to easily slip their way out of the ropes out post-launch, meaning they wouldn't be stuck inside the escape pod forever once they landed back down on Earth.

Then, the security guards escorted the captives into escape pods that were mainly located down the hallway, some in the other direction away from them, others around past where Skye and the others stood. These pods were connected via airlocks down the length of the mainly empty hallway. Whereas these locks had been locked completely ever since the Red Day, now they were functional. When the right buttons were pressed in the control room (which would be done shortly) then escape pods would launch off to the flight path down to the landing pad of the American shuttle station from which Skye had come into space. The flight path itself had been pre-programmed by one of the flight crew who stood by Fritz's side. Whether or not this woman had been coerced into cooperation, or had been persuaded, Skye didn't know. It was nice, however, to have someone to rely on, because she felt she could trust Fritz, and watching this didn't shake her confidence. It did, however, hurt her to watch.

Eventually, the security guards must've run out of the escape pods in the other direction, because a few people were brought towards them, each of them secured by two security guards who walked them with their own arms locked around their arms, or, in some cases, practically dragged them against their will.

Skye had to almost double take when she first saw the children accompanying the parents. The security guards didn't tie up their hands or drag them the same way they did the adults, but they tailed near their parents, often holding their parents' hands.

One of them, a girl who couldn't have been older than six or seven, was tugging on her mother's blouse asking her mother, who Skye recognized as one of the VPs, whether they were going home.

"Yes," the mother said, although she was crying as the guards took her down the hallway.

"Sheesh," Madison mumbled under her breath once they passed by. "I know their parents are a security threat... But those are *kids*."

"They wanted to go, as a family," Graham said quietly. "Skye... We... gave them an option. Frees up resources that way."

That's their choice, Skye assured herself, as if the kids were deciding to go on their own willpower, and not being forced down with their parents. *This isn't my fault. It can't be.*

Skye recognized some more faces but only that until a few had been walked past them did she recognize someone by name. It was Ron, the man who had proposed to her recently. He was kicking around and flailing like a petulant child in a tantrum being forcibly carried by their parents into their room. His eyes flicked around the hallway desperately, and his face, which already had been scrunched in fear and panic, seemed to somehow grow more animated when he saw Skye in his vision.

"You bitch," Ron growled at Skye as he flailed in the security guards' grip. "You could have had me! You had to go and kill everyone, you vile cunt! We're all dead! *Dead!*"

Skye shook her head, looked away. Graham slipped his hand into hers, and she squeezed it. Madison saw the gesture from where she stood, but she pretended to not notice. In that moment, it finally clicked to Madison that something had happened between Graham and Skye.

Ron's shouting grew quieter, and eventually silent, as he entered through a doorway to the airlock and the escape pod beyond.

"I never got to thank you," Skye murmured to Graham once Ron was out of sight, and, at least somewhat, out of mind.

"What?" Graham asked, not letting go of her hand.

"You saved my life. It didn't really register, but who knows what would've happened if you hadn't been there? The man could've taken the gun, killed me."

"You act like I was acting so brave," Graham commented. "I acted spontaneously. But I was trying my best, to make sure they didn't hurt you. Not after everything we've been through."

"What happened?" Madison asked. Graham looked away, but Skye responded.

"He saved me earlier today," she managed, leaving out the part about Graham shooting and killing the enraged Mr. Bertrand.

Am I so desensitized with the end of the world, that killing someone feels not only hardly impactful, but right? Graham really didn't know, but he didn't want to know, either. Who he held in his hand was real, and beautiful, and as long as they were on the right side together, he knew he wouldn't second guess himself.

Madison choked out a cry of protest when she saw who was taken down shortly after.

"This can't be right," Madison said. The woman was someone Graham had seen before around in the ship. The same person who, their first evening in space, before they would have ever thought the Earth could be destroyed, had led a concert for energetic fans aboard. It was Eva, and she was walking confidently despite the ropes bound over her wrists, although one guard had his arm wrapped around her elbow just as a precautionary measure.

The Laser from Above

Skye shrugged. "The decision was made by Fritz. She was associated with undesirables, and had no familial relations with anyone on board. We have no reason to believe that she wasn't conspiring with Lusky to some extent."

"*Fuck*," Madison said, looking away.

Eva's entire look was rough, with frazzled hair, wrinkled clothes, and black mascara that ran down her cheeks. But it looked like she was over crying now, as she quietly strolled by without another word until Madison spoke up.

"I'm a big fan," Madison said as Eva passed by. "I'm sorry this had to happen."

"Really?" Eva asked, craning her neck back, but still walking forwards. "Can you tell these guys to lay off? This is clearly a misunderstanding. I was just performing. I mean, come on."

She managed a forced chuckle, and Madison turned to Skye with pleading eyes to reconsider the judgment passed onto Eva.

"Skye?"

"Take her away," Skye told the guard, and, like the rest, Eva was gone. Madison recollected herself, sighed.

"Boss knows best," Madison mumbled.

Lastly, it was Lusky who marched by. Lusky moved with dignity and grace, far unlike the Chief Information Officer a few minutes before. Lusky strutted slowly and confidently. He didn't struggle at all, but his eyes locked into Skye's as he walked.

"This is our final goodbye, I suppose," Lusky said.

"Yes, it is," Skye commented. Lusky broke into a smile as he walked past her.

"Thank you for letting my child and wife stay. Believe it or not, I always liked you, Skye Calvert," he said as he walked past

51

her, and looked straight ahead in the hallway. "Time will tell if you have what it takes. I don't know. I really don't."

Skye wanted to open her mouth, fire back some snarky retort of some kind, but it was as if her tongue was tied, and by the time she thought to speak, Lusky was gone.

It was only a couple of minutes after that the escape pods propelled off the ship with a loud click and a rumble. Skye and Graham could look through the windows and see the large white orb-like escape pods flying back down to Earth, a trail of fire following the thrusters that directed them down through the atmosphere. Fritz had told Skye that the escape pods would have burned through most of their fuel by the time they landed back on Earth. All of their interfaces were programmed to be locked, meaning they could not take control of the ship, even if they wanted. They were, ultimately, never coming back.

Chapter 6

"*I know their parents are a security threat… But those are kids.*"

"*You vile cunt! We're all dead! Dead!*"

"*Do not run away, or my colleague will be forced to pull the trigger of that gun.*"

There was a gunshot. Then more. Then there were pools of blood forming on the ground. Dead, blank eyes. Unmistakable, fragments of grey matter, all over the ground.

Grace Elliott was lying gurgling on the ground, the attempts to resuscitate her all failures.

And then she held a syringe, plunging it through a man's neck.

"*Lucas is dead.*"

The sequence of the images were memories, not distorted, but the truth.

But there was something else. The Noxium gas was here, and it was suffocating Skye, reaching down into her throat. Skye saw two dead corpses walking towards her, their hands outstretched: a man, Benjamin Mosi, and a boy, Oswald Bertrand. They were dead from the gas, because of *her*, and she could feel their grip tightening around her arms and a quiet voice in her ear, a voice with the cadence and tone of another deceased person she knew. It was Lucas.

"How much bloodshed will you cause? How many lives will you ruin?"

"I... I had to... protect," Skye tried mouthing out, but she couldn't breathe, her lungs empty of air. The Noxium, she must've been drowning in it.

Skye woke up screaming, drenched in sweat. She looked around, swatting her arms as if there was a swarm of insects harassing her. After a few moments, she regained her wits and recollected her heaving breathing, although her heart was pounding so hard, she was legitimately concerned for her own well-being.

"I can't be like this," she said aloud. "Why am I so anxious? Why? I was okay... It's over now..."

Skye found herself crying for a few moments. Then she turned over to the clock.

It was only 11:17 in the evening, and she'd been asleep for not even an hour.

"I'm not letting anyone hurt us again," Skye said. "No matter what, no one's going to harm the ISH. Ever."

***

"Would you like me to buy you a drink?"

The question came from Marcell's side. Seated at the bar, Marcell had developed an appreciation of alcohol as he recovered from being bedridden to being able to move around with a cane after several days.

Marcell looked over and saw the person who had asked the question. It was a man around his age, maybe several years later, and for a few seconds, didn't believe it. He looked to his side, wondering if there was a woman next to him who was invisible to him but not to the other man. But there was no one but himself.

"Sorry? Who are you?"

"Oh, sorry," the man replied, extending his name. "My name's Jordan. I'd like to buy you a drink. Unless you're busy waiting on someone else?"

"Oh, no," Marcell responded. "No, no, that's great. My name's Marcell, by the way."

"Great, Marcell," the man replied. "Do you have any preference for my drink?"

"No," Marcell responded. "Surprise me."

The man walked up to one of the few automated spouts, pressing his keycard in front of one of the beer taps once he set the drink right below it. Usually, the scanner would automatically charge the guest's account, but that was not the case right now. There was, however, an automatic cap placed for two drinks a day per keycard. With multiple keycards, however, people could easily get extremely intoxicated, especially considering it was easier to get drunk in space. Jordan finished filling a glass full of a golden beer before the spout automatically stopped near the edge.

While the food reserves on board were squeezed to their limits, their supply of alcohol was seemingly endless, and, with the regime of leadership changing, open for business. This had led to many on board binge drinking, which presented a different security issue entirely. If anything positive did come of this, however, it was the fact that it did distract people enough that the news of the rations being cut to one meal a day had been received much better than anticipated in the ISH. There were no riots or widespread looting, just a lot of drinking. Marcell was more than buzzed right now.

"Tell me, Marcell," the man said, sliding over next to him and handing him the drink. "You are out here with your girlfriend? Family?"

"Me? Girlfriend?" He chuckled. "No, I'm gay."

The man seemed pleased by the answer. "Me too. Well, bisexual, with a preference for men. I... Well, let's just say I shot my shot based on your outfit, but I couldn't be 100% sure if you were just an ally."

Marcell looked down at the rainbow flag necklace that dangled around his neck. Marcell was amused, if anything.

"Your gaydar went off?" Marcell asked, smirking.

"Yeah, call it an educated guess," Jordan replied. "It's just, only a couple of hundred people on board, but it seems like I'm the only non-straight person. I know I'm not, but that's how it feels sometimes. Like, isn't it supposed to be 2048? Or did we pass through a time portal to 1948?"

"Oh," Marcell said, managing a laugh. "Tell me about it. I work security. Don't even let me get started about my colleagues. They're straighter than parallel lines."

"Security. Figures why you have such a good build."

Marcell blushed, shook his head.

"What about you?" Marcell asked after a couple of seconds. "What do, or, did you do? I've never seen you around here. I barely recognize you."

"Me?" The man asked. "I was a client, obviously. Got up here just a few days before everything happened. I was up here on the trip of a lifetime. I was a senior VP at a fortune 500 company."

"Wow, senior VP, impressive," Marcell commented. "You're young, too. You must've made a lot of money."

"I look a bit younger than I am," Jordan answered. "I'm in my early thirties. I did make a lot of money, though. I prided myself on it... Not that it matters at all anymore. I won an award for my performance and won a short trip up here, and the rest is history."

Jordan looked down. All of a sudden, and Jordan looked slightly concerned. Marcell followed where his eyes had gone and saw what he must have been looking at.

"Yeah," Marcell said, holding his cane up in the air. "This is my cane. Sorry if it comes as a bit of a shock."

"I thought you said you worked in security," Jordan replied.

"I did," Marcell replied. "Workplace accident. Does this change anything?"

Jordan thought for a few moments before shaking his head.

"Not at all," he answered. "How did you get hurt?"

"Gunshot wound," Marcell answered, and Jordan's eyes widened. "It hit my torso, and it hurts to walk now. At least I can move about with a cane, although I'm slow."

"What are you, James Bond?" Jordan asked, and they fell silent for a few moments until Marcell laughed. Jordan broke out laughing with him, until Marcell had to stop, clasping his side in pain. Marcell felt something he hadn't in a long while. He felt charmed. Romance was budding on board the International Space Hotel in more places than one.

Chapter 7

The council was pressed with a difficult decision around this same time.

A woman in her forties had been at the hotel with her pre-teen aged daughters and sons, and had sacrificed some of her own rations to keep them full. However, she'd been caught stealing rations from the storage facilities, and the way she'd defended herself made it sound like she'd stolen before. Now the five members were deliberating in the meeting room, deciding what punishment should be dealt while the woman remained imprisoned in the holding cell.

"We need to set an example," Skye insisted.

For everyone we've lost, she almost added.

"I agree," Fritz said, nodding.

"Yes," Dr. Chetana said. "Stealing is really bad. Honestly, I could understand why it could warrant the death penalty, in some cases."

"Yes," Marcell said. "But what kind of example do we set? We can't just give her a slap on the wrist. People will break the rules, steal food like her. But we can't be too harsh, either. We can't be like Lusky, set a bad precedent. We threw them over with the image that we're going to be democratic, then we're not going to be despotic and certainly won't kill people over offenses that kill no one."

"Perhaps, we educate them," Nathan offered. "About the common good with man, and we will promote a sense of brotherhood among everyone. That will make it less likely for people to steal. After all, scalping food hurts everyone, and if we encourage the common good, then no one will be motivated to commit a crime."

Skye said nothing about scalping extra food with Marcell, because that was ancient history.

"No, we're not doing that," Fritz said in response to Nathan's plan. It looked like he was struggling to conceal himself from laughing and Marcell shook his head in disapproval at the man's immaturity. "We're not about to fire up a propaganda machine. Things are done differently here, and I'm all about fair laws."

Dick, Marcell thought.

"I say, we sentence her to three days in isolation," Dr. Chetana said. "We don't give her any food, only water and a toilet. A second infraction, then we consider the death penalty."

"Fair," Fritz said, nodding. "I don't think it's public enough, though. We need to get the memo out. Public flogging. That's the good ole fashion way."

"How about," Skye offered, "we publicly execute her?"

The council was silent.

"Skye, girl..." Marcell started, but Skye didn't let him lecture her.

"Look, I never did support the death penalty in the past," Skye said. "But in this case, stealing food from someone else, that's basically killing them. It isn't a statement just against someone else, either, but about the entire ship. It's choosing yourself before the community, at everyone else's expense. That's not right."

"What are you saying?" Dr. Chetana said, her voice almost a shriek. "We shoot her?"

"No," Skye replied. "We eject her through the garbage chute into space, open up the blinds to space and let people watch. Say if anyone steals food from the ship, then they die."

"Wow," Fritz said, blinking in surprise. "Skye, that's... That's a little bit despotic, no?"

But Skye shrugged, and she was quiet for a while as others advocated for their ideas.

In the end, the council ended up voting by a count of 3-2 in favor of Dr. Chetana's plan, with only Skye and Fritz voting against it in favor of their own plans. In doing so, the council sentenced the woman to three days of starvation in a prison cell. In addition, they agreed to deliver a public announcement warning strictly about the consequences and penalties of stealing (as well as a double jeopardy death), posting a trusted security guard in the food section of the storage facility, full-time. But Marcell couldn't believe what Skye had said. Skye was cutthroat when it came to running a tight ship.

***

Madison wasted no time confronting Sarah once she'd recovered. It'd only been a few weeks that she'd been hooked on it, but it had been enough that she had experienced some symptoms of withdrawal. Fortunately, they hadn't been serious, although she'd spent a couple of days in the infirmary just to be safe.

"Hello, Maddie," Sarah greeted her as she approached the front of the desk.

"Hi," Madison replied.

"Why are you here?" Sarah asked. Madison was properly dressed and had the ID necklace hanging around her neck, as if she was reporting to a shift of work during her internship back before the Red Day.

"I came looking for work," Madison responded. "I'll come through the door in a sec and get to work."

"Oh, no," Sarah politely declined from behind the desk, waving her away. "You don't have to worry."

Madison stopped in her tracks before she even reached the door.

"Are you sure?" Madison asked. "I have my job to do."

"No, it's okay," Sarah responded. "You know, with everything having happened, your internship is a little bit expendable. We don't need the help anymore, unless there's a medical emergency on board. I appreciate all the help that you've provided."

"Look," Madison replied. "About the bag... about the drugs. Please don't fault me for that."

Sarah fell silent and then crossed her arms. It looked like she wanted Madison to fess up.

"*God*," Madison groaned. "Fine. It was me. I'm the one who stole the drugs. I was emotionally broken, and in a bad place, and I'm sorry."

"I had counted inventory," Sarah recounted slowly, sighing. "I thought I was crazy, but I knew we were short. Then I was telling myself, maybe something happened. There was an accident of some kind, and the front office was being all *hush hush* and they took it. But then I noticed something else. The keys were slightly misplaced, which I found interesting. I mean, it's easy enough to miss, if you aren't careful, but I am. This seemed like too many red flags to be a coincidence.

"So, I went and I asked Dr. Chetana herself that day. She'd know if there had been anything that required those drugs. There was nothing of the sort. Of course, I lied for your sake and didn't throw you under the bus. But I knew it was you. Even though I had to accept your help after all the medical emergencies, don't think I didn't know."

"I'm sorry," Madison replied, and her apology did sound genuine. "It'll never happen again. I had some problems... Have some problems... But I'm better than that now. I want to help."

"I believe you," Sarah responded. "Still, you didn't return everything you took."

"I know," Madison replied. "I used some of it."

"Please leave. You're no longer needed here."

"I just want to learn from you," Madison begged. "Learn from the doctors, sit in with them. I'm not proud of my actions, and if you want me to turn myself into the authorities running this ship, I will. But please, please, let me help. There's nothing to do anymore and I'm driving myself crazy sitting around. I'm sure Fritz Nussbaum would vouch for me on this."

"Fritz, huh?" Sarah asked. She sighed once again. "You're hard to turn down, Maddie. Fine. But mark my words... If you steal anything more, you'll never even sniff this pharmacy again, and I'm sure the doctors will blacklist you. Go ask Nurse Steward if she needs anything right now."

Madison practically skipped out of the room. Only when she exited into the hallway did she finally let herself grin.

***

Graham and Skye sat together underneath the covers that same night that Madison had reconciled with Sarah. They were still, however, almost completely clothed. The bed had been set with the electronic controls to be very soft, as Skye had preferred.

"This bed feels so soft. Makes me feel like I'm a graham cracker on a bed of marshmallows," Graham commented before he frowned. "Did I really just say that?"

"Oh, I love it, I love it." Skye laughed. "You're turning into Maddie, with that pun."

"Yeah... I'm not on her level yet. I hope I never will be."

Skye stared into his eyes, and her hand slowly stroked his chest. Graham looked back at her, unsure of how to proceed. "Have you ever done this before?"

"No," Graham said. "Last time I shared a bed with someone of the opposite sex was with my cousin on some family trip like five years ago."

Skye snorted.

"Don't you dare go there," Graham warned, shaking his head. "Don't you dare make an Alabama joke."

"I know, I'm kidding, I'm kidding," Skye promised. "It's kind of cute when you're mad, too."

Graham nodded, before looking like he was thinking. "Now that I remember, I think I've shared a bed with someone else since being up here. Maddie."

"You *what*?" Skye asked, her eyes growing wide.

"It's not what it sounds like! It was a hospital shift and she stumbled into my room at some point after I let her in, and she passed out."

"Oh really? Was that all that happened?"

"Yes! It was after one of her big hospital shifts around the Red Day. She passed out on me."

"You're blushing."

"No," Graham said. "No, I'm not."

"Are too," Skye replied, grinning.

Some people might get jealous at the idea of their friends sharing the same bed as their boyfriend: but Skye very clearly believed him, in any case, and it was pretty obvious that Madison wouldn't have ever done anything with Graham, who she treated like a brother. The runt brother sometimes, but the brother nonetheless.

"Lalala," Graham said, pretending to plug his ears.

"Blushing like a tomato," Skye said, smiling. "Speaking of red, do you notice anything that's different with me?"

Graham had a faint idea, and he carefully caressed her hair, finding what he was looking for, a red streak.

"This!" He exclaimed enthusiastically, carefully brushing a bunch of strands of her hair, as if he'd discovered a piece of treasure.

"It'd faded out," Skye said. "I got it dyed again. Do you like it?"

"I love it," Graham said, nodding. "Adds a lot of flair. In a good way."

"My best friend and I had been dying a streak in our hair since we were thirteen," Skye explained with a grin. "She got a blue streak, and I got a red streak. We said, even when we move on from each other, she went to college at the University of Minnesota, we'd keep doing it. But it faded away. Y'know, like a lot of memories… but I didn't want to forget. Her face, or what we had together. I decided to keep it."

"Good for you. Did you bring the hair dye up here?"

"No, I got Marcell to find some on board."

"That was nice of him."

"Yes, yes it was. I have to ask. Are you… ready?" Skye asked, her expression turning serious.

"Yes," Graham answered. "I mean, aren't we moving a little bit fast? I mean, I'm totally into it. I'm not going to pretend like you're not the most beautiful person on board, but… It's only been like a few days now."

"Yes. Yes, Graham, it has," Skye admitted, nodding. "Do you think I'm moving too fast?"

"No, it's not," Graham replied. "I have felt like with all this surviving… We never got a chance to *live*, you know? I do want this. And I need this. Bad."

"Yeah," Skye agreed. "That's my thought exactly. I wonder how Maddie feels though. We're all super tight, and now you and I are suddenly dating. I've seen that ruin friend groups before."

"I don't know," Graham replied. "She's a very nice person, and I'm sure she'd have no problem finding a partner if she looks for them. She doesn't seem desperate for one though. I respect that. I know she talked about her former boyfriend. Seems dedicated to him."

"You're right," Skye responded. "Remember what she said about Marcell? She saw him walking with some dude, holding hands. And not in a platonic way."

"I know," Graham. "It seems like everyone on board is partnering up."

"I'm not Minnie," Skye clarified. "For the record. Which means if it happens, I need protection."

"Yes, yes," Graham replied. "Speaking of which…"

Graham leaned over into the bed, where he had his wallet. He opened up the wallet, pulled out what he referred to as his lucky condom, and read the small print on the backside.

"Ah, darn!"

"What's wrong?"

"The condom expired… In 2047."

"Geez."

"You'd think with the advancement of technology we'd have condoms with a better shelf life, but here we are."

"Wow. Unreal."

"My parents got them my freshman year of college. My dad told me to use them responsibly. As you can tell, I didn't need them. Lucky condom my ass. More like unlucky condom." Graham stood up, throwing on his shirt. "I'll stop by the pharmacy."

"I'll wait," Skye replied. Skye pulled off the covers. Unlike him, she'd been wearing a pajama shirt and pants, and she started unbuttoning her pink stripe pajama top, starting at the top.

Graham's eyes widened, and he froze for a second. Now he was as turned on as a wild animal in the peak of mating season, and when he reached the door, he was practically sprinting.

"Be a good boy and get a non-expired pack, okay!?" Skye called.

The words were maybe meant to tantalize him further, but Graham felt like he was trapped in quicksand, immediately immobilized by the words before he reached for the handle.

Good boy.

Then, slowly, the memories hit him, memories which seemed like with all the events of the past month, he'd completely blotted out from his mind. Of him looking through the blueprints, seeing a weapon with that same name.

The Good Boy. The laser weapon had almost eluded him and slipped from his mind completely, but now it was there, more tangible than anything else.

Nathan Xiong had taken the blueprint, and Nathan would now be accountable to *him*. He could finally get answers, no doubt about it.

"Graham?" Skye asked, concerned by his silence and lack of movement near the doorway.

Graham fished through his pocket to confirm that he still had the master card Marcell had lent him, and then he rushed over to the nearest registry, leaving the room without another word.

Chapter 8

There were a few registries that Graham was aware of, but he had a spare copy in his room, so he first stopped next door before flipping through and finding Nathan Xiong's room. According to the registry, he lived in room 227, which was a decent walk, especially with no escalator track (the ISH's power conversation plans had remained constant through the leadership change), but Graham felt that he reached the room in record time.

By the time he'd knocked the door the third time, the door flew open.

"Graham," Mr. Xiong said, rubbing his eyes. It looked like he had been sleeping judging by the t-shirt and shorts that he wore, as if he'd just thrown on the clothing.

"Sorry for the late call, Mr. Xiong," Graham apologized. "Can I come in?"

"Oh... Sure... Sure..."

Mr. Xiong flicked on the lights, revealing a messy room. Clothes were strewn all over, along with a few boxes, and a suitcase. A chair in front of his desk had simply tipped onto the floor, and he'd left it there. That wasn't even mentioning the bottles and cups which were littered about the room, making Mr. Xiong's room appear as if it had been the site of a college party, and not a grown man's living quarters.

"I apologize for the mess," Nathan commented sadly. "I've been trying to motivate myself to clean my room... I have not."

The Laser from Above

"I don't mean to bring this up, but... Will anyone be interrupting this visit? Any guests, anyone else living here?"

"Huh?" Mr. Xiong asked, a little bit alarmed. "No... My family, they were all down on Earth when it happened. I had just reached a temporary two-year contract extension three months ago. Two years, $920,000 total. I was going to visit Earth twice a year, two weeks at a time."

"Wow," Graham managed.

If only this apocalypse had happened ten years later, maybe I'd have struck it rich, he thought.

"Why did you come here, Graham?" Mr. Xiong asked, clearing a spot on the sofa for Graham to sit on.

"I'm sorry," Graham said. "I know it's late, and I won't stay here too long. But I have some questions to ask you."

"What's that?"

"The good boy. That space thing... Tell me everything you know about it."

Mr. Xiong fell silent. He paced around for a little bit before sitting down on the bed and sighing. "I knew you would ask at some point."

"Well, can you tell me?"

"I signed an NDA about this stuff."

"Well, Lusky is gone! I demand as your superior to tell me everything you know."

Graham felt guilty for using such a harsh tone.

"Superior? I thought I was on the council," Mr. Xiong replied, confused.

"I'm speaking on behalf of Skye," Graham blurted out.

Improvise. Adapt. Overcome.

"Oh, I see..." Nathan replied. "Well, if it's coming from her, then I guess I have no choice but to tell you. I don't know a lot about it."

"But you know more than me," Graham said. "Just tell me, please, Nathan."

"Okay, okay," Nathan relented. "Do you know what Ascendant Technologies is?"

"Yes," Graham replied. "They're a giant corporation, right?"

"They're one of the three largest military contractors in the whole world. Or was. You know what I mean."

"What about them?"

"The International Space Hotel, it was one of the subsidiaries, or, they were, you know? Sponsored by Ascendant Technologies. They were the top financier of the project, outside of the United States government."

"Okay..."

"There were other projects that Ascendant helped with. That Lusky and the others in management played an advisory role in. The Space Armament Stations. The first one designed was nicknamed the *Good Boy*. Kinda funny right, like it's a dog... But it wasn't."

"They... They built these things? What even were they?"

"They were weapons," Nathan explained. "Much like in the mid-1900s, when there was a race between the Soviet Union and the United States as they stockpiled on nuclear weapons... It was like that, except now it was mainly China and the United States in a race for space dominance. You've read some news articles; you probably know about the escalating conflict. But these weapons, they were so much more powerful. Unlike nukes they didn't deteriorate over time or leave the same adverse effects of radiation lingering on the world. They harnessed the power of the sun and used nuclear-powered fuel cells to supercharge these giant lasers. They were capable of unleashing great devastation to something as small as a house, or as large as a city."

"So I was right," Graham mumbled. "The schematics that I stumbled across in the engineering facility. They were for a weapon."

"Yes," Nathan replied. "We held them in the engineering facility, and the U.S. always had some researchers and consultants on board here, too. Launching the ISH wouldn't have been possible without their help. Lusky requested me to bring those blueprints to him shortly before the Red Day, I don't know why."

"Okay," Graham replied, "I think I'm starting to finally understand. But what the hell happened that led our country to war? To everything being destroyed?"

"I don't know," Mr. Xiong replied. "Mr. Lusky was confused as you were when the world went to war… The stations weren't supposed to be so close to the Earth. They were launched well into orbit, and yet they went closer near the surface. That's what the news said. Mr. Lusky and management were so confused why they were close. We had no idea, had no communications we could connect through, either."

"Who controlled those things? Who ran them? Was it the United States government as a whole? Or the CEO of Ascendant?"

"I don't know," Mr. Xiong asked. "That information was above my pay grade. I'm sure Lusky and his board knew."

"Yeah," Graham muttered. "That ship has sailed. Thank you, Mr. Xiong. Is that all you remember?"

"I think so," Mr. Xiong replied. "I will tell you if I remember anything else."

Graham nodded, thanking him before walking into the hallway. He slowly lumbered back towards his room. Earlier, he'd felt so much energy he felt like he was projecting rays of sunlight, but now he wasn't in the mood, not anymore. He went to call out to Skye through her door, tell him he was going to bed and was suddenly feeling ill. Then he headed back to his own bed in his own room, alone, his mind moving a million miles a minute.

***

The next day, Graham quickly spilled his guts.

Skye knew something was off by the way that Graham had brushed her off so abruptly. That morning, she knocked on his door, and he opened it up. It only took some prodding and he confessed how he'd remembered something that had rubbed him so wrong, how he'd confronted Nathan Xiong and learned the truth about Ascendant Technologies, and the giant space weapons that had helped spur the unraveling of the entire planet.

"We're so close to learning the truth of what happened," Graham concluded when he had finished telling his rambling account of the last night. "I hardly slept last night. It felt so surreal."

"We're alive," Skye said, patting his shoulder. "This isn't your fault, and it's not mine. It's a tragedy, but you don't need to get so worked up over it."

"I don't know..." Graham hesitated. "I feel like we'll have to document this, you know? It's up to us. Especially if we're one of the last organized groups of survivors in all of Earth."

Skye fell silent once again, reminded of her family and friends back on Earth, her school and home state of Minnesota. The land of 10,000 lakes was likely now the scorched land of 10,000 acid pools.

Despite the pain of the truth impacting Graham, the next couple of days also marked a major step forward in the relationship as they took things to another level. On the other side of the ship, Marcell, who now still visited Skye, Madison, and the others every couple of days, was also developing a blossoming relationship. He had told them he had met someone wonderful. But most of his feelings and processing happened away from his younger friends, alone, with Jordan.

"I told myself, never again," Marcell insisted at one point while he sat on the sofa in his own room, sitting next to Jordan in front of the television. A gaming system had been hooked up into the television, but now had been turned off. Marcell had confiscated the system from the gaming room, and had sat down more than a few times during his free time. But now it sat, idle, the polar opposite of his thoughts.

"Why?" Jordan asked, concerned.

"I was hurt," Marcell admitted. "Not to be dramatic, but it hurt more than this wound on my side."

"Are you afraid?"

Marcell was silent for a few moments.

Of course, I am, he thought, *and yet despite that, I'm more eager than ever.*

"I'm ready to be hurt again," Marcell answered.

Chapter 9

A few days later and the food reserves were stretched so that only three more days remained until they dried up completely, even having cut down to only one meal a day. This included the supplementary plant production from the garden and the meat generation of the lab, both of which offered insufficient calories to sustain anyone at their current numbers. The garden employees had plucked every remaining fruit from their branches, dug up every root, and cut every leaf. Some of the plants would take only a week to replenish, others a month. Either way, it was too long.

A deep hunger had set in throughout the ship, one that now even the most hardcore binge drinker complained about. Skye felt rather weak and tired, as if she was slogging through mud. The night before, she had experienced a great deal of difficulty concentrating during the council meeting, where Dr. Chetana had accused Skye of making the International Space Hotel "a glittering, false mockery", whatever that meant. The council meeting itself had been rather unproductive. There were no viable alternative solutions proposed to the draining resources, and the pressure was mounting. It was looking like within a week's time, that they would probably be forced to do exactly what Lusky and his management had pushed for, remove people off the ship, except they would certainly be much more transparent about the process. Skye had already started to shed weight decently. She could tell that just by feeling and looking at her belly fat, which by now had diminished significantly. She looked quite slim, although not extremely thin, to the extent Skye thought she looked better than she'd ever looked, but she felt like garbage and knew that within a couple of weeks she'd be looking like a breathing skeleton.

Despite Dr. Chetana's recommendations to the whole ship that they conserve energy by avoiding unnecessary exercise, Skye went out on a stroll with Madison. She wore an earpiece now with a direct pipeline to Fritz, Dr. Chetana, and Nathan if any emergency arose. This came in handy as she heard something from Fritz.

"There's something I need you to see, Skye," Fritz said over the line.

"What's going on?" She asked.

"We're within range of a Space Armament Station," he said, and Skye paused her walk, aghast.

"What's up?" Madison asked. "Someone talking to you?"

Skye raised her hand to quiet Madison for a second, and then she spoke again.

"Excuse me?" Skye asked. "Correct me if I'm wrong, but you just said there's a Space Armament Station nearby?"

"Yes," Fritz replied, "Come quickly."

***

Skye walked to the control room at a brisk pace. The Space Armament Station. Through Graham she had learned what they were, and but she was able to see one through the screen of a monitor, which was surrounded by some of the flight crew and emergency personnel, who were now on high alert.

Over a backdrop of space, she could make out the slender shape of a cone, almost like a giant needle, floating slowly in orbit, the beautiful blue ocean of Earth, with wispy strands of cloud, visible underneath it.

"It's breathtaking," Skye observed. "High quality image, right there."

"Why, yes," Fritz agreed. "It's also a security threat."

"Why?"

"Why?" Fritz asked. "This is the closest we've ever gotten to one of these stations. We're on course to almost collide, or be approximately a half mile away from them, in the next hour, if we don't adjust ourselves. They might shoot us before then."

"I've heard about these things," Skye responded, recalling what Graham had explained to her. "Why would they ever shoot us?"

"I don't know," Fritz replied. "For starters, we heard these may have been a primary cause of the mass destruction of the Earth. They're unpredictable."

"I say we broadcast a message to them," Skye replied.

Madison covered her mouth, shocked.

"What?" Fritz asked. By now he was so bewildered, it looked like his eyes were going to pop out of his head.

"You got some *cojones*," Madison whispered from behind her. Madison may not have been invited, but she had followed Skye all the way out of curiosity.

"There's been no signal received from their direction," one of the flight crew explained from over Skye's shoulder. "We don't know whether or not their intentions are positive."

"We're within range, if not in range," Skye reasoned. "They haven't shot at us, or warned us. I would say that they aren't."

"Or, perhaps they are out of energy," another one of the flight crew speculated. "Incapable of harming us, even if they wanted."

"That's true. It has been well over a month since the incident, and they depend on a supply chain of fuel cells being transported via shuttle," Fritz responded. "If they were used during the Red Day, then… There's no way they aren't out of energy. It's desolate."

"If we're not willing to compromise our ship by getting in range, I understand," Skye replied. "I also understand maneuvering the hotel to get away from a crash course. Do it, right now. You don't need me to sign off on that."

"Good," Fritz replied, mumbling something over to the woman standing next to him, who walked out of the room hurriedly. Some of the flight crew positioned themselves throughout the room in front of their various substations, clearly preparing active thrusters to adjust the ISH's course.

"Of course," Skye continued, "I also intend to get into contact with them later. If we have to, we'll send an escape pod to go close."

"No," Fritz replied.

Skye raised her eyebrows, while Madison covered her mouth again.

Who does he think he is? She thought.

"No?" Skye asked. "Excuse me? You appointed me the leader, and now you're defying my order?"

"This is a critical decision," Fritz replied. "It's a decision that could save lives, or kill us all. We need to hold an emergency council meeting, stat. Put our decision to a vote."

"Think of the food," Skye said. "If it has food, it could save us. Our rations are getting low. We can't sit around here."

"Call all able-bodied council members here, right now."

"And what if there's a tie?"

"Then I guess we'll have to go to Marcell. Again."

***

Nathan and Dr. Chetana were both busy, but promised that they would make their way to the front cabin of the ship within the next fifteen minutes. Dr. Chetana was there in a crisp twelve minutes. Mr. Xiong, on the other hand, was far less punctual, failing to arrive until almost a half hour later.

"Apologies for my tardiness," Nathan replied. "Maintenance is time-consuming, and I was helping oversee some maintenance on the Oxygen Center."

"Nothing severe, I hope?" Fritz asked.

"No," He said, nodding. "The Oxygen Center is in fine condition. It just took a couple of bullets during Operation Exodus, that's all."

Skye nodded, remembering back to the night of Operation Exodus and the killings that had ensued. She'd have guessed the strays were from Marcell, although she wasn't going to tell them that.

"Sure," Fritz said, nodding, although Skye had grown so impatient, that she was tapping her foot on the ground, and on the verge of blowing up. Nathan fortunately arrived in the nick of time before Skye seriously considered screaming.

They better support what I have to say, or I'm going to raise a shitstorm. And does Nathan really not care? Skye wondered.

A couple of bystanders, meanwhile, stood watching their impromptu meeting. Among them were the crew members who had apparently first alerted Fritz to the Space Armament Station nearby. There was also Madison, still intently hanging around to see what would happen.

"Should we move the meeting to a more private location?" Dr. Chetana asked, leaning against a support beam as the four huddled together. "We're in earshot of all these people."

At that, a couple of the crew members turned away, although Madison still kept staring at their conversation, smirking.

"What do you think?" Fritz asked.

Fritz seemed to be deferring to Skye, which Skye imagined might've looked weird for the others, considering it was common knowledge that he was the one in charge.

If only they knew, he's the figurehead, the puppet, I'm the ventriloquist.

"I say we stick it here, and hurry up and make a decision what to do with this," Skye answered.

"Of course," Fritz replied.

Fritz explained the situation to Dr. Chetana, although he clearly didn't need to for Nathan, who was asked by Fritz whether he knew about them once he'd finished filling in Dr. Chetana of the situation.

"Yes, I know all about them," Mr. Xiong replied. "I've done my research on them, courtesy of Mr. Lusky."

"Well…" Skye started. "If you're an expert on them, then tell us, which one exactly is it? Is it special?"

"I don't know," Mr. Xiong said, and Skye sighed. "What I mean to say is, there are multiple of them. I need to look at it more closely to identify which one it is."

"Never mind this shit," Fritz mumbled. "That's not what's important. I don't care if it's type 1 or type 2, this isn't diabetes. What is important is that there's a dangerous space weapon that we're headed towards, and I think we're going to be obliterated if we don't get the hell away from it, and ASAP."

"Dangerous space weapon?" Dr. Chetana asked. "Mr. Xiong, will it attack us?"

"We have no idea," Mr. Xiong replied. "Firstly, it depends who's manning the station. These weapons aren't autonomous and don't think on their own. Secondly, it very well could be abandoned. There's no reason to believe that anyone would've stayed on it so long."

"I watched the television, the Red Day," Skye admitted. "They said something about them... Not to mention I think we saw one of them in action in the gazing lobby, on the Red Day."

"So I heard," Mr. Xiong replied.

"The question is, why is this even a question about going there?" Dr. Chetana asked. "There's nothing good that could come could from this. Let's just chart a new course, and stay away from it."

"Seriously?" Skye asked. They all turned to her, waiting for her to speak up. She glared at all of them, shaking her head.

"What? I'm not a mind reader, what is it?" Fritz asked.

"We're running out of food," Skye said. "There's a non-zero chance that there's all sorts of rations on board. Is that not worth checking out?"

"Is that really worth the chance, though?" Nathan asked. "I've seen the carrying capacity for those Space Armament Stations. The largest ones house maybe a dozen or a dozen and a half crew. Even if they had weeks of food stored, and we assume it's been abandoned during this time, that might be only a few days' worth of food for us, tops."

"That's not negligible," Skye said. "Even if it's only a couple days' worth of food, I would say it's worth checking out."

"I wouldn't," Dr. Chetana replied.

"Me neither," Fritz replied.

"Look..." Skye said. "It's not just about the food, even though I think that's something we ought to consider. The Red Day, the Space Armament Stations, it's all connected... I think there might be some key information there, some closure for everyone on board. If we can learn more about what happened that day, then we could get answers. Not only about why this happened, but about when it could be safe to return."

The others fell silent for a short while, considering her proposition.

"You know what they say, about curiosity killing the cat?" Nathan jumped in.

"I believe the saying goes, and satisfaction brought it back," Skye countered, and Fritz snorted.

"We don't have nine lives, Skye," Fritz said.

"I *am* interested," Dr. Chetana interjected. Fritz turned to Dr. Chetana.

"Doc?"

"I think every now and then, about the vaccines that were never developed, the diseases that will never be cured, because of what happened on the Red Day," Dr. Chetana said. "I know it's silly, everyone always thinks about far more personal things like their family and friends. But having that lack of closure, knowing any medical progress is stopped… It's truly horrible. The worst part is, we might never even know what caused it. Not that anything would've ever justified it. I think that if we do as the girl says, then we might get answers. That's worth risking a life for."

"I'm on board, too," Nathan agreed. "Let's check out the station."

"But what if they open fire on us? We need to stop pretending like everyone out there would be our friend," Fritz said. "We haven't prepared for the event that there are hostiles."

"Why would they attack us?" Dr. Chetana asked. "We'll come in peace."

"Don't be naïve. Not everyone would be so friendly, especially a Chinese or Russian military group."

"Then we'll play it safe," Skye said. "First sign of danger, we'll run."

"You say that like it's easy," Fritz said. "It's possible they lure is in, like a trap. What do we do then? Even if it's the U.S. military, they might take no chances with outsiders."

"We prepare," Skye said, "no matter what."

"Glad that's resolved," Dr. Chetana said. "As I said, we have to do this."

"Very well. Fine," Fritz relented, sighing. "We don't have to hold a vote. It's clear where you stand, Skye."

"That's right."

"Now then," Fritz continued, "I suppose it's a matter of finding who-"

"I'll do it," Skye interrupted.

Fritz looked like he'd been slapped across the face.

"What? Why? How?"

"Well, is that possible?" Skye asked.

"Hypothetically, yes," Fritz answered. "Why we would do that, however, I don't know."

"We'll send a pod close to them," Skye replied. "I'll volunteer myself. I can do it. I just need someone qualified to steer the escape pod."

"Skye," Madison said from behind her. "Listen to what you're saying."

"Listen to your friend," Fritz advised.

"Who are you?" Dr. Chetana asked, turning to Madison, but Skye was rambling on.

"I know, Maddie," Skye replied. "But I'm determined to do this. I know we said we don't know which particular station this is. Would we know what crew is running it? Whether they speak English?"

"I don't know," Fritz answered. "We could send someone to look through our archives to confirm which one it is, but that might take some time."

"I can do that," Nathan agreed.

"Great," Skye replied. "In the meantime, do you have anyone who can help fly me up close?"

Fritz shrugged. "I can spare one qualified professional… But that's it. I think I know the perfect woman from the flight crew."

"Okay. Tell her about this, and I'll go with her, then," Skye consented.

"And I will be sure that our medical team is on standby… just in case," Dr. Chetana promised.

"That would be appreciated," Skye said.

"We can't just let you … I mean, they could shoot you," Fritz replied. "Even if their active laser system is down, they might have different turrets, depending on the model. It could be a suicide mission. I believe in the freedom of choice 'til the day I die, but I don't think the council's going to let that slide. Not with you, a council member, in such a dangerous position."

"I volunteer myself," Madison interrupted. Both of them turned to her, Skye's mouth widening.

"Huh…?" Skye asked. "Maddie, what are you saying?"

Don't you do this to me, girl, Skye thought. *Not this time!*

"You want answers for this whole death ray situation, right? I'm your girl," Madison replied.

Fritz nodded with a half-smile. "Now that, I can get on board with. She's not a part of the council, and she's actually volunteering to do this dangerous mission."

"On one condition," Madison added. "You have at least one security guard to protect me."

Fritz shrugged. "Fine. But if something happens, the blood will be on your hands, and not mine."

***

A few of the spots in the archives of the ship had been oddly enough, scrubbed. There was no way to restore the information lost in the database regarding Space Armament Stations, so that the information as to the crew and their nationality, was lost completely. From what conversations Skye had with Fritz, and some of the flight crew, it appeared that the station probably either belonged to the American government, the Chinese government, or Ascendant Technologies. It didn't exactly narrow down the field of options very well.

However, despite their lack of information about this ship, Mr. Xiong was able to identify which station it was. He had hurried over to the nearest computer in the back of the room, sorting through the archives. Dr. Chetana, meanwhile, returned to work in the medical wing. It was around this time that Graham, who had been working repairs in the back of the ship, accompanied Nathan, having completed his tasks in the morning alongside Yusef.

Based upon the curvature, color scheme, and size, Nathan was able to definitively identify the station.

"Station 2," he replied. "I have good news, and bad news."

"Bad news first," Skye replied. "I want the bad news first, always."

"Okay, well, there's one turret on the station. If it activates and hits you, you would probably be punched into little pieces."

"What about the good news?" Graham asked.

Yusef looked at Graham, silently, wondering in what world he thought it was proper to speak up like this.

"The good news is, I would say that it looks powered off," Nathan speculated. "No lights are on. It looks used, which means the turret might not even activate."

"What if we can't get in?" Madison questioned. "We go there, and no one responds. They don't listen to us, or are dead."

"Then you leave," Mr. Xiong suggested. "Better luck next time. Come back to the docking bay, and we'll be ready to welcome you back."

"Is there any way we can bypass any defensive locks they may have? Forcibly enter the ship?" Madison asked. Skye smirked.

"That's exactly what I was wondering," she said. "Great minds think alike."

Mr. Xiong nodded. "Yes. It's possible."

A loud voice began the countdown from the flight crew as they all readied on their stations, a few of the people pressing a couple of buttons. It seemed awfully complicated for such a simple plan, but it was important to sync their direction of orbit with the Space Armament Station. That would make it much easier to travel between the two locations.

"T-minus 10. 9. 8. 7. 6. 5. 4. 3. 2. 1. Proceed!"

Graham straightened his back. He could feel the ship moving as the Hotel's thrusters fired, and the building lurched backwards before smoothing off. For a second, it was so intense that Graham bent his knees down, almost falling backwards. He could imagine people yelling in the hallway, and knew that Skye was probably going to be announcing an apology to the whole ship in ten minutes for what felt like major turbulence, although in the void of space there was no such thing.

"Maddie, what you're proposing sounds like breaking and entering," Graham offered once the movement concluded, and the flight crew stepped away from the controls, high-fiving each other.

"I know what it sounds like," Madison replied. "But I want to do my job, make myself useful. I think discovering the source of what started all of this and maybe getting some crucial information is well worth the risk. Especially after... Well, what I did back you-know-when."

Is that it, then? This is some kind of redemption for her? Skye had numerous reservations about Madison endangering her life on the ship, but she knew that she would not be able to take this away from her. Skye sure was going to do everything to make sure she survived unscathed.

"There are three ways of entry I can think of," Nathan told Madison. "The first way is to simply dock with the ship. They have a clear section on the side of the structure to do so."

"We can do that?" Skye asked. "That sounds easy."

"Yes, but they'll know we're coming," Nathan countered. "The second that the girl opens the door to step in, and there's a good chance she gets shot in the head."

"Yeah..." Madison responded, voice trailing off. "I'd rather not die today. Or tomorrow, for that matter."

"What are the other two options?" Skye asked.

"The second option, blow the whole thing open. I'm assuming that's a no-go," Nathan said.

"That's a no," Skye agreed. "The point is that we want to be able to access it, see if we can find any survivors, any food, anything useful. That defeats the whole purpose. What's the third way?"

"I figured that; it was simply an option. The third way is exploiting a structural weakness. The hatch. We can rip the hatch off. It won't be easy, but it will be possible. It was an oversight that wasn't patched until the third of the four SAS stations."

"Simple as that, huh?" Madison asked. "That might work."

"The cabin will depressurize," Nathan said. "You will have a brief moment of time before the airlock automatically seals. But if you hurry, you should have no problem. At that point, you should be inside. Any obstacles inside, we help you with our perspective on your camera, and you on the line."

Madison nodded. "Thank you."

"Well, I think our plan going forward is clear," Skye offered.

"What's that?" Nathan asked.

"If you are welcomed, then feel free to dock to the ship," Skye told Madison. "If you get no response, or, are given a hostile response, then you rip off the hatch."

"I think, if there's any hostile response, you ought to turn around and leave," Nathan replied. "We're not trying to start a battle."

"Yes," Skye said. "If they tell you to leave, you probably have to."

"Why do we have to rip off the hatch if we get no response?" Madison asked. "Can't we just dock onto it?"

"It doesn't work like that," Nathan explained. "The docking bay is extremely secure. You can't access it unless it opens up for you. If they don't, you can't force yourself through the docking bay. The hatch would become your best bet."

Madison nodded, although she knew anything could happen. There were so many possible outcomes, it made her head spin.

***

Within an hour, Madison was standing in the entrance to one of the airlocks leading to one of the space pods. It had been prepped with the equipment necessary, and right now, the last steps were being finalized from inside the escape pod, where, dressed in a full astronaut outfit, was a woman called Olivia, who would be crucial in the next couple of hours. There also was a man called Sylvester, who was there with the sole purpose of protecting Madison. Fritz had been a little bit grumpy to risk yet another security guard, what with Marcell being out of commission, and Joshua and Audrey having been killed within the last couple of weeks, but in the end gave in to Madison's ultimatum, which had been quickly backed by Skye.

But even though Fritz had followed through with her demand, Madison wasn't exactly happy.

"Oh, it's you," she said, displeased upon meeting the man. "Seriously?"

"What?" Sylvester asked. "What did I do?"

"You restrained me, took me from my bed, and threw me into a holding cell the night Lusky was going to evict everyone from the ship."

"Oh," Sylvester said, nodding. "I see."

Sylvester was tall, dwarfing her by almost a foot, but his chubby cheeks led to an oddly baby-faced yet warm look. Madison was having none of him, however. No matter how kind he may have appeared, she remembered Operation Exodus vividly, and that made her despise him.

"I'm not proud of that," Sylvester admitted. "But seriously, I was just following orders, and I've made peace."

"Yeah, I bet you'd have followed his orders to walk the plank, if he'd told you to," Madison retorted.

The Laser from Above

"Come on," Olivia whined. "Let's put aside our ill feelings for just one day, please. The mission depends on it."

Despite Madison's misgivings with Sylvester, she knew he was right, and soon she'd finished zipping on her astronaut outfit, silent all the while. All Madison had left was to put on her helmet, which she carried by her side and would have Olivia help put on shortly. Sylvester, meanwhile, was already wearing a similar full astronaut outfit.

Madison had used to say that she wanted to be an astronaut when she grew up. Now that she was in a full suit, and about to embark on an expedition which may or may not have been the most dangerous thing she'd ever done in her life, she wasn't so excited anymore. The suit was warm, bulky, and heavy, which, coupled with her recent starvation, Madison figured would make an awful combination in a few hours. Even now, she silently cursed at herself for her bold plan. She knew she was impulsive, but didn't think it would lead her to this position. But now that she was in for it, she wasn't going to let them down.

"You don't have to do this, you know," Skye offered. "Now that I think about it, I actually would recommend you don't do this. You can just swoop by, see if you get any signal."

"Don't worry," Madison replied, even though she herself *did* worry, so much so that she was struggling to maintain her composure. "I have Olivia to watch over me, no matter what happens. And you'll be watching through my head camera and essentially be with me, too."

"Yes," Graham agreed. "The comms should work. Mr. Xiong and Fritz will help. And they timed and angled the thrusters such that our course should follow their course. If bad things happen, we'll save you."

"Thanks, guys."

Madison hugged Graham and Skye. At the exact same time, the door to the escape pod opened, and Olivia stepped out.

"Hey Madison, I think it's time to go."

Madison sighed, muttered a prayer under her breath. "Okay, I'm ready to go."

Chapter 10

Madison hadn't experienced much in her flight up to the International Space Hotel, because, as the vast majority of guests were, she was unconscious for it. Now she would have a little bit of experience of actual flight through space, rather than simply being in orbit. And unlike being stationed on the International Space Hotel, there would be no artificial gravity. Apart from being in a zero-gravity chamber once, Madison had absolutely no experience in that environment.

Now that Madison was taking in this experience for herself, and was awake to tell the story, she was mortified. Unlike Olivia, however, she was not a certified space navigator, nor did she have the confidence of one, because Madison was strapped onto the seat, clinging onto the railing that enclosed the walls. Olivia sat in front of the control panel, buckled up as well while Sylvester, seemingly unfazed by the lurching, was standing, although he too was in a sort of buckle connected to the wall. You had to: with all the motion, you had to be strapped in or you'd faceplant almost instantly.

The ship itself was spacious. Spacious enough to probably house a dozen or so individuals total, if you packed them together like sardines. What the ship had in size, however, it lacked in comfortability: the frame felt rickety, and was constantly shaking, akin to the movement of some sort of old rollercoaster. With each bump, a gun which had been slung over her seemed to oscillate about her back and forth in an irritating manner.

Madison had no idea how to even reload a weapon, but Fritz had strongly recommended coming prepared.

The front window allowed her to gaze to space beyond and the blue world. It was astoundingly beautiful, although it wasn't her source of focus over the brief fifteen-minute flight. As the escape pod approached a dot in the horizon suspended over the Earth, it soon grew larger and larger in the horizon. The whole time, Olivia lectured Madison on some of the dos and don'ts of being out in space, in the event that the ship looked abandoned and they breached the whole station to explore what was inside. Sylvester, meanwhile, was staring through the window at Earth, so engrossed that he may as well have been a dog eagerly awaiting the mailman.

"Did you hear what I was saying?" Olivia stopped to ask at one point.

"Yeah, yeah," Madison managed, although it felt like half of the words were in through one ear and out the other. "There's going to be a wheel on the hatch, use the strong fiber hook, winch, to latch on, since it's almost impossible to do it completely remotely. You'll use the full thrusters to take the door out, and then I'll head inside."

"Exactly," Olivia answered, nodding. "Good. Like ripping a lid off a can."

"I don't know what cans you use, but I've never done that," Madison quipped. "I hope it doesn't come down to doing that."

"I don't know," Olivia admitted. "Also, very important, if, I don't think it'll happen, but if we rip off the hatch, then you'll need to use your thrusters. There are little thrusters on the back of your life support system, that's the backpack thing behind us. It'll help you go down the chute."

"Yes," Nathan agreed.

"Gah!" Madison said, impulsively touching her helmet. "You scared me! I had no idea you were listening in already."

"Apologies," Nathan managed. "As I was saying, it's like in movies, air will shoot out of the station once it's opened. It's due to the pressure differential. Space, of course, is an empty vacuum."

"Right, right," Madison said. "Kind of like osmosis, except not."

"Yes," Olivia agreed. "You have a red and green button on your wrist for that stage."

Madison looked at the red button and green button. They looked the same.

"Yeah, I'm colorblind," Madison said. She could feel the sweat building up on her face, and figured with her clumsiness she was going to mistake them, even though the tint between the colors was slightly different.

"The green one's on the right," Sylvester explained, pointing at her wrist. "Other one, that's red."

"That's right," Olivia agreed. "Right goes forward, the left one reverses."

"Oh geez," Madison replied, shaken. "This is going to go awfully wrong, isn't it?"

"But you have the others communicating to you via earpiece, along with streaming through that camera on your shoulder. They should be able to help guide you if you get a bit confused."

"Don't worry about everyone watching you," Skye explained. "There's just a few of us in the room. It's me, Mr. X, Marcell. And Dr. Chetana."

"Hello, Madison," Dr. Chetana greeted.

"Uh, hi," Madison replied. "I'm glad to hear you're all present."

"Indeed," Olivia agreed, revealing by pointing to her ear, that she, too, was on the line. "We're all on the line, together."

"I see," Madison said. She turned to Sylvester. "You know, I've just been thinking, with all this information... I'm not a professional. Maybe you can have him do it instead, Olivia?"

"Me?" Sylvester asked, turning around. He laughed, but it was clearly a superficial laugh with no sense of humor. "I'm already upset enough that I was pawned off to this potentially deadly task. No, lady, this is your responsibility. My orders were to protect you at all costs. That is the bare minimum, and the bare maximum, I'll be doing. All of this space shit... That's on you."

"Oh, come on," Madison whined. "Is that true? Wait, is Fritz on the line?"

"No," Skye answered. "I'm sorry Maddie, but those were his conditions. He's the one who recruited Olivia and got Sylvester. I think we have to abide by his rules. Everything will work out, though. I have a good feeling."

"You owe me this," she told Sylvester. "After how you treated me."

"Nuh-uh," Sylvester said. "I owe you nothing. I already told you."

Madison mumbled for a couple of seconds, and sighed. Olivia seemed to read her discomfort.

"How does it feel?" Olivia asked. "The helmet, and the earpiece?"

Madison touched the outside of her helmet, praying it was securely fastened on. She was in no mood to become a martyr.

"It feels like I'm in a fishbowl," Madison answered.

"That sounds about right," Olivia chuckled. "You'll get more used to it. It gets better with time. Same thing goes with the nerves, too."

Up ahead, the Space Armament Station was coming into full view. Madison could make out the outline of the ship, and then, within the next minute, the various parts that constituted the whole, the cabin, the barrel, and the antennae that protruded from the side. Reality was truly sinking in now.

"So, let me ask you something," Madison started, "how come an escape pod comes prepared with a winch? It seems strange."

"This isn't an escape pod," Olivia clarified. "This is a work shuttle. It can also double as an escape pod. Same thing, except it's got some extra tools with it. It's usually used for external repairs on the ISH."

"Ah," Madison commented. "I see."

It was closer now, and Olivia started pressing a few buttons and adjusting some sort of slider. Even Sylvester had now taken a seat, apparently anticipating some sort of movement.

"I hope you know what you're doing," Madison remarked, and Olivia shushed Madison, who listened and fell silent as Olivia pressed a button to broadcast a signal.

"Hello, my name is Olivia. I am currently in a work shuttle launched from the International Space Hotel. I come in peace. If anyone is there, then please respond. Over."

A voice buzzed over Madison's headpiece, and it took Madison a second to register that it belonged to Mr. Xiong.

"Look at the ship," he was saying. "There are no external lights. It looks off, inactive. My guess is it's drained of energy. Antigrav chamber's probably off, too."

"There's gravity on board?" Madison asked.

"I doubt it," he replied. "All four models can turn on artificial gravity, but it drains energy."

"Then what about the freezer with all the food? Are we sure that would have remained on, if it's abandoned?"

"You'll have to go and see. As soon as you board safely."

By now they were within striking distance of the ship, and Olivia pulled a couple of levers to slow down the ship to a near standstill.

There was more speaking again, except this time it came from the radio. It was static, and Madison perked up for a few seconds, wondering if they were receiving a message from the station. But after a couple of seconds the voice came through clearly.

"Hi Olivia," Skye said. "I suggest you try again, and then you can go through with the plan. It looks inactive right now, so I think you should be safe to proceed."

"Yes," Olivia agreed, out loud, pressing down the button once again to patch herself over to the station's radio system.

"This is Olivia, once again," she replied. "Again, we mean no harm. We are sending a scout to assess the situation. The lights on the ship are out. Please let us in once we have sent them out. Respond once you have received this message. We can't enter the docking bay without your cooperation, and if you do not respond, then we will have to enter through the hatch. Please unlock the hatch, or otherwise respond to assist in docking. Over."

A couple of more minutes passed in anticipation, as the ship's thrusters stabilized the ship so it hardly drifted away from them. But there was no response, and soon Olivia was radioing back to the ISH.

"Are you sure they are receiving the message?" Olivia asked. "I did everything right, followed my training precisely, and transmitted the signals straight in their direction. But there's complete radio silence."

"I'm not there," Fritz offered. "But I trust you, and that's why I handpicked you for the job. Send the girl in."

"Are you sure?" Olivia asked. "This seems brash. They could just be busy."

"You can wait a few more minutes for a clear conscience. But we sent you to scout out the SAS, dammit, so you're going to have to enter through the hatch if the docking bay doesn't open."

"Okay," Olivia asked. Nothing happened within the span of the next five or so minutes, and she turned around to Madison.

"Looks like it's your time to shine. Remember, I've got your back."

"You got this!" Skye cheered on over her earpiece, but it sounded shrill and forced, Madison swore she could hear Graham sighing.

"Don't do anything brash," Dr. Chetana warned. Madison felt like screaming.

Chapter 11

Madison really wished she had been well versed in space training. She didn't know next to anything, apart from the few details she'd picked up on when planning to leave and listening to Olivia on the flight here.

What Madison did know was that first things first, she needed to be connected to the proper space line. After they had all unbuckled, the work shuttle maintaining a relatively stable position in space, Olivia hooked Madison up to the inside of the ship. This step was perhaps the easiest in the process, for obvious reasons, and was a very fleeting arrangement.

Madison next needed to get onto the ladder that flanked the side of the orbiting station, and hook herself in. When she would complete this step, then the back line would be disconnected, and Madison would be able to scale the distance to the hatch easily. The winch would be launched in her direction (softly, and not straight at her) and she would catch it and connect it to the wheel. This was, of course, on the condition that the door wasn't unlocked already, since they'd notified any potential passengers of their presence and had already asked them to unlock the door.

Then Madison would simply enter in, be welcomed with open arms to the passengers alongside Sylvester, and finally get to the bottom of what the hell had happened on the Red Day. They'd also hopefully learn when, and where, it would be safe to return to Earth.

It would be a clean ride back straight to the ISH, and Madison would never have to do any of this spacewalking business ever again.

Or so, this is what Madison and the others hoped for.

Olivia directed their pod close to the station, so close, in fact, that Madison worried they were going to crash into the metal structure of the ship. All the while, the ship tilted upwards to match the angular momentum of the rotating station. Olivia then adjusted the thrusters to hold their position, spaced out several feet away from the SAS.

"This is close," Madison observed, standing near the doorway, one hand still attached to the railing inside the ship. She felt she had to keep her hand there, even though she knew with a lack of gravity it wasn't the case.

"That's as close as I go," Olivia replied.

"Yeah."

"What are you waiting for?"

"Huh?"

"Just jump out... And land on the ladder. If you miss it, don't worry. You're connected on a line, and I can pull you back."

Madison could feel her heart rate picking up fast. Every single instinct in her body was telling her not to go along with this. Yet she had a duty she also didn't want to shirk.

"Come on," Skye encouraged her, but still, she couldn't move.

Madison turned to Sylvester. Sylvester was sitting now, impatiently, his arms crossed. He was tied to the line, but was positioned behind her.

"You go," she said, but Sylvester shook his head.

"No," he replied. "Look at the way she connected the line. If I go first, you get dragged behind me. You have to lead."

Madison panicked.

"Nuh-uh," she said, shaking her head. "No. I'm not doing it."

Madison couldn't move. She looked down on Earth. It looked like it was a million miles above, making the whatever brownish landscape they orbited over look puny. But assuming that the station was a similar height above Earth as was the International Space Hotel, then they were more likely around three hundred miles above. Not that that did anything to ease her nerves.

"Madison, we need you," Olivia said. Dr. Chetana said something over the line about how this was perfectly medically safe. And Graham said something about how she had come in the clutch with her own brilliance, and that she was following through again.

Madison closed her eyes for a second, deeply exhaled. Her mind was set. Truly, this was one giant leap of faith surpassed by none other. She crossed herself for good measure.

Then Madison sprung up and jumped across a chasm of space.

Chapter 12

Madison was flying for a whole lot longer than she expected. And, unlike her irrational fear, the forces of gravity were not there to pull her down. It was as if Madison was gliding on the clouds, although judging by the look of Earth she was hundreds of miles above them, and then, the metal was right there in her face.

Madison surprised herself by the fact that her hands did actually loop around the metal bar that she reached for, and somehow, she found the grip strength to latch on, rather than bouncing back off the metal. Within only a couple of seconds, she could hear Nathan Xiong congratulating her on her "gymnastic jump," and a whoop from Marcell. She quickly hooked up her line to the nearest hook on the side of the station, turning around to see Sylvester mid-leap, his legs stretched out like he was long jumping. He seemed extremely graceful, and, much like Madison, managed to catch onto the bars during his first attempt, just this time several rungs below her (although with her messed-up sense of direction, Madison really couldn't tell which direction was which).

Madison undid the other line along with Sylvester and turned around to see Olivia standing there, reeling the line in like some sort of fishing line and raising her thumb up from the doorway.

"Good job," Skye congratulated her. "Great job."

Madison snuck a peek back down on Earth, and realized that she was dizzy; the ship was slowly twisting around, and that was messing with her head. She decided to not look around, lest she somehow stare into the raging sun and go blind on the spot (she always was scared of that), but instead she put one hand above each other, rung by rung, clamoring up. To calm her nerves, she pretended that this ladder was one of the mere ladders she scaled in her childhood on the playground, except even safer, because unlike back then she had a rope that would prevent her from falling in the event that she somehow slipped off.

Before, Madison had heard about how it was silent in space. Whenever no one else spoke, the only thing she could hear was her own breathing and pounding heart. It was an extremely surreal experience. But it was also oddly empowering. She thought that maybe if shit hadn't hit the fan, maybe her childhood goal of being an astronaut wasn't so horrible after all. Because between the glistening stars in the distance, and the Earth from space… There was nothing else she'd ever seen as beautiful as that. Where she had been extremely anxious when she started climbing the length of the thirty or so rungs of ladders, by the time she reached the top, she was more awestruck than anything, although the spinning of the station did still throw her for a loop a little bit.

"Well done, well done," Olivia lauded them. "You're on the top."

Madison looked to see that Sylvester was right beside her once she had reached the peak of the ladder. The only difference was that he now clung to the right side of the ladder, and she nudged over to the left. The hatch was right in front of them. It was a circular hatch with a giant twistable wheel, like a bigger version of the faucet handles used back on the hose at her house.

Madison looked at Sylvester. Of course, she couldn't see any of his features. Much like her helmet, his astronaut helmet had been tinted to minimize the effects of any excessive solar radiation. Of course, Madison didn't know that fact, but Sylvester could tell she was staring at him, and his next words seemed thick with annoyance.

"What are you looking at?" Sylvester asked. "Try the door."

Madison hoped her grumbles were quiet enough to not be heard over the line, as she positioned herself so that her feet were firmly on one of the top rungs of the ladder. Then she turned the wheel to the right as hard as she could, but it didn't move at all.

"Lefty loosey," she stated aloud, before trying it the other direction, pulling with all of her strength and loudly grunting over the communications line. This time, the results were identical.

"No luck?" Olivia asked from inside the spacecraft.

"No," Madison stated matter-of-factly. "I can't catch a break."

"Move aside, weaksauce," Sylvester commanded. "Let me handle it."

Madison was reluctant, but stepped out of his way, adjusting the sling with the gun which had been almost wrapping itself around her neck before hanging down on the bars and looking up.

She could hear Sylvester straining himself as much as he could over the line. Yet the wheel, much like when Madison had tried, didn't budge one bit.

"Dammit. It's stuck completely. There's no way we're getting through like with our brute strength."

"Told you," Madison mouthed, but didn't say aloud.

"All right," Olivia said. "Heads up for the winch. I'm sending it your way."

Madison turned around as a rope extended forwards in their direction, shooting a couple of feet above her head. Madison climbed up a couple of rungs, catching the winch and hooking it around the wheel. Sylvester put his hands on the wheel, tugging at the winch to make sure it was attached. It was clear that he didn't trust Madison's quality of work, but Olivia sounded impressed.

"Good work," Olivia said. "I'll pull back now and remove the hatch. Looks- *oh shit*! Get down!"

The next few seconds were a blur for Madison, startled by whatever commotion was happening. Sylvester yelled for Madison to get down, and started climbing down the ladder, rung by rung, as fast as he could. In the process, whether intentionally or not, Sylvester's leg kicked at Madison from above, sending her flying downwards relative to the ladder, plummeting down towards the Earth. Madison felt like she was in freefall, screaming, and her earpiece was flooded with the desperate and confused cries of Skye and the others back in the International Space Hotel, so loud she thought her eardrums were going to bleed.

Despite her flight downwards, she looked up to see Sylvester, who seemed to have strategically kicked Madison, the rope now dragging him down with her, although at a slower velocity now.

Then, off to the side slightly, Madison saw the source of the commotion, what Olivia had spotted on the Space Armament Station, and felt her body wince, like she wanted to retreat into her suit, but couldn't.

A turret had popped out of the side of the ship, angled off in their direction; two barrels pointed straight out at them. Although she couldn't exactly gauge the size of the turret, she would've guessed the barrels were at least a couple of feet long, and likely shot projectiles that would eviscerate her on contact.

There was no sound in space. What there was, however, was sight, and Madison yanked herself to the left to use the body of the station itself to shield her from fire. The turret's placement looked like they were just almost out of range, but it would be close. The most ominous thing of it all was the silence apart from the cries of everyone panicking over her earpiece.

There was light flashing from the barrels; the surrounding area was still silent. There were sparks flying off the side of the ship, and it was still silent. As Madison neared the bottom of the ladder, she desperately reached forward towards the rungs, hooking her hands around one of the bars only several from the bottom and managing to snag herself on it. As she did, her body slammed into the metal structure of the ship, so hard that she was worried her helmet would crack.

She looked up, saw Sylvester on the line still flying down towards her, and then she was screaming, as his body, contorted in agony, haphazardly flew away from the ladder and towards the open space away from the structure of the SAS. Unlike Madison, he had been unable to grab onto the ladder in time.

"Ugh! I'm hit!"

Indeed, Sylvester was drifting into the line of fire of the turret and away from the safety of cover: Madison could see him clutching what appeared to be his right hand, almost completely sheared off apart from the lower portion, which was practically a stump. A few droplets had been propelled out into space, freezing into red crystals, and it looked like a jagged, red icicle slowly extended around his wound as Madison watched, choking up. The space was so cold that it was freezing his open wound instantly, and she knew in that moment, that no matter what she tried, he was a goner.

"Ow! Ow God! Pull me Madison! Pull-"

Madison grabbed the rope, pulled him towards her with her one right hand, since her left hand was still fastened around a ladder rung, and yanked with all of her strength.

Madison reeled him towards her as fast as he could, which was much slower than for her liking, and Sylvester reached his one single functional arm towards Madison, ready for her to grab his hand. Madison was only a couple of seconds away from getting him to the ladder, but in that moment, a couple more shots from the turret's direction must have connected, shredding the line between them.

Another shot somehow must have grazed Sylvester, because his helmet shattered like a fractured lightbulb. Madison was helpless as his body catapulted through the void of space, down towards Earth and away from her. Madison only had a couple of seconds to see his helmet, and his face, ravaged by shrapnel and resembling an uncooked, smushed meatball, which quickly froze into a solid crystallized blue.

Then he was gone, too far away to be nothing more than a faint shrinking dot falling towards the Earth.

"Firing! Firing now!" Olivia screamed.

Madison barely managed to get her other hand on the ladder before looking up around to see a missile connect with the turret and erupt into an explosion of flame that was quickly quenched by the vacuum of space. The force was so strong that the station was knocked off course of its orbit, lurching strongly, and Madison was thrown off the ladder itself despite having two hands locked hard around a rung. This was where the line to the station had saved her life. Sylvester had been behind her; if it had been the other way around, then she wouldn't have still been connected to the station. Nothing would have stopped her from being thrust into space and flying off to burn up in Earth's atmosphere. The line stopped her with a jerk, and Madison grunted in pain.

"Madison! Madison! Are you okay!? Madison!? Tell me!" The scream from Skye sounded like a half-sob.

"I'm okay!" She called back over the line, gasping for breath. "I'm okay! I'm okay! But Sylvester's dead!"

The shouts of surprise made it clear that amidst Madison's spinning and falling, they hadn't seen Sylvester's tragic end. They were luckier than her.

Madison could hear something about Marcell moaning how Fritz was going to kill them. And then there was Olivia.

"The turret is out of commission!" Olivia was saying. "The station is heavily damaged: but the hatch is coming loose!"

For the time being, Madison was like someone on one of the zipline parks who had lost momentum and was stuck on the line. Fortunately for her, she had her trump card in the form of the thrusters.

Madison slammed the right button, and her thrusters launched her forward to the ladder. She began scaling the rungs, detaching her rope from the connector on the station.

I didn't mess up the thruster button! I didn't! Madison was celebrating internally for almost a second, until the image of Sylvester flying away in space wiped any minor semblance of joy she might have felt otherwise.

"I don't know why you have a missile," Madison told Olivia, as she clamored up rung by rung. "But I'm grateful."

"Yeah," Nathan said over the line, his voice shaking. "Our work shuttles were all designed with the help of Ascendant Technologies. That included developing weapons to protect the International Space Hotel in the event of a f-foreign takeover."

"Fascinating," Madison sputtered, but she was hardly focusing, now trying her best to assure herself that Sylvester's death wasn't her fault. *Sylvester just died, and this man's lecturing me about equipment?*

The entire time she scaled the ladder, Madison was rapidly breathing, so much so that she was worried she was somehow going to run out of oxygen, but there were more pressing concerns, such as Olivia screaming for her to stop in place. Madison looked up, noticed that only several rungs above was the hatch, and then it was gone, ripped off, and she looked back and saw Olivia in the work shuttle, the hatch flying off with the winch.

Madison knew she had little time to act. She crawled on the top, and then leaned into the hole. There was a ladder leading down to what looked like the plain gray floor, likely of the airlock area, but air was being sucked out of the ship, so much so that even trying to pull herself down the ladder, she could hardly progress. She remembered her thrusters and pressed the buttons again, and then she felt truly like was flying, flying headfirst down into the ship.

There was a significant issue, however. Madison had received a lot of information about the ship itself, but she hadn't ever seen the layout for the ship, and neither had she anticipated that there had been an antigrav on board. This meant she was plunging headfirst towards the floor, and a fall could be disastrous.

***

Despite her thrusters no longer firing, Madison could feel gravity pulling her down fast, and she reached forward for the rungs of the ladder. Nathan was wrong. The antigrav chamber, somehow, must have been on.

Madison flipped head over heels a few feet, but managed to right herself enough that her arms reached out and caught a bar, and even though she couldn't secure her grip, it slowed her descent enough that she caught the next couple of bars down. She had to conceal a scream, as there was a pop on her shoulder and pain radiating throughout it once she latched on. Her assault rifle, meanwhile, which had been over her chest in a sling, had simply fallen off towards the ground, and as she stopped on the rungs, she could hear the sound of a nearby shout tinged with a British accent and approaching footsteps.

"Die, you bastard! *Ahhhh!*"

Madison didn't know how what happened next, but she looked down to see her machine gun slamming into the ground, abruptly firing in a chaotic semi-circle on the ground. There was the sound of a scream, and a gun clattering to the floor. Then, nothing but a low groan.

"Madison! What's going on!?" Skye asked, and Madison dropped to the floor with a thud.

Madison tried to land gracefully, but she ended up collapsing on the floor, her head spinning as she looked up and saw a man in a blue uniform, his back up against the wall, clutching his right knee. Blood was running down his shins, and his face was scrunched in pain. In the meantime, she could hear a hatch close from the chute she'd leapt down, sealing off, and Madison knew she had just scraped by the airlock in time, before it had automatically sealed.

"Don't kill me! Don't kill me!" The bleeding man pleaded.

The man was crawling on the ground, towards something in the middle of the room. Her vision adjusted, and she saw the metal object that appeared equidistant from both of them. It was a black pistol that the man in the airlock had evidently been carrying, positioned far closer to him than the machine gun was.

Madison was scrambling, reaching the gun only a second before the other man did and kicking the gun way out to the side and out of reach of either of them. The man slunk to the ground in defeat, clasping his hands together in supplication.

"Please don't kill me! Please!"

Madison removed her helmet, and the man's jaw dropped, his face turning from panic into confusion.

"Huh?"

"What are you doing?" Skye and Marcell were asking. In the background, it sounded like Fritz had barged onto the scene and was in a screaming match over his dead team member.

Madison was too annoyed to bother with them. Madison went to reach up and hit the mute button with her left hand, but then her arm cramped up and spasmed in pain. She used her right hand to mute it instead.

In the meantime, Madison was wincing in pain. She could feel her left shoulder swelling, and knew she'd need Dr. Chetana to reset her shoulder afterwards. She could do it herself, but that could end badly. But somehow, she'd made it here. Only now did it start to sink in the severity of the situation, and how Sylvester had died in space.

"What am I doing here?" Madison asked, confused. "Didn't you hear the broadcast...? We're with the International Space Hotel. I'm a scout who was looking for survivors. Why the *fuck* would I kill you?"

"Huh?" The man asked. "I... You really aren't going to kill me?"

"Relax," She touched her shoulder. "My shoulder's fucked. Your knee is hurt. Maybe we can help each other out."

"Oh God," he said. "I don't know how I can help you."

"Is there anyone else with you?" Madison asked.

"What?" He asked. He looked around for a little bit. "Why?"

"I don't know, I want to know whether or not anyone's going to be running in with guns blazing and kill me."

"No," he said, his face falling before lighting up again. "You would know, if you were with *them*."

"Why?"

"Because… Because they killed us. Slaughtered almost everyone aboard this station."

Chapter 13

A couple of minutes later, Madison had taken the injured man up into the main quarters of the station, where he now sat down on a sofa that was nailed to the ground. The process had been onerous, since the man couldn't so much as walk on his injured knee, so he had bunny-hopped with only one leg, with Madison almost having to lift him up onto the couch.

Only in the last minute did she unmute her earpiece, and talk to Skye and the others. She told Olivia that she was okay for now, and Olivia said she had a few hours until they had to go, lest the work shuttle run out of energy, so she was patrolling in the vicinity. On the way, Madison and the man had stopped by the control panel, which had been marked by various red warning signals lit up all over the board. Madison had also caught a glimpse of the layout on a piece of paper on the control panel: there were five rather spacious rooms inside on one floor, making the internal section of the Space Armament Station as big as a large house back on Earth.

"Are you sure the station is okay?" Madison asked the man once again.

"The condition is stable," the man said, wincing in pain. "The hatch, ruined, since you took it off. The turret is destroyed. The ship is damaged, but it shouldn't be at risk of falling apart, at least in in the short term."

Madison nodded, and then she was silent. In her earpiece, Fritz was directing her to chide him for shooting at him. She wasn't about to listen to everything he was saying, but he did have some points.

"You killed the man with me," Madison said, shaking her head. "You activated the turret."

"I'm sorry," the man apologized. He looked up at her, and his gaze showed genuine regret. "I… I had to. The way they treated us last time, I wasn't going to bloody let that happen to me."

"You just said "they"? Who are you talking about?"

"It's a long story," the man said.

"I guess we should introduce ourselves, then," Madison said. "My name is Maddie. I'm a survivor from the International Space Hotel."

"Could you please get me some painkillers? I'm in some serious pain, and I think I'm going to need them." His face was scrunched in pain, and he was sweating bullets, so Madison definitely believed him.

Madison stood there for a few seconds. Something about the request made her nervous, even though it was completely understandable.

"Okay," she said, now holding her gun in her hands. "I'm just being cautious, okay?"

The man managed a nod.

A couple of minutes later she had returned, with her machine gun slung around her chest once again and the pistol hidden away. The man had directed her to a nearby cabinet in the room over in the bathroom, and she soon quickly returned. She also found some stitches, a needle, bandages, and hydrogen peroxide, all of which she brought over as well.

"Thank you," the man said as he popped a few pills in his mouth. He looked at the other supplies she set on a nearby table and turned to her with a confused expression.

"Are you...? Going to...?"

"Yes," Madison replied. "I can perform a little surgery. Although I need a knife or something to dig out the bullet first, I'd reckon."

"I can help," Dr. Chetana said over the line.

"Relax, relax," Madison responded. "I've done this before."

"You're on the line with someone?" the man asked.

"Yes, sure am," Madison said. She stood up, walked across the room, and spoke quietly over the line.

"You've done this before?" Skye asked, confused. "How? When?"

"Yeah, you never told us that," Graham replied. Madison frowned. Graham must've somehow butted in on the line, even though he had no part of the council of leadership. Judging by his absence to this point, he seemed to have been spared the chaos of the turret and Sylvester's demise.

Madison huffed. "Long story short, my boyfriend, Fuego, once was in a drug deal gone wrong. He got shot in the arm. He didn't have insurance so he asked for me to help dig it out while he got high. I did so, and it left nothing but a scar. And funny enough, that's how I really got into medicine when I was sixteen."

"My gosh," Graham sputtered. "That's hardcore. I mean, *Maddie*..."

"Where is this bullet?" Dr. Chetana asked. "Removing it depends on so many factors."

"It's in his knee area," she said, before turning around. "Look, I'm going to help him, but first I'm going to get some information out of him."

"Good," Fritz replied. "This better be worth it. I want you to get as much information about Ascendant and whoever the hell he was talking about as possible. If we're down another man then this better have been worth it."

"We're going to have to recruit some more security members to maintain order," Skye told Fritz from the other side of the line. "Tap into the pool of able-bodied men on board."

"Oh yeah," Madison added. "Please mute your side of the line unless you have something important to tell me. Not to sound bitchy, but it was really loud. I thought your screams were the last thing I was going to hear, which is not what I would ever want."

The line went mute on the other side of the earpiece, and Madison headed over to sit near the man.

"All right, I'm back," she said.

"Okay," he said. "Am I going to bleed out? I'm worried about my knee."

"You're fine," Madison replied. "I'm… I'm trained. I'll be able to help you, but first I have some questions I need to ask. I promise I'll try to be as quick as I can."

"Are you a doctor?" he asked. "You look so young, though."

"Yeah, I'm twenty-one," she replied. "I was pre-med, an intern at the ISH. About to go into my final year of undergrad."

"I guess that's as good as I can ask," the man said. "My name is Cole Caldwell. I was a technician on this station, and an employee of Ascendant Technologies…"

"There were more of you?"

"Yes. There were seven of us." He pointed over to the corner of the room. "You can find some traces of them over there."

Madison strained her eyes and saw what he was talking about. It was a deep red stain in the corner of the room.

"It's a bloodstain," she said.

"Yes," Cole agreed. "I tried scrubbing them out all over. But what was the point? There was so much blood, liters and liters of it."

"Who did that?"

"I don't know, but they were wearing camouflage. Dark camouflage, you know, a full get-up. They got on board under a false pretense. They pretended to be from Ascendant and on a supply run, so I just couldn't trust you. It's not personal."

"That sounds like an army," Fritz interrupted from over the line. "Ask him if it was the army."

"Was it an army?" Madison asked.

"Maybe," Cole replied, wincing the entire time. "My mind was jumbled, for what it's worth. I didn't really hear them, or see them. All I got were a couple of glimpses of skin, they were pretty armored up. I'm pretty sure their skin color was white, at least the person I saw, not that that narrows many countries down. I got away, ran to a hiding spot. I almost died. They killed everyone else on board."

"How? Why?"

"I don't know," Cole replied.

"There's got to be more you know."

"Well, of course. I go to my hiding space amidst some of the electrical wires. I'm terrified for my own life. And then the entire station shakes. I can hear the entire thing shaking, and the laser being activated. I don't know why, so I cower there for a full day until they leave."

"The Red Day," Madison replied.

"The Red Day, huh?" he asked. "I haven't heard that phrase before. Of course, this is the first conversation I've had in over a month… How is Earth? Is it safe to go down?"

"It's… It's not good," Madison replied. "Tons of nuclear fallout. But there are survivors. We were advised to wait a month or two after it happened. But going back to your story, what happened after this?"

"Well eventually, the next day or so, they left," Cole replied. "I was dehydrated, starving, had pissed my knickers. I looked around and found their bodies. All dead… All dead…"

Cole put his face in his hands. "I was left alone the past month. I was too scared to leave, even though I have a pod I could go down to Earth with. I was too scared to trust anyone. It's been awful. Awful. I powered down most of our systems so any passerby would assume that the ship was dead. Just left the anti-grav on to preserve my sanity."

"Ask him about the food," Fritz said.

"I'm sorry to ask, but…" Madison hesitated.

"What?"

"Do you have any excess food, supplies? Things are starting to get desperate on the International Space Hotel."

"I have a little bit of food. Might be several dozen meals total or so. I don't know. I haven't been eating a lot, I've been skipping some meals out of guilt. I can't sacrifice it though, unless you admit me on board wherever you're from."

"Dammit!" Fritz roared over the line. "Sylvester, for several dozen meals!?"

"Okay. That's fair," Madison responded to Cole. "I guess we will see about that, I'm not sure though."

Madison looked around the room, back to the bloodstain.

"What did you do with the bodies, anyway?"

"I launched them through the garbage chute," Cole said. "What else was I supposed to do? I couldn't remain with them on board, I would've lost my sanity."

Madison nodded. She felt bad for the man, wanted to say something comforting, but was left tongue-tied.

"Ask about Ascendant," Nathan said over the line.

"You worked with Ascendant Technologies, you said, right?"

"What?" Cole asked. "Yes, why?"

"Do you know anything more about that, and what happened?"

"No," Cole replied. "I know about the global tensions a bit. Conflict over ownership of the stations. You see, our ships, they're all staffed with different employees. The Chinese, Russians, Americans, all had their own. And then there's Europe, and we were the ones residing on this one. Station 2."

"I see," Madison replied. "Well, Ascendant Technologies is an American company, right?"

"Yes," Cole answered.

"So, were there any conversations you had with the government? Or with the company in the days leading up to them attacking this ship?"

"I'm a technician," Cole replied. "I also was the newest member of the team, and was only here for a few weeks before it happened. If there was anything deep happening, my captain would've known. Torild Kristiansen was her name. But I didn't hear anything personally. There were conversations on board leading to the day. People stressing out over whether everyone will nuke each other or somehow use one of the Space Armament

Stations to do damage. We never believed it would happen… We were wrong."

"Is there any documentation for this?" Madison asked.

Cole managed a smile, pointed straight at the table in front of them, which, much like the sofa, also was nailed to the table.

"With only free time in my hands, I've looked through our records to find something. Anything. To make their deaths clear," he said, choking up a little bit. "To make their deaths meaningful. But I've found nothing. It's a bloody waste."

Madison dug through the records, flipping through the pages.

"I'll bring these papers back to the ISH," she told Cole. She was about to set the stack down before something caught her eye. She pulled out the paper, stopped, and read through it.

It was some sort of contract for a work order on board the ship. Scanning through provided details about the defense system in the turret, how they were planning on reinforcing the hull of Station 2 and putting in a repair order on the "electrostatic chamber", whatever that meant. It was from about ten months ago, but it was one of the printed signatures that caught Madison's attention.

"Amelia Melero," she read off the contract. "She was the head of the SAS program, it says."

"Yes," Cole said. "She visited all of the stations; I think. The sister of one of the top members of the American Congress, if I remember correctly."

"No," Madison corrected him, "Bruno Melero is now the President of the United States. Or whatever is left of it."

***

Even though Madison was now safely aboard the Space Armament Station 2, Skye had a new task to do, now that the plan had resulted in a fatality.

She was extremely relieved that Madison was okay. In the event that something worse had happened, worse than Madison getting minorly injured as it seemed she had, then Skye would've been devastated. She never would've forgiven herself. She might've given up right and then, ejected herself through the garbage chute into the vacuum of space.

Tragically, a man had died. But the plan had worked, and it seemed that they were on the cusp of learning some crucial information. It may have been a shame that there had been a death, but if anyone had to go, then it was Sylvester. She was a leader, after all, and Madison, her best friend, which meant that she was a priority. Sylvester's life, as cruel as it sounded, was expendable. Skye hoped he was in a better place now, although she didn't quite believe in the afterlife.

Fritz is never going to let me hear the end of this, Skye thought, *but learning what we've learned, securing those supplies and the station, might make it worth it.*

Skye stepped up to log the death. By now, she'd mastered this routine, and felt like she was so comfortable with it that she could do it in her sleep. That was a slightly terrifying realization.

"Sylvester Barker. Date of Birth, November 4th, 2012. Time of death, July 22nd, 2048, 3:32 p.m. UST. Place of death, space. Cause of death, gunshot wound."

***

Despite Dr. Chetana warning Madison that, with her dislocated shoulder, there was no way she should be treating Cole, and that she should wait, transport him back to the ISH first, she did so.

It wasn't an easy process, especially considering that, despite the presence of painkillers coursing through his veins, Cole was antsy. The first thing she had to do was find the location of the bullet. That was easy enough. The bullet was clearly visible underneath the skin near his own knee.

"Looks like a ricochet," Madison replied. "It hardly broke the surface. You're lucky."

"That's right," Dr. Chetana said over the line. "I'm impressed."

"Are you sure?" Cole asked. "Is that a good thing?"

"Yes and yes," Madison answered. "The good news is, since I know where it is, then I think I can dig it out. And it looks like it's a bit below your knee, so I don't think it lodged in any bone."

"Are you sure it didn't hit an artery?"

"The femoral artery is a little bit higher, above the knee," Madison replied. "If it had hit your artery, you'd probably already be dead. Looks like it missed any veins or nerves. I think I can dig it out."

"Thank God," he mumbled, and nodded. "Okay. I'm ready."

"Stay still," Madison commanded him. Dr. Chetana directed her during the whole time, although her words were not particularly necessary. Before she knew it, she was digging into the man's leg, who was screaming, kicking her off of him.

"Stay down!" Madison screamed, and while the man tried his best to stay still, he pounded his arms down on the sofa, which naturally shook his lower body, and to a lesser extent, the cushions they were on as well.

Within a minute the bullet clattered onto the ground, and with it, there was a collective sigh of relief from her, Cole, and a couple of other people over the line; then Madison sutured the wound, which was a surprisingly smooth procedure but took a few minutes longer. Madison figured that the painkillers had been kicking in to a greater extent. Finally, she poured on hydrogen peroxide. At this stage, Cole flailed around wildly, screaming, knocking the bottle over and spilling it all over the ground. The deed had been done, however, and Madison couldn't care less.

"Oh God, it's fizzling!" He yelled, tears running down his face. "My leg is melting! Fuck it hurts!"

Madison had held up her end of the bargain. She took up the contracts, telling Olivia how she was ready to go. Somehow, she felt the mission had been a success, although remembering back what had happened to Sylvester put her back into a more somber mood.

"Ummm…. One other thing," Cole said. "Can I go back with you? Like I said, you can have the food if you let me join you."

Madison told Cole she'd ask them, and she did. Discourse, soon breaking out into an argument, followed over Madison's earpiece. Fritz didn't want this, but Skye did. As the argument continued, Madison stepped away from Cole telling him she'd get back to him.

"I say we bring him in," Skye jumped in.

"He *killed* Sylvester!" Fritz fired back. "The only thing we should be bringing in, is his food."

"I know," Skye replied. "I never said we let our guard down… As a matter of fact, I think we don't. I have a plan. I think we can make it work."

"And how's that?" Mr. Xiong asked.

"We lure them in," Skye replied. "Maybe we can find the people responsible for killing the Ascendant Technologies employees on deck."

Chapter 14

One day later, Graham was working on the escape pods and preparing in advance for the potential danger waiting ahead.

Systems Check Complete, the A.I. voice over the escape pod comms system announced. *No Issues Detected.*

"Is it good?" Yusef asked from outside the ship. Graham stepped out through the airlock doorway and back inside the hallway.

"Yes," he replied. "Escape Pod 26 is functional, no issues detected."

Yusef carried a clipboard, and etched down notes on it, nodding.

"Just a few more, and then we're done," Yusef said, yawning. "Finally."

"Good," Graham responded. "I know I've done enough of this for my life, and I'm sick of it."

"We have to help, somehow," Yusef offered, as the pair continued down the hallway.

On the way to the next one, however, he saw Fritz emerge from an adjacent hallway. He stepped closer, and saw Marcell, still using his cane, but limping oddly quickly, following behind Fritz.

"Come on," Marcell was saying. He appeared agitated.

"It's not up to me," Fritz said. "We have to take whatever we can get at this point. It's not my fault that everyone's gotten killed off. Soon enough we're going to end up with a higher casualty rate than the Minnesota's 1st Infantry Regiment. You think I'm proud of this? But this is what happens. I trusted you so much I didn't even look at the camera footage from that night. I ask that you trust me on this, and chill out."

"Not him," Marcell begged. "Anyone on board, but not Jordan."

"He's at the firing range," Fritz replied. "With ten others. All of them are perfectly capable of choosing what's best for themselves. They're adults, goddammit."

"Just... find a way," Marcell pleaded. "Make him protect Skye or something, I don't care. I don't want him to get hurt."

Fritz huffed, and he didn't say anything. He then noticed Graham tailing them, and he turned around.

"What do you want, kid?" Fritz barked. "I'm busy."

"I was just wondering whether or not you've received any updates about what's going on."

"No," Marcell said, turning to him with a miserable expression. "No updates on whether we've received any word. All I know is that my boyfriend is being enlisted for active defense duty on the ship, and I'm pissed."

"The distress signal from the Space Armament Station was activated one hour ago," Fritz replied. "I think it might take longer than that, if they even show up again at all."

"And Maddie?"

"Madison and the others are there," Fritz replied. "A couple work shuttles are cycling out every couple of hours to protect them, just in case. Now if you don't mind, I've got to get back to the firing range."

The Laser from Above

Graham thanked him, turned around, and he could hear Marcell's whining slowly fade away as he walked back. Yusef was standing back where he'd left him, arms folded.

"Sorry about that," Graham apologized. "Just had to ask for some updates on the current situation."

"You have some balls," Yusef said, and Graham looked confused.

"Huh?"

"That was Fritz, right? Fritz Nussbaum? The guy in charge of the ship?"

That's right, Graham thought. *This guy doesn't even know who's really running the show.*

"Yes, I know," Graham replied. "We've met on more than one occasion."

"That's insane," Yusef commented. "How?"

"I don't know," Graham said, shrugging. "I knew the right people at the right time. I have my connections."

"Ugh," Yusef replied. It was clear by Yusef's frustration that the jealousy was palpable, and Graham had to conceal a smile. He never could've said back at home that he knew people, so at least he could appreciate that one aspect of his life. "The only way I knew how to connect with people was on LinkedIn."

***

Convincing everyone to get on board with her plan with the SAS had been easier than Skye had expected.

For starters, now they knew about the fate of the ship, and who had attacked the SAS. That, of course, brought serious questions, questions as to whether the soldiers who had breached the station would come for the ISH if the signal was activated.

But Fritz had promised his security forces had been ready: and besides, their docking stations would be locked until further notice, meaning there was no way that anyone could easily board the ship. Nathan seemed to go along with him, confident that triggering the distress signal would bring in the help of the U.S. Space Force, who would certainly assist the ISH.

Dr. Chetana had actually disagreed vehemently with the plan.

"We don't know," she had said. "Who's responsible for this whole mess on Earth. I don't want some space pirates raiding us."

"This isn't Star Wars," Skye retorted. "There's no such thing."

"You overestimate how kindly anyone would take to meeting us. I don't care, even if it's the U.S. government that comes, I don't trust them."

But a majority was a majority, and Marcell, who was consulted according to Dr. Chetana's insistence (although the three of them voting in support of the plan constituted a majority no matter what), ended up abstaining from voting either way, letting them sort the voting amongst themselves. And so, it was settled, Skye presiding over the plan now.

Skye was in the front control room, along with many of the flight crew, when she first got the news that they had spotted another ship.

"Look! Something's showed up on our radar!"

Skye rushed over to the man who'd yelled the news, as a crowd of the flight crew gathered to assess the validity of the claim. Nathan was supervising the preparation of all of the escape pods and an evacuation plan, Fritz was helping training recruits, and Dr. Chetana was who-knows-where. That meant that Skye was in complete charge, and by now everyone recognized that she was on the council, although next to no one outside the council and a select few knew that she actually ran it, and not Fritz.

Skye first called the other council members over her earpiece, saying they'd spotted a ship. Soon enough, the flight crew used their telescope function to bring the ship into sight. It looked like a small scouting ship, some of the flight crew said, and Skye reiterated that to the other council members. It looked like their strategic effort to bait someone into exploring the signals and drawing close to the SAS, while being in sight of the ISH's radio range, had paid off.

"Yeah," Skye said over the line. "Looks like a scouting ship. I don't know where it's from or anything, but it's here all right. I can look at it on our monitor."

"On my way," Dr. Chetana replied.

"Me too," Mr. Xiong added, although Fritz and Marcell explained that they were still busy.

"I hope you're right about this," Fritz managed. "I know I voted for this, but it was out of necessity. This could go very wrong, too."

"Don't worry, Fritz," Skye replied. "We've gone over this. We're pleading ignorance of anything to do with the distress signal on the SAS, and there's only one of us on board there. Maddie is smart. She'll remain hidden, as will Cole Caldwell."

"Got it. It's just..." There was a faint crackling of static before the audio of Fritz's breaths returned, indicating that he was hesitating.

"What?" Skye asked, annoyed.

"Nothing, but..."

"Spit it out."

"You seem awful willing to put Madison in the line of danger."

"How *dare* you," Skye replied. "This is my best friend we're talking about. She knew the risks when she volunteered for this mission. Don't you *ever* question my care for her."

With that, Skye signed off, Fritz muttering some sort of half-hearted apology.

Skye turned her attention back to those around her.

"I need you to send out a message to them," Skye directed the flight crew. "I'll speak with them."

"On it," One of the flight crew responded, pressing buttons to activate a signal of their own.

Within a minute, Skye got the green light to talk, and she leaned down over the microphone to speak.

"Hello, my name is Skye and I'm with the International Space Hotel," she said over the line. "We can see your scouting ship. It's good to see someone. Please let us know if you receive this transmission. We come in peace. Over."

There was nothing for a couple of minutes, and then there was static. Skye and the others who had been bustling about in the front cabin fell silent. Then, there was something.

"Hello...." The voice faded in and out, and it sounded like static for a couple of seconds before coming through with a newfound clarity. "I said, can you hear me?"

"Yes," Skye answered. "Who is this?"

"This is Sergeant Rutherford of the U.S. Army," he said. "I'm on a scouting ship for the S.S. Washington."

"The S.S. Washington?" Skye asked. "You guys are okay?"

"Yes," the man replied. "We received your broadcast. You're with the International Space Hotel? That's... That's excellent. We didn't think you would have made it so far."

There were some voices speaking in the broadcast, like multiple people were in the background, and Skye caught some of them talking in the background asking about what they should do.

"Yes," Skye replied, trying to keep her voice level through the next part of her statement, which was a lie. "We came across an empty station in orbit. Some sort of weapon. There was nothing inside but dead bodies."

"I see," the voice said. "Did you activate a distress signal? It's what we were sent to scout out."

"No," Skye replied. "Must've gone off when we broke into it."

"Okay," the sergeant replied, satisfied with that answer. "Look, I think I'm going to have to ask my commanding officers what to do next. This is our first time ever finding any survivors in space."

Skye frowned, not entirely convinced.

"Okay, but please, listen carefully," Skye said. From behind her, Dr. Chetana showed up, standing next to her. "We're running out of resources. We're only one day from running out of food completely. There are women and children on board, and we all need your help desperately."

"Okay," Sergeant Rutherford responded. "I'll be sure to communicate that information to my superiors."

Skye temporarily muted their line as they stopped speaking. She turned to Dr. Chetana.

"Looks like we might be saved, after all," Dr. Chetana offered, smiling, although Skye couldn't let herself feel optimistic, not until their safety was guaranteed.

***

Marcell knocked on the door of the forensics lab for around ten seconds before the door opened. Beside him, Ariel, the final surviving female security guard from before the Red Day carried a cardboard box packed full of various documents that Madison had brought back from on board the SAS.

The door flew open, and a small, spectacled old man, wearing a button-up shirt and slacks, answered the door.

"Oh," the man said, scanning his new guests. "I was hoping I was being delivered a second meal. I haven't been this hungry since I was stranded at sea when I was twenty-six."

"No," Marcell said, smirking. "I'm sorry, Mr.... Sorry, I forgot your name. I don't believe we've ever worked together directly. If anyone worked with you, it was Fritz."

"McFarland," the man replied. "I'm sure Fritz has his hands full, running the ship and whatnot. What are your names?"

"I'm Marcell, and this is Ariel," Marcell responded. "We were both security guards before this happened."

McFarland looked at their nametags on their black armored uniforms and smiled. "Of course."

"May we come in?" Marcell asked, and the man nodded, beckoning the pair in.

"Where should I set this down?" Ariel asked, and he pointed to an open surface on one of the tables. One half of the room was full of various equipment, such as the fingerprint scanner which McFarland had used to analyze the fingerprints in the Grace Elliott case, cross-referencing them with the U.S. database, unsuccessfully.

Marcell was aware of McFarland's background. McFarland was a former FBI, as well as CIA agent who had stepped down from his job a long time ago before becoming a private investigator. After that, he had decided to retire in space a few years ago. However, as wealthy as he was, that wasn't a feasible situation since the housing market on Mars wasn't set to be established for another decade. Instead, he landed a job on the International Space Hotel, where he would willingly offer his services by working in a Forensics Lab when needed (which, was only usually a few times a year, and usually on suicide or natural cause cases) and in exchange would be granted a room on the hotel for as long as he lived. McFarland's wife had died around five years ago, and this was a great gig for him to start anew.

On the other hand, there was also a variety of rumors about this man, which Marcell was significantly less likely to believe. It was said that he'd committed espionage in Russia in the '20s, as well as had a hand in assassinating not one, but two African dictators in 2034. Marcell was far likelier to buy into the recent rumor that he'd slept with one woman from every nationality on the globe (despite being married) than he was to believe the latter.

"These are all the documents we brought back," Marcell explained, slapping them on the table. "I hope this is enough to discover... I don't know. Something."

"Okay," McFarland replied. "What evidence have we found right now? Could you please enlighten me?"

Marcell looked to Ariel, who stood there awkwardly.

"Oh, do you want me to leave?" Ariel asked, but Marcell shook his head.

"No," Marcell replied. "But it goes without saying that this conversation is confidential."

Ariel nodded, and Marcell hurriedly explained the gist of the situation. He told McFarland about the Space Armament Stations, how there were four of them orbiting Earth, and how they'd recently crossed paths and even gotten into contact with one. Without giving details about Sylvester's death (it had been written off as an accident, and the last thing he needed was a reason to turn Ariel against him), Marcell explained how there was a survivor who had been working for Ascendant Technologies, how everyone on board except for him had been killed, the laser activated on the Red Day. He said how the same person leading the SAS program was the sister of the current president.

"It's fishy," Marcell said. "Our leader Sk- I mean, Fritz, suspects that they might be connected. It's unbelievable to believe but it's possible that... that..."

"That the United States had a hand in the Red Day," McFarland finished. "I understand, now."

"Yes."

"I'll check it out," McFarland promised.

Marcell was about to leave with Ariel, when an announcement came over the line. It was Skye.

Attention, everyone on board. I have good news. The good news is that we have made contact with the S.S. Washington. Our hope is for them to arrive either in the middle of the night, or sometime tomorrow. I don't know whether or not they will be able to rescue us, but I hope this meeting will entail a restocking of our food. I will keep you all updated. In the meantime, business continues as usual. Thank you.

The P.A. announcement turned off, as Marcell waved the announcement away with his hand.

"Oh, disregard that," Marcell stated. "You might be working with a bit of a deadline... Especially if the people on board that ship were the same people who killed those on the Space Armament Station. Just tell us if, or when, you learn anything."

Marcell and Ariel left the room. The security of the ship, including the new recruits who had been recruited over the course of the past twenty-four hours, were on high alert.

Chapter 15

"Ow!" Graham exclaimed, pulling his hand away from the engine of the space pod. He tried retracting back into the main chamber, but in the process hit his head on something. "Ow, darn…"

"You okay?" Yusef asked him. "What's going on?"

Graham sat up, now within the main body of the escape pod. They had been working underneath a crawl space, and Yusef followed him from underneath to slither back into the main chamber when he heard no response from Graham.

Graham looked down, and saw a deep red cut on the left side of his left hand. He was grateful it was his nondominant left hand; but the wound stung, and he couldn't keep working like this. Not without painting the entire scene red and making the space look like a crime scene.

"I cut myself, on an edge," Graham winced. "I didn't even know I was grazing it, until I nicked myself."

"Here, let me look," Yusef said, pulling his arm towards him a bit. "That's a bit gnarly."

"Do we have a first aid kit?" Graham asked, looking around, even though he figured he didn't need one. They had brought tool boxes here, but there was no first aid kit to be seen.

"I don't think so," Yusef replied. And with that, he turned back to looking at the circuitry inside and started crawling back into the crawl space underneath the dashboard and. "This is our last escape pod, man. That's some bad luck."

"*Darn* bad luck," Graham agreed.

Graham figured there was a first aid kit stored somewhere inside on board with them, and certainly out in the hallway. But he figured he may as well have it checked out professionally. He figured he had paid his dues plenty with all of the repairing and maintenance he'd worked on over the past few weeks, and he trusted Yusef to the task.

If Madison was there, then he'd have had her check out his hand in a heartbeat. He'd attended Skye's meeting by convincing security to let him past the double doors that kept the meeting room separate from the public, and had been able to catch part of what had been in the Space Armament Station. He hadn't seen Sylvester die (which, in his mind, Skye had taken quite easily, Madison, not quite as much), but he had seen her literally extract a bullet from the employee at Ascendant Technologies and stitch it, to boot, using only one hand. Dr. Chetana had ended up resetting her shoulder when she arrived back after the expedition.

It was Dr. Chetana who he, by some miracle, ran into in the hallways again. Graham, clasping his hand, had used an old rag from the toolbox to cover up his wound and prevent it from bleeding all over the hallway. He had just turned the corner and was about to go into the pharmacy and ask for a bandage when he caught Dr. Chetana leaving the pharmacy. She carried some medical supplies in a box.

"Oh, hello," Dr. Chetana said. "You're Skye's boyfriend, right? Graham?"

"Yes," he said.

Dr. Chetana looked down at his hand. "You're hurt."

The Laser from Above

"Yes," Graham responded. "I wanted to get a bandage. Figured I may as well make the walk to the pharmacy instead of using a first aid kit, when we might need them in the future."

"Come in," Dr. Chetana said, running into the pharmacy. Inside, Sarah was working the desk, but he didn't see Madison, at least for now, and Dr. Chetana invited him to sit down in the small, vacant waiting room area.

Dr. Chetana evaluated his wound briefly.

"That laceration looks like it hurts," Dr. Chetana commented. "But it should be okay. You don't need stitches."

"I'm glad to hear it," Graham replied. "I didn't think so, but I wanted to be sure."

Dr. Chetana opened up her box of supplies and dug through until she found a proper medical bandage, using it to cover up his wound.

"Perfect," Graham replied, pressing his arm on the armrest, ready to lift himself up to his feet. "Thanks for helping me, doc."

"Yes. Funny I should run into you, of all people, at this time."

"Okay?" Graham asked. He sat back down.

"I think there's something you should know. Being Skye's boyfriend, and all."

"What is it?"

"At our first council meeting a while back," Dr. Chetana said, "I had a conversation with Skye."

"Yes... And what happened?"

"I told her that if anyone should be leading the Space Hotel, it should be me," Dr. Chetana said. "If not me, then perhaps Fritz Nussbaum. I've thought about this, you know, and she's what, twenty right?"

"Yes. Twenty-one in the next month."

"Okay, sure. Well, I asked her to do the reasonable thing and overturn the position as head of council to me. She could retain a spot on the council, I said."

"What'd she say?"

"She said no."

"Why are you telling me this?" Graham asked. He didn't understand what Dr. Chetana's angle was here, but whatever she was doing, he didn't like it.

"I just thought you should know," Dr. Chetana replied, standing up on her feet. "I hoped you could maybe talk some sense into her. You understand where I'm coming from, right?"

"Yes, I do," he said. "But I don't think her age is a big deal."

"I know," Dr. Chetana said. "I'm a little bit... How to put it. She just... I don't want to be too harsh, but she seems to be growing slightly more unhinged."

"She's fine!" Graham insisted. "It's a lot of pressure on her. She can handle this."

"I don't doubt it. But there was a time shortly ago, where someone committed theft of food. The council had to make a decision. We were discussing things like a public whipping, or solitary confinement. And all of a sudden, Skye says we should launch her out into space, while everyone watches. Let her freeze solid and die."

Graham's eyes widened upon hearing this.

"That's... That's messed up. I had no idea." Graham said. "She never said anything at all about that. That doesn't sound like her."

"She's a tough girl. But I'm worried this is too much for her. That's all."

Graham nodded, and he walked out of the room legitimately concerned.

***

"You push yourself too hard," Graham told Skye. He sat, legs crossed, on her bed, while she was under the covers. The lights were still on, but it was approaching ten o' clock in the evening.

Over the last few days, their relationship had escalated to the extent that they were comfortable staying over at each other's place and sharing their beds for the night. It was magical, but like every bit of magic, it came with its limitations. In this case, Graham had been busy thinking about what Dr. Chetana had told him.

"I think you need to... slow down a bit," Graham continued.

"Really?" Skye asked. He leaned in for a kiss, and Skye reciprocated, tilting her head and her lips meeting his.

"Yes, really," he responded.

"How?"

"Take today," he said. "You activate the distress signals, and then you run around for hours. You make contact with a scouting ship, great. But then you keep on running around. You even log the death of that guy that Madison was with, right? Why?"

"Someone had to do it," Skye replied. "Just because the world is... the way it is, doesn't mean that we shouldn't keep an active history of what's happened."

"Yes, maybe you're right," Graham replied. "But not you. That's beneath you. You don't have to do this. You look really stressed, and tired."

"I'm... not tired," Skye said. But even as she did say that word, her eyelids appeared to be drooping.

"I just think you should dial it back, you know?"

"Huh?" She asked, yawning. "How so?"

"Maybe you should let someone else take the reins a bit with this whole leadership shebang."

Skye's eyes widened, and she perked up. "What are you talking about? Don't you believe in me?"

She looks pissed. Is she going to bite me?

"Of course, I do," Graham sputtered. "So much so that I'm trying to look after your best interests."

"No," Skye growled, sitting up in her bed, her voice escalating in a gradual crescendo. "Who the hell put you up to this, anyway? Was it Fritz? No, let me guess, Dr. Chetana!?"

"Stop!" Graham pleaded, more terrified by Skye's pure mask of rage than he would've liked to have admitted. "Don't fight with me. I didn't mean to hurt your feelings."

"Never… suggest that to me again."

Graham sighed, shook his head. "Okay. It was just a suggestion."

"I have to be something, and do this," Skye said, much more quietly and calmly. "I have to prove I am something, you know? A leader. Since my dreams of ever being something in the real world have been squashed…"

"You've already proven yourself," Graham said from his side of the bed. "You've proven yourself so many times."

But Skye didn't respond. Another word was not spoken in that room for the rest of the night, and Skye turned over in the bed to face the wall.

Chapter 16

For a short while, Skye wondered whether or not the S.S. Washington would come after all. After all, it had been well over a month since the Red Day, and yet they never had even so much as radioed in with them.

According to what Mr. Xiong said, the ISH had apparently activated their distress signal, hoping to get into communication with other spaceships. But there had been nothing. No signs at all from the S.S. Washington. That made the situation even more suspicious and nerve-wracking. It was only after that they sent a scout ship to check out the signal, and, going into range with the ISH's communication, that they finally established communications with them. Where they had been before, no one in the flight crew or on the council seemed to know. It was as if the S.S. Washington had been a ghost the entire time.

Yet despite the shroud of mystery that covered them, the scout ship certainly did inform their superiors, and must have ended up listening to their pleas, because the S.S. Washington ended up showing up.

Skye didn't trust the U.S. government. Not with how much they must have butchered their diplomatic ties to let the world descend into total havoc on the Red Day, and not with the strange connections between the Melero name and the Space Armament Stations. But she felt that there was not much choice. Everyone was starving, and food supplies were going to run out. Even if they were responsible for the situation they'd been put into, if they could save their life, then Skye would have to take any aid they would provide.

It wasn't until the next day that the S.S. Washington was detected, but when it was, it came in a blaze of glory. First there was beeping on the monitor, one of the flight crew ushering Skye and the others to come see what was happening. And then, the telescope was aimed to zoom in on the ship and project it onto a large screen for everyone to see.

The ship was colossal, so big that it was over half the size of the International Space Hotel. Only it was high instead of wide, and extremely long. It looked almost like a sort of cruise ship you would see in the ocean back on earth, except with thrusters instead of propellers lining the ships, and except for the fact that there were giant turrets along the side, and what looked like rockets resting underneath. The entire thing was well lit, as unlike the ISH, it didn't look like they turned off a lot of their lights to conserve energy.

Skye was still in the control room with Marcell and Dr. Chetana when the ship first registered on the monitor. And she was there when the S.S. Washington sent out their broadcast to ISH, asking a question.

"May I speak to Alan Lusky?"

Skye looked at the others, who were unsure how to proceed.

"What should we do?" Dr. Chetana asked. "Lie?"

"I don't know why we'd have to lie," Marcell responded.

"I... We don't need to go into details," Skye said, "but we'll tell them the truth. Partially."

She pressed the button to turn on her microphone and broadcast back to the S.S. Washington.

"Can you hear me? This is the International Space Hotel speaking."

The Laser from Above

"Yes, we can hear you," the voice, an oddly regal bass, replied.

"You cannot speak with Alan Lusky," Skye responded. "Don't get the wrong idea, though. You cannot speak with Alan Lusky because he is no longer with us."

"Oh," The voice replied in a disappointed tone. "That's unfortunate. My condolences. May I speak with the next-in-command, then?"

"Yes," Skye replied. "You're speaking with her currently. My name is Skye."

Maybe I should have let him know that Fritz was in charge. Too late.

"Great, Skye," the voice responded. "Then, full disclosure, I should let you know upfront… This is Bruno Melero that you are speaking with. President of the United States."

Skye's jaw dropped, and her finger lifted from the communications button so that he couldn't hear the audible gasp that escaped from many of their mouths.

"This is… The President?" Marcell asked, shocked.

"My God," Dr. Chetana said, shaking her head in disbelief.

Skye gulped and pressed the button again.

"It is an honor to be in your presence," Skye managed. "We had no idea… I mean, no idea that you were in space."

"Yes," President Melero replied. "As far as timing goes, I couldn't have been luckier. I was meeting with some generals in space when everything happened… Now I'm in charge of the greatest country of the world."

Greatest country, my ass, Skye thought. *More like the greatest mound of ashes now. My whole family probably died.*

Skye's hands balled into fists, her knuckles growing white. She couldn't even begin to imagine how furious she would be if she learned that if this man was the one responsible for everything. He would have hell to pay. Of course, they were the ones with the military spaceship, and potentially dozens, if not hundreds, of soldiers, and the International Space Hotel only had five seasoned security guards plus ten new recruits. They wouldn't stand a chance.

"Is the Earth not safe to return? We've had many discussions about whether or not it is, but the truth is, we don't have any access to any accurate, stable information about what's going on."

"I'm not taking any chances," Bruno admitted. "The United States is in a stage of... disorganization right now, to say the least. It's a mess. I have coordinated with the majority of national emergency bunkers throughout the country. It's a long road to recovery, and we intend to stay in space until we have to land. With our self-sustaining power resources, that might be in a few weeks, or a few months. I can't really say."

"You hold active communications with Earth? We have barely gotten through to them, and it's been weeks."

"Yes," he answered. "The communications systems of the S.S. Washington is unparalleled."

"That's... that's amazing," Skye said. "Look, I know we mentioned it earlier, but we desperately need food. Today we've used up our last portions. While we can produce some of our own food, what we have produced is not enough to be even close to sustaining all of us, and we've all been starving the last couple of weeks... We need food. Please."

The President was silent for a few moments as he pondered her statement before he replied.

"I understand your need," he said. "Of course, I'm not heartless. And of course, I know there is a need for you all to get food. I will help with your food situation. We can get you a good, healthy number of supplies, at least a week's worth."

"Thank you, thank you so much," Skye replied.

A week of food. That isn't enough. That definitely isn't enough, she thought.

"Your ship is huge," Skye observed. "Are there a lot of people on board your ship?"

"There are around four hundred of us in total," he answered, and Dr. Chetana and Marcell looked even more surprised. "And unlike the International Space Hotel, which was designed for to sustain less folk, we have more than enough in terms of food production to sustain our population. The ship was designed to hold people in the long-term, for space expeditions."

"You seem knowledgeable about the International Space Hotel," Skye remarked, hoping to glean some information from his response.

"Of course," he answered. "I… was a big fan. As I mentioned, we'll give you a weeks' worth of food. No, make that two."

"Well, we thank you for your generous gift," Skye replied. "From the bottom of my heart, thank you."

"Oh, don't get the wrong idea," The President said. "I'm not doing this out of the kindness of my heart. We expect a little something in return."

"What do you have in mind?"

"Well, you have to understand, our ship… it can handle more people than we already have. We're the best shot of survival anywhere, I'd reckon."

"Okay…"

"First things first, I'd like to inquire about the people in *your* hotel. How many people are on board? I'd like a demographic breakdown as well."

***

"I'm nervous, I'm so nervous," Cole said. He had shrunk into a ball in his wheelchair near the electrical room which, over a month before, he had hidden in for over a day. Only now, Madison was in the room with him. She had convinced him to show where he had hidden from the forces that had infiltrated the SAS on the Red Day, and, unfortunately for him, now it looked like he was perhaps suffering from a bout of PTSD.

Skye had pushed for Madison to return back to the ISH and stay there after Dr. Chetana had reset her shoulder. But Madison had insisted on returning almost immediately to Space Armament Station 2 in the hopes of being able to learn more information from Cole.

Madison looked over at Cole, offered him her hand.

"I know," Madison replied. "We'll protect you from anything that happens. I just wanted you to show me where the hiding area was, it was my mistake."

Cole accepted his hand, and Madison pulled him back up so that he sat upright. He wheeled alongside her as they hurried back into the living room.

"Blimey, Maddie," Cole exclaimed. "Why are we doing this? What's the point?"

"We had to see if they could help us," Madison replied. "The situation's out of control on board. We're out of food. Everyone's starving."

"I have some food reserves, why don't ya go and take them? Why did you say I might have to hide?"

"We'll take them back after, for sure," Madison agreed. "Issue is, right now, your food reserves were designed for 7 people. The rations you have left, I don't think they're even a day's worth of food for a couple of hundred people. They might be half a meal for everyone."

"Geez," Cole said, shaking his head.

Madison made her way over to the control room. They moved past the living room, where a couple of volunteers peeled through various documents and drawers looking for any important information that might help discover what happened on this ship, or in the Red Day. In the control room, they found Olivia at the controls with another one of the flight crew who'd been assigned on board, Jace.

"They're talking with the S.S. Washington," Olivia said glumly, turning to them. "It sounds like they got a couple of weeks of rations."

"That's great!" Madison responded, practically jumping for joy. She turned to Jace and Olivia, who were solemnly staring through the window, and laughed out in a confused tone. "Guys, why so down? You're acting like this is a funeral. This is great news."

"There are terms to this deal," Jace replied.

"What?" Madison asked. "What do you mean?"

"The price to pay, Maddie," Olivia explained, "is fifty women."

Chapter 17

"What?" Skye asked back over the microphone. "I'm sorry, I think there might be an issue with the microphone. If I didn't hear you correctly, then it's because I thought you said you wanted us to turn over fifty women."

"I did," President Melero said. "You heard me right."

Skye lifted her finger off the button to mute their side of the line, and turned to the others for input.

"Oh god," Marcell mumbled.

"Yes," Skye replied. "I can't believe this. That's really the offer."

"That's bad," Dr. Chetana agreed. As much as she always seemed to take opposing stances from Skye, it sounded like they were all in mutual agreement.

"This has to be some kind of weird human trafficking deal," Marcell speculated. "He could've specified fifty people, but he had to go out of his way."

"Yes," Dr. Chetana responded. "It's a military ship. The U.S. military doesn't exactly have a good track record vis-à-vis treating women."

"Fuck," Skye mumbled. "This is bad. Let me respond."

Skye pressed the button for the microphone, hesitating.

"That's concerning," Skye spoke back into the microphone. "Why women specifically?"

"Our ship is not like the International Space Hotel," President Melero replied. "It's designed to sustain a population in the long run."

"I thought you just said five minutes ago that you plan on returning to Earth whenever you have to."

"Yes, if issues arise, we might be forced to land," President Melero said. "But my point stands. The S.S. Washington holds some important government officials, military personnel, and researchers. People who are integral to rebuilding the foundation of our country."

"What are you getting at?"

"As you can imagine, there's a gender imbalance among this population," President Melero explained. "There are significantly more men than women. As part of our rebuilding our culture and heritage, a more even gender split is desired. That's where you would come in."

"Let's tell it like it is: you want us to volunteer women to be your sex slaves."

There was a loud exhale, like as if the President was shocked. "That's... despicable. That's not what this is about at all."

"Really? And you think people will willingly sell out their souls, and their bodies, just for a little bit more comfort? You really think people would agree to do that?"

"I think people will be willing to do what it takes to survive," The President replied. "And yes, that would include selling their body, although that's not what this is about at all."

"It doesn't sound like we have much of a choice," Dr. Chetana blurted out.

There was silence for a few moments on the other side of the line, until the President spoke up once again.

"Hey, who said that?"

"Dr. Chetana, Chief Medical Officer and Head Doctor of the International Space Hotel, at your service."

"Well, Dr. Chetana, you absolutely do have a choice," President Melero insisted. "If you say yes, I will provide you with two weeks of food-"

"Three," Skye interrupted.

"Fine, three weeks of food," he ceded, "in exchange for fifty women, under the age of fifty."

"Oh, now you're adding an age limit, huh?" Skye replied in a snarky tone. "You aren't one for subtlety."

"Those are my terms," The President said. "Like it or not, that's our offer."

"How do we even know you honor your agreement? How do we know you're not just going to pillage and rape the entirety of the ISH?"

"Fair point," The President responded. "Well, what would it take for you to trust us?"

"Proof," Skye said. "I want to see your food reserves for myself. Show us your ship."

The President paused. "Very well. I think I can do that. We'll approach your ship, peacefully, and send out a connector to your docking bay. From there, we will show your leadership, whoever you all are, the ship itself, and our food reserves. I'm sure some residents aboard the International Space Hotel will also be eager to even come on board to the S.S. Washington. I'll even be willing to host a celebratory banquet, conditional on your acceptance."

"And what am I supposed to tell everyone on board the hotel about the deal?"

"I don't know," President Melero admitted. "You're the captain of the ship. That's on you."

"What if I say no, after the tour? Will you destroy us then?"

"No," President Melero promised. "There is no coercion, that I swear to you. If you say no, then we will peacefully exit, retract our connector, and our business between us will be done, permanently."

Skye looked at the time in the corner of one of the monitors. It was around 9:30 in the morning.

"This is an extremely difficult decision, you understand," Skye replied. "It takes time... and a lot of hard work to decide something like this."

"I know," The President replied. "I'd be willing to cut you some slack. I will give you a day to make up your mind. Tomorrow by midnight, we expect a final decision. In the meantime, we will remain connected via the docking bay."

"Okay," Skye replied. "Show us the ship, and we will have our decision by midnight space-time."

"Okay," he replied. "According to the flight crew, our ship should be in position to dock in the next half hour."

Skye lifted her hand off the button once again to mute their microphone.

"What do we do now?" Skye asked.

"I don't know, I don't know," Marcell repeated.

"We can't accept the deal," Dr. Chetana replied. "The toll on human life is more than any amount of food they can provide."

"We need the food," Skye stated. "Without it, we'll all slowly starve to death, or have to go back to Earth, which might be a death sentence. You heard what they said about the Earth."

"Dr. Chetana's right," Marcell responded. "Although maybe Fritz and Nathan will see it another way."

Skye groaned in frustration. "I just wish there was a third way."

"There always is," Dr. Chetana offered. "We just need to think of it."

***

Marcell went to check on McFarland's progress within the next couple of hours. He knocked on the door, and McFarland yelled at him to come in.

Many papers were spread out across one of the tables, and McFarland hovered over all of them, scanning his eyes from paper to paper. In his hands was a small notebook, in which he scrawled notes with his pencil.

"Sorry, I know that it's only been a couple of hours," Marcell apologized once he closed the door behind himself. "I just wanted to check in on you."

"No, not at all," McFarland stated. "It's just, there's a little bit more I want you to tell me about this whole incident."

"What? Why?"

"You said that there was a survivor in SAS 2, right? Did he happen to describe who came in and shot them up? All you said is some people in camouflage."

"Yes," Marcell replied. "He said that he saw one of them and their skin color, and that at least one was white. That's all he recalled."

"That's very interesting," he said, nodding. He tapped his pencil underneath his chin, smiled. "That might be a very key clue."

"Really?" Marcell asked. "How so? Tell me."

"Well, I still need to look a lot more, but here's what I've gathered. Yes, the Melero connection is sketchy. Amelia Melero led the entire project, and Bruno Melero, well, he was one of the fiercest advocates for investment in space weaponry in the world."

"Really?"

"Yes, although that knowledge comes from what I know of him elsewhere," McFarland explained. "The news before everything, you know? What I found particularly interesting was the Emergency Clause that was wedged in one of the contracts. It clearly outlines something crucial."

"What's that?"

McFarland pointed at one of the papers, and Marcell narrowed his eyes, reading through the dense lines as McFarland explained what looked like word salad at a first glance.

"Space Armament Station 1 could be repossessed in the event of an emergency by the United States," McFarland explained. "Space Armament Station 2, by mutual consent of the United Kingdom or the E.U. Space Armament Station 3, Russia. Space Armament Station 4, by China."

"And this was Space Armament Station 2," Marcell remembered. "Right?"

"Correct. Ascendant Technologies was a globalized corporation," McFarland said. "Part of their purpose in being in charge was to help preserve world peace, as twisted as it sounds, by placing these neutral people in control of the ship. As a matter of fact, Station 2 was only used once in its six-year history of being operated. That was to assassinate a small enclave of terrorists in Somalia. It was a real demonstration of the weapon's power."

"But someone took over the ship."

"Yes," McFarland replied. "And by my deductive reasoning, it couldn't have been the EU and the UK, because they simply could have exercised their emergency clause to repossess it. There was no reason to deceive them and kill everyone on board."

"I see."

"If what you said about the skin tone was true, then it most likely isn't the Chinese, because why would Chinese Special Forces be white? I don't think this is a job you entrust to foreign mercenaries, either. Which leads me to my final conclusion: either Russia or the United States was the ones who operated that station during the Red Day. I can't rule either of them out at this stage of the process."

"The United States... I mean, that's impossible, isn't it?"

"We nuked Hiroshima and Nagasaki... Is it really that difficult to believe that we'd take over and use a space laser?"

Marcell sighed. "Got me there. Okay. Well, is there anything else?"

"I want to learn more information... I think I want to go and see the station for myself. Try and see if I can uncover any information from the weapon itself."

Marcell looked away.

"About that. There's an issue."

"Huh? What?"

Marcell explained the situation with the S.S. Washington, how they were now preparing to dock within the next couple of minutes. Sending an escape pod would likely draw attention and suspicion, and Marcell figured that suspicion was the last thing they needed right now, what with a giant military spaceship right on their doorstep, and what with them potentially depending on them for food.

"We simply discovered an abandoned Space Armament Station, and are checking it out more closely for supplies," McFarland said. "That's what you tell them if they ask. I need to go."

"Okay," Marcell relented. He pressed his earpiece.

"Council members. Are you here?"

"Yes," multiple of them affirmed at once.

"How's the boarding process going?" he asked.

"The connector is extending to the docking bay as we speak," Nathan replied. "I think it is a couple of minutes away."

"About that," Marcell responded. "Just an FYI, I'm going to be sending McFarland out. I'll get someone to take him and get them dressed up for space and the SAS, and then I'll be there afterwards."

"Why?" Dr. Chetana questioned.

"It's important," Marcell said. "I'll tell you in person, it takes too long to explain right now."

"I trust you," Skye replied. "Go for it. I'll have it covered on my end."

McFarland followed Marcell out of the room as he limped along with his cane at incredible speed, hobbling along like his life depended on it.

***

"Tell me a little bit more about how this weapon works," Madison said, pointing at the interface of the SAS 2. Cole, who was still in his wheelchair, hesitated.

Earlier, Olivia had been standing at the controls, but right now she was sitting in the living room, reading some book, and they were alone, at least until Jace returned from a restroom break. Cole had said he was pretty sure Jace was raiding the fridge right now, but it didn't matter in the grand scheme of things in Madison's mind. Either they were getting a bunch more food soon, or they were probably going back down to Earth.

"I... I don't know..." Cole hesitated.

"Come on," Madison pleaded. "Don't flake out on me. Don't you trust me?"

"I do," Cole replied. "It's just, this is not something I should be explaining. They threatened me, and yes, I know, Ascendant Technologies probably doesn't exist anymore."

"I cleaned your bandage and everything."

"Okay. Well, I'm not going to demonstrate. This right here, it's the charge." He pointed out a particular panel on the control board.

"It's at 17%," Madison observed. "That doesn't sound good."

"Yes," Cole admitted. "Most of the battery was drained. You see, this system uses solar rays, as well as nuclear fuel cells, to charge. But the solar energy is hardly enough and replenishes the energy very slowly. It was almost completely out of energy after it was used. That was over a month ago."

"How much energy does it require to fire a blast?"

"It depends," Cole replied. "On a number of factors. Distance, the size of the beam, the longevity. I would say that it was only fired for around twenty-five minutes on… what'd you call it, the Red Day."

"Forty-five minutes for 100%," Madison said, doing some mental math. "So, 17% would be what, between four and five minutes?"

"Yes," Cole said. "Although I would've guessed that beam was bloody huge. The entire ship was shaking. It was much different from a more concentrated beam. You could probably shoot that for twice as long."

Madison frowned, wondering why he'd know the difference.

But of course, she thought, *he probably went through a bunch of training, as well as virtual simulations. Just like I've done all the VR medical simulations back in college.*

"Could you, theoretically, shoot that spaceship that's docking over there?" Madison asked, pointing at the ship that was adjacent to the International Space Hotel. "Without hitting the ISH?"

"Yes," Cole replied. "Now controlling for any fragmentation is different, but I guarantee the laser could hit it. The range of this is approximately a thousand miles, and to put that into perspective, we're about three-hundred above the Pacific Ocean right now."

Madison looked down at the Earth, where there was a vast array of blue and very few wispy white clouds. It was a sunny day over the ocean.

"See that island?" He pointed at a random green island that appeared to have been spared from any nuclear or laser strikes due to its coloration.

Madison nodded.

"We could hit a target as small as a house on that island, if we only knew the exact coordinates," Cole claimed. "At its peak, meanwhile, we could scorch a square mile within a second with a huge beam."

"That's insane," Madison responded. "That's… amazing. And terrifying. So, what you're saying is, you'd have no problems destroying that spaceship, or our hotel, if you wanted."

"Yes, no question," Cole answered. "I've been trained, and this station has the power."

A button on the dashboard lit up.

"What's wrong?" Madison asked, as Cole rolled up in his wheelchair to press the button.

"Nothing," Cole answered. "It means we're receiving a transmission. Let's hear what this bugger has to say."

Cole pressed a button to unmute.

"This is McFarland speaking," the voice said. "I'm on my way to help out."

Cole's finger hovered over to activate the microphone of his own.

"No," Madison stopped him, his finger inches away from hitting the button.

"What?" he asked. "Why not?"

"Nathan Xiong told me to not risk anything, and for us to avoid broadcasting any confidential information."

"Who's that?"

"Never mind," Madison replied. "Look, when we send out radio signals to communicate, it's possible that other ships could intercept it. Including the S.S. Washington."

"Fine," Cole replied. "Let's tell the others about what's going on."

Madison's stomach rumbled. It had been doing a lot of that recently, and as Cole explained what was happening to Jace and Olivia, she went to scrounge through the freezer herself. The crates had been searched through thoroughly, although next to nothing had been taken out. However, deep in one of the boxes, Madison found a small box containing ice cream sandwiches, and as the others planned for the mysterious visitor, of which they had no understanding of why he was coming, Madison engorged herself on the entire box of four ice cream sandwiches. When she was finished, she belched loudly and emerged back into the control room, wiping the smear of chocolate from her face and licking her hand. She made a mental note to dispose of the box when she found a chance.

Chapter 18

Meanwhile, back in the International Space Hotel, the connector had finally been set into place and pumped full of the ideal amount of oxygen, meaning that now, there was a complete metal hallway that connected the S.S. Washington to the International Space Hotel. Given that they were the ones to dock, Skye found it fit for them to wait for their new arrivals, and lined up in position.

A squadron of four soldiers in uniform were the first to pass through the connector. However, it was not as scary as one would have thought. For they were marching in formation, saluting and grinning as they walked through the long connector that extended all the way to the docking bay. The four soldiers emerged to find Skye, Nathan Xiong, Fritz, and Dr. Chetana, flanked by a few newly trained security guards (they had been clothed in spare uniforms that Marcell and Fritz had dug out of the armory). A small crowd of former clients and employees also gathered behind, and they cheered and clapped as the soldiers passed through and waved them welcome.

After entering into the lobby area, they were soon followed by a couple more soldiers, except these were higher ranking. They had an assortment of badges; their skin was far more worn with age. Among these men were a couple of bodyguards, not dressed too differently from secret service members, and one man who stood out far more than the others.

"It's President Melero!"

The man stepped to the front of the crowd, revealing his pristine black suit and red tie. President Bruno Melero was above average in height, although not towering tall; his skin was smooth and a light brown, with a clean complexion that reminded Skye of something she'd see from a Hollywood actor. Atop his head was a fine head of hair, with black curls that looked like he'd hardly shed a hair despite his age in his forties. Indeed, aged at around 42 and a half, he barely edged out Theodore Roosevelt for the youngest president-elect in history, and Skye knew that if everything hadn't gone to down the drain down on Earth, the paparazzi would have doted all over him. She could have imagined the headlines: *the hottest president of all time, the golden boy, straight-arrow Melero*. It was hard to believe it was really him.

"Greetings, residents and leaders of the International Space Hotel," he said, stepping forward.

If it had been different, and they were back on Earth and the Red Day had never happened, then the crowd might have applauded or screamed for autographs. In this instance, the crowd was pretty quiet, however, except for one of the clients who seemed to speak everyone's mind.

"Are you giving us food? Please, Mr. President, everyone here is *begging* you to give us food."

"Don't worry about that," President Melero promised, calling out to the crowd. "I will be working this out with your leadership immediately! I ask you all to have patience as we organize the logistics with your leaders. I am sure your leadership will be able to communicate the situation to you clearly within a couple of hours."

Even though it'd been weeks now of meager rations, and now only a day of nothing, judging by the murmurs and a couple of boos from the crowd, it appeared that a couple of hours was far too long for them. But no one stepped forward or protested. With an armed military guard, and as well as a few hotel security guards spectating the scene, nobody tried anything stupid.

He turned to Skye, Fritz, and the others. "I presume you are the leaders?"

"You presume correctly," Fritz affirmed.

"All right," President Melero said, waving them over to the connector. "Come with me."

Skye, Nathan, and Dr. Chetana followed him over to the connector, and yet Marcell and Fritz hesitated, hanging back for a few seconds as they looked at each other. Marcell didn't trust this man. Alarm bells were ringing in his head. Besides that, if they were somehow taken into custody, or worse yet, eliminated, the ship would be thrown into total disarray. No, it was crucial that one of them stayed.

"You thinking what I'm thinking?" Fritz whispered to Marcell.

"Yes," Marcell replied.

"You stay back," Fritz offered. "You're the cripple here."

The words were blunt, but Marcell understood, and agreed with the sentiment.

President Melero stopped in the doorway and turned around to see Marcell and Fritz lingering back in the hotel, before Fritz walked up towards the President. The entire time, the nearby generals, bodyguards, and soldiers stood only a couple of feet away, staring him down, as if they were ready to tackle him at a moment's notice should he make the wrong move.

Fritz cleared his throat. "Marcell here is one of the leaders. However, he's made the executive decision to stay back and supervise things on our ship while we are absent."

"Okay," President Melero replied understandingly. "I see you have a cane. No purpose to over-exert yourself. I'm sure everyone here can report what they see."

Marcell nodded and muttered something of a thank you.

"Are you Skye?" He asked, turning to Dr. Chetana. "The current leader of the International Space Hotel?"

"No, that would be me," Skye answered.

President Melero frowned, turning to Skye. He sized her up for a few moments, unsure whether or not she was bluffing. "Is that so?"

"Yes," Fritz replied. Now that they were in the connectors and a short walk from the other ship, Skye was worried. Worried that something would go wrong, the connector would break, and they'd be cast out into space like that one man had been with Madison. Each word in the hallway did the opposite of echo: it seemed to almost stop in her mouth, stifling her words.

"How old are you?" Melero asked. As he asked the question, he seemed to be scrutinizing every detail on everything above her shoulders, including the red streak in her hair and all of her face. It made Skye uncomfortable.

"Does it matter?" Skye fired back.

"No," President Melero replied. "You look young, however, so I am simply curious."

"I'm twenty," Skye answered. "But ages can be deceiving, so I suggest you don't discredit what I have to say just because of it."

"You surely weren't the second in command before this all happened?" The President asked. By now, they were almost at the end of the hallway, and close to entering the S.S. Washington. "I mean, I've heard of prodigies in academia, and they're a novelty, but in the business world, people your age, they just don't lead. Not that they are all incapable of doing so, but they just don't. They don't have the life experience to run the show."

"There was a tragedy," Fritz said. "She assumed command of the ship single-handedly, and has guided us to where we are. We can thank her for that."

Don't you speak for me, Skye thought.

"A tragedy?" Melero asked. "How unfortunate."

Finally, the group reached the end of the connector, and the airlock of the S.S. Washington beyond. They emerged to find several soldiers at ease, brandishing their guns. If this all wasn't a show to flex the forces stationed on the ship and strike a little bit of fear into their hearts, then Skye didn't know what it was.

Melero continued walking for a few moments until they had reached the hallways of the S.S. Washington. Whereas the main hallways of the International Space Hotel were cozy, filled with all sorts of amenities like bathrooms, water fountains, and escalator tracks which had served to entertain all of the tourists, the hallways here were narrow, sterile, and cold, with more metal surfaces than Skye could count. Skye thought that this was much more what she had in mind when it came to space travel, probably because of all the depictions in the media she'd consumed over the course of her life and the fact that this was a military spacecraft.

President Melero walked a little bit ahead of the group, whispering to some of the generals with him, who soon nodded and walked away, the four soldiers trailing behind them before slowing down a bit and speaking with them. Now it was just the four of them, the President, and two bodyguards.

"Forgive my entourage for accompanying me so far," The President apologized. "These guards, they're assigned to me at all times. Unfortunately, I can't just tell them to leave. It's their sworn duty to watch me, 24/7. Especially with what's happened to the world."

"It's okay," Skye replied. "We have no issues with all of the armed security. This *is* the S.S. Washington, after all."

"You're taking us to show the food reserves, right?" Dr. Chetana inquired. "As proof of your proposition?"

"Indeed," The President affirmed. "As a matter of fact, I can give you a whole tour, if you so desire. Well, at least a short one. It shouldn't take more than an hour or so."

"That would be very nice," Skye replied. Dr. Chetana turned to her and gave her a strange look, unsure of why she'd taken up the deal. Skye figured if there was any funny business going on the ship, then it would behoove them to inspect every place they could.

The conversation dried up for a few minutes as they neared the storage facility. Before they reached their destination, however, Melero had another egg to crack.

"So I observe that there are a lot of you," Bruno Melero responded. "You must be on top of things if you've made it this far. If I may ask, what is your leadership structure?"

"There are five of us," Nathan responded. "The council."

"Ah, well, this can't be how things typically were run," President Melero observed.

"No," Dr. Chetana answered. "Desperate times call for desperate measures."

"I see," The President responded. "That's one way of putting it."

"I know you're cynical," Skye stated. Melero's eyebrows raised at the comment. "But I can assure you, our intentions are pure. We've heard your deal, and we are considering it."

The five of them, accompanied by the same two bodyguards who had reached the threshold for the storage facility, stopped immediately once President Melero turned around on his feet. His hand covered his face, which seemed to reflect a certain exasperation on his part.

"Look, I'm not going to ask many questions. I want to, but I don't know if I want to know the truth. Alan Lusky. Ron Wills. Ai Hamasaki. They may not have been close friends of mine, but they were all acquaintances. Acquaintances who, for whatever reason I cannot fathom, are not standing before me as representative leaders from the ISH. I can guess that they didn't willingly relinquish their roles as leaders, so I can only assume the worst happened. We don't need to talk about it. But don't count me as a fool."

The group was struck silent. Fritz started to speak, but Skye cut him off. As rude as it may have been, she knew that whatever lie he was going to concoct was not going to be adequate.

"They say the best captains go down with their ship," Skye said. "Unfortunately, I don't think he was the best captain. The little pickle we were in, the sparse food situation, was management's fault. They took a chance to land on their tropical island with half our food supply, and we were left out to dry. I stepped up to the plate. That's all there is to that story."

Fritz raised his eyebrows, but nodded, as if to accept this lie. The others didn't speak up, and tried their best to employ their relatively poor acting skills to play along with Skye's charade.

"I understand now," President Melero said, nodding. "Yes. I can't say it's out of character because, again, they were merely acquaintances. Now, if you may follow me."

President Melero wasn't lying when he said that they had food in the reserves. There were crates and crates of food in both refrigeration and freezer sections. Nathan asked if he could take a glimpse for himself, and President Melero encouraged all of them to take some peeks in. Unless the food they were looking at was somehow fake and made of wax, their frozen reserves of food were not depleted at all, but were amazingly abundant.

"This is great," Skye commented at one point. "You came well-stocked."

"As you can imagine, the U.S. government always comes prepared in the event of emergencies," President Melero said as he led them out of the storage area. "Wait until you see our laboratories and gardens. They are capable of growing at speeds of up to twenty-five times of what you could see in nature. Our protein laboratories, meanwhile, churn out pound after pound of various synthetic meats spanning from chicken, beef, lamb, to pork and even shrimp."

"Twenty-five?" Dr. Chetana asked. "That's extremely impressive."

"I'm fairly certain our plants on board the hotel don't even do half that," Nathan added.

"Indeed," President Melero said. "Our researchers on board used to specialize in perfecting some of the techniques that have come in handy over the past couple of months. The situation is so well that our reserves have only slowly drained over time."

Skye frowned over the next few moments, thinking about how convenient it was that this ship was well-stocked. She knew it might have been like he said—that they simply came well prepared—but something about the whole situation didn't exactly sit right with her.

President Melero showed them the laboratories and gardens, although only through some windows in the hallway (he claimed to not want to disturb the workers with such a scene), before showing them one of the sleeping quarters on board. There were a few dozen bunks on board, and President Melero mentioned how these were only one of ten identical quarters spread throughout the ship.

"This is where the soldiers sleep," President Melero said. "Researchers and civilians have a different designated sleeping area."

"Just how many of them are soldiers?" Fritz asked.

"Over two hundred and twenty," President Melero replied without missing a beat. "Over half the individuals on board. All of them are either with the U.S. Army or the U.S. Marines, although some of those Marines are technically within the Space Force subdivision."

The tour continued over the course of the next few minutes, and Skye was growing frustrated. On the one hand, she had seen the evidence firsthand that Bruno Melero would honor the deal, hence strengthening that side of the argument. Yet despite that, her overall worries hadn't dispelled, but had even grown. Could she seriously be considering a deal as wrong as this? Skye knew that asking for women specifically could mean only one thing, and yet everything on board seemed perfect. Almost *too* perfect.

It wasn't like there were no women on the ship. At one point, the President directed a tour in a different laboratory, where Skye saw several women at work in lab coats, yet again behind glass panes. They appeared to be calm, and set on work. She tried making eye contact with them, but none of them seemed to even acknowledge her at all. Skye asked to walk in and maybe ask them some questions, but the President did not allow it.

"There's no reason to distract them," Melero brushed her off again. "Any questions you have, I can answer them, and if not, I certainly can refer them to the necessary individuals."

He wasn't budging on this stance, and it was extremely suspicious. And while there were a great deal of soldiers patrolling the hallways during the course of the tour, they weren't flooding the hallways or overwhelming the occasional civilian or researcher present during the tour the same way she would have expected. At one point, the President even showed them into a "rec room", where over a dozen women, a handful of them in uniform, were working away in some sort of knitting club crocheting various multi-colored scarfs, blankets, and other things that Skye couldn't quite catch.

Staged, Fritz mouthed to her at one point, and she looked away from him. He didn't need to spell it out for her. There was a very real possibility that this was all staged, but that would beg another question: why? Why, unless the food in the reserves wasn't real? It *did* look real, but there was really no way to know for sure unless she inspected the contents of each sealed bag or container of food that they were gifted.

"Many of the soldiers are in the gym for their daily training," President Melero claimed at one point. "They all adhere to a strict regime, and we haven't let off on them."

The final straw that broke the camel's back, however, and convinced Skye that there was something nefarious going on behind the scenes, didn't occur due to anything President Melero said, or the restrictive nature of the tour. Rather, it happened during the final leg of the tour, when he was showing them the large kitchen that served an even larger mess hall.

Many of the chefs were actively preparing lunch, and the smells of cooking (grown) meat, rich cooked sauces, and freshly roasted spawned vegetables and herbs was almost enough to make Skye's mouth water. She'd expected most of the cooks to have been soldiers, and hence wearing the same old uniform, but they all wore chef's outfits. The only thing missing from them to complete the picture of their gourmet position was the fancy froufrou chef's hat.

"As you can see," President Melero stated, "there are five high quality chefs-"

He seemed to stop abruptly, and Skye froze in the back of the room. She saw a chef looking down at the food, stirring a pot, and Melero seemed to be staring at him, before turning back as the other man scampered out the back door.

"Is everything okay?" President Melero asked.

"Yes…" Skye sputtered, turning back to him and forcing a smile. "I never thought I'd smell something like this again, and it's so refreshing. Makes me feel alive again."

"I'm glad to hear it," President Melero said. "Now, I think we're just about done…"

President Melero's words were in one ear and out the other. Because the person she'd spotted in the back of the room was someone she'd seen long ago, before the Red Day, near the start of the internship. Even though the mustache was gone, there was no mistaking the man she'd spotted.

The man who killed Grace Elliot, and whose identity had eluded all the authorities on the International Space Hotel, was the chef who had been standing in the back of the room. It seemed like there had been some sort of miscommunication, and perhaps he'd worked on a shift he shouldn't have; regardless, President Melero's reaction had been a dead giveaway.

Skye was now determined to not let President Melero get away with this. She would do whatever it took to find out his connection to the Red Day and uncover his dirty secrets.

Chapter 19

McFarland was one piece of work. When the man arrived and was dropped off at the SAS 2, gaining access through the port area through Olivia and Jace's cooperation at the control panel, Madison had no idea what to expect. He hadn't even disclosed who he was, let alone what he would be doing on the ship. But it became abundantly clear within a matter of minutes just how serious he was about his job. He set down a large suitcase before pacing around.

"I'm here to look around," McFarland stated upon arrival, walking through the various rooms throughout the ship and examining them closely, as if he was some sort of inspector.

"We're not in trouble, are we?" Cole asked. He looked around for a couple of seconds, as if assessing whether or not this was a trap. "You're from the International Space Hotel?"

"Of course, I'm from the International Space Hotel," he answered. "Where else could I possibly be from?"

"The S.S. Washington, of course," Madison speculated.

McFarland sighed for a couple of seconds, as Madison stepped forward to block his path into the refrigerator.

"What? What is it?"

"What are you doing here?"

McFarland dodged the question and peered into the refrigerator, humming as he walked in. She turned around to look for help. Olivia and Jace were still manning the controls, and the only other two people on the ship were still pouring through some of the extensive paperwork, so she groaned in frustration. It had always had to be her.

McFarland walked into the freezer, checking out some boxes, still nonchalantly humming the entire time.

"Come on now," Madison replied. "I just… want you to tell us what you're doing so we can help you."

McFarland leaned down into the box that Madison had searched through less than an hour before, uncovering four wrappers and pulling them out of the box.

"Well, well… What do we have here?"

"There's nothing in here," Madison claimed, stepping forward, her hands on her hips now. "We're looking for evidence pertaining to Space Armament Station 2. I don't know why you're here, but I suggest you come out and help us investigate."

"Oh, oh, but this is evidence," he said. He looked at the wrappers, then looked back up at her. "Evidence of a thief."

Cole rolled his wheelchair into the room.

"What's going on here?"

"I was just telling the lady that we have an ice cream burglar."

"*What?*" Cole asked. "Really? Ah man, I was saving those for when I was really feeling desperate."

Madison shook her head, turning red. "This is ridiculous. I demand you leave this room immediately."

McFarland reached out, grabbed and pulled her hands. Madison tried pulling away, but despite the man's old age, he still possessed respectable strength.

"Your hands appear to be slightly sticky," he said, touching the palms of her hands, "and this appears to be a small fragment of a chocolate cookie in between your index and middle finger on your left hand. Traces of the crime."

"What?" Madison asked, like she'd just been punched in the gut, "Do you even hear yourself? You freak."

"This is your ice cream thief," McFarland claimed, turning to Cole and pointing to Madison.

Cole turned to Madison. "Maddie?"

"Fuck you," Madison spat through gritted teeth, before turning back to McFarland.

"If you aren't responsible, then perhaps you would let me check these wrappers for fingerprints and DNA evidence."

"Come on," Madison responded. "Why the *hell* are you really here?"

"Dammit Maddie," Cole replied. "Even though I'd only known you a day, I trusted you, and you went behind my back-"

McFarland coughed. "All right, all right, settle down. There's no reason to get this worked up over ice cream. This was merely a demonstration."

"A demonstration?"

"You can call me Investigator McFarland," he said. "I'm the forensics expert and private investigator for the International Space Hotel."

"Investigator…?" Madison asked, and then it clicked. "Oh yeah, I remember Skye told me about you, something about how you helped clear her name in the Elliott case."

"Yes, I was the one who spearheaded the onboard investigation," McFarland said. "The feds sent a couple of people to investigate afterward, and they didn't come to a single conclusion that I hadn't already."

"Didn't you not solve the case, though?" Madison asked. "No offense intended, of course."

McFarland fell silent for a few moments. "You don't need to remind me. Yes, with limited available resources, I wasn't able to find the man responsible. Worst of all was the fact that despite lifting his fingerprints, there were no matches in the ship's database, or even any in the national registry."

"His fingerprints?" Cole asked. "Who?"

"The man who killed Elliott, right?" Madison asked, and McFarland nodded. McFarland led the two of them back into the living room.

"I've been dispatched here, but right as I was about to exit the ISH I was stopped, and received some big news. The same person who assassinated Elliot was spotted on board the S.S. Washington. Or at least Skye and Fritz believe so."

"No way," Madison replied.

"Do you have any tapes I can take a look at? Footage from the massacre?"

"Yes," Cole responded. Madison turned to him, surprised.

"Wait, you're telling me this entire time, that you had footage, and yet you couldn't even tell me who it was that infiltrated here?" Madison asked.

"I'm not about to look back at the murders!" Cole replied defensively. "I was traumatized, and you're asking me to look back at that? I will never relive that again. *Never*."

"I'm going to want to take a look at that," McFarland said. "I need to analyze the tapes and ascertain the identities."

"What about the bodies?"

Cole shook his head. "Uh... No. It was over a month ago; after a couple of days, I gathered the courage to dispose of them through the garbage chute, launch them out into space."

"Were they all members of your crew?"

"No," Cole responded. "There were seven deaths. Maybe a couple of their guys were wounded, I don't know. But there were seven fatalities that I came across on the ship. All six from my crew, and one of the invaders, a white man."

"Now here's a question for you," McFarland inquired. "Do you recall where the body of the assailant was found?"

"Over there," Cole said, pointing over to the corner of the main living room, the same blood splotch that Madison had first noticed yesterday. "I don't know who got him. I think it was Torild. She always was a fighter. She was the captain, and I found her in the next room over."

McFarland nodded. "Now let's take a look at these tapes, and get to the bottom of this."

***

"I can't be the only one who saw him, right?" Skye asked. She found herself now in the fancy Meeting Room 01 with the rest of the council. They had just told Marcell what had happened, and now they were debating over how to proceed next.

"No," Fritz responded. "I remember what you are talking about."

"Who are you talking about?" Nathan asked, confused.

"The man in the kitchen, the chef," Skye said. "He was the man who assassinated Grace Elliott. I'm certain of it. The way the President acted, too, it was as if he wasn't supposed to be there."

The room fell silent.

"I don't know what in the world you are talking about," Dr. Chetana replied. "I, for one, found the tour to be an excellent one. With that in mind, I think accepting the deal is a no-brainer. They seem to treat their women well."

"Me too!" Nathan proclaimed enthusiastically. Fritz looked at Skye. It looked like this was going to be a 2 v. 2, with the exact same teams as when they had argued over kicking Lusky and management back down to Earth. Skye wondered if Marcell would be the tiebreaker, again.

"I'm telling you, I don't think Skye's wrong, now that I look back on it," Fritz said. "I think we should err on the side of caution."

"How would you know?" Dr. Chetana replied. "Surely you're looking for a coincidence when there's nothing to be found."

"I was there," Skye responded. "I was detained and a suspect in the assassination, because I was working as a hostess and delivered the poison, unknowingly. I saw the man, and I'm telling you, this guy is the same. There's no way I was mistaken. Especially with how Melero waved him away."

"I trust you," Nathan said. "But what can we do?"

"Why would they kill Elliott?" Marcell asked. "That's what I don't get. You're telling me an American politician ordered the assassination of another? And for what?"

"He became the Speaker of the House, right?" Skye asked. "Therefore, he moved up one line in the U.S. government succession, and was next in line for the Presidency after the Vice President, in the event of the President's death. Sure enough, after the Red Day, he was anointed as President."

"And don't doubt this man's boldness," Fritz said. "I've heard about the tragedy that struck his family before. Bruno Melero lost his entire family, autonomous driving accident, if I remember correctly. He might have had nothing to lose after that."

"Shit," Marcell mumbled under his breath. "You're right. Oh God, if what you're saying is true, then... Then President

Melero might be the culprit behind everything. Including the Red Day."

"I wouldn't jump that far," Dr. Chetana responded. "That's crazy. Even if it's true, which I don't believe, by the way, then we still are waiting on McFarland to conduct his investigation. Now if he comes back and tells me that the soldiers were American—which they won't be; for the record, it was the Russians, I'm certain—then we'll reconsider this theory. For now, I think you're getting way ahead of yourself."

"We have less than 36 hours to make our decision," Skye said. "We can't sit around."

"That's exactly what we're doing," Nathan responded. "We're pretending like we're in charge, like we know what we do, and yet we're doing absolutely nothing, no?"

Fritz grunted in agreement.

"How would this impact our decision?" Marcell asked. "Let's say that we find out Americans were the ones that breached SAS 2, and come to a consensus that the assassin was the same person. Then what?"

"Are you that big of a dunderhead?" Fritz asked. "Then we tell them to go shove it!"

"No," Skye replied, and Fritz looked stunned.

"Huh?"

"There's no point," Skye responded. "At pissing them off. They have hundreds of soldiers, and we have less than a dozen. And most of ours are new recruits, who probably couldn't hit the broad side of a barn with their guns if they tried."

"Don't doubt my ability to coach them up," Fritz growled. "They will be ready. They've shown steady improvement at the range."

"Even so," Marcell asserted, "My point stands. Either we go along and accept their deal for the food, or we refuse it, and we take our chances down on Earth."

"It doesn't have to be so binary," Skye said.

"Well then, what do you propose?" Marcell asked. "Because right now, I see two options: accept the deal, or reject it. And I don't think we have any leverage for bargaining in this case."

Skye sat still for a few moments. Then, something flashed her brain. Before she knew it, she was rapidly scratching down notes on a notepad in front of her, brow furrowed in concentration.

"I don't like the look on her face," Fritz grunted. "It means we're going to do something dangerous that will probably get another security member killed."

"What's going on?" Dr. Chetana asked. "Skye?"

Skye looked up. She didn't know why, but she felt like she'd had a knack for devising plans ever since she assumed her position as leader on the ship. It was exactly what needed to boost her confidence, what with the way she'd felt incompetent handling Operation Exodus. She felt like could finally prove her mettle.

"What if there was a way to get the food, get some answers, and maybe not have to give up all of those women?" Skye asked.

"Then I'd call you either batshit crazy, or a genius," Fritz answered. "What are you thinking, young woman?"

Chapter 20

Madison didn't want to watch the tapes of the bloodshed that had taken place when invaders rushed into the SAS 2, killing almost everyone inside. So instead, she stared at McFarland's blank expression while he watched. Cole wasn't even in the room during the entire process, since he said it would be too hard on him. Even though Madison didn't look at the footage while it streamed, the audio was on. Screams and gunshots played loudly from the monitor. It was enough to rattle Madison.

Madison and McFarland were in the security room adjacent to the front control room to rewatch the footage. When it was finished, he played it two more times. Finally, he turned the screen off, and beckoned for Madison to follow him back to the main quarters.

"Did you watch it enough?" Madison asked, voice dripping with sarcasm.

"Of course not," McFarland responded. "I'm a former FBI agent. In our investigations, we'd watch tapes like these thousands of times over the course of weeks or even months. But I can safely conclude that our answers to this question don't lie in the tape. Sure, if you listen closely, they speak in English, and with an American accent, but it's possible that their leaders specifically instructed them to do so on the guise of being American. I want to assess the blood."

The Laser from Above

McFarland went out and scraped some of the blood from a corner of the room; then, using a swab and coating the end with the aforementioned blood, he inserted the tip inside some kind of metal machine that looked a little bit like an old calculator or one of those credit card machines Madison had seen in antiquated stores.

After a couple of minutes, he set the machine down on the table, and sat out on the sofa. By now, the other two who had been looking at the contracts, whose names Madison didn't know, had walked over to inquire about the situation.

"Sir, any word from the ISH?" one of them asked. "I feel like we are sitting ducks here."

"No, ma'am," McFarland said. "Nothing."

"When do you think we'll hear from them?" the other questioned.

"My guess is as good as yours," he admitted. "My goal here is to get some more intel, which might take as little as whenever this machine is finished analyzing the blood, or could take several hours."

"Ugh," Madison groaned. "At this rate, then, the S.S. Washington's going to grow impatient and leave us all in the dry."

"Oh, we have until tomorrow night, at the latest," McFarland clarified. "Our deadline is tomorrow night."

The next hour passed slowly. Most people picked up a book to read, as the majority of books on the bookshelf that Cole pointed out were written in English, or otherwise translated into English.

After around an hour, the machine sitting on the table beeped. McFarland looked at the screen with interest, and Madison closed in on him, sitting next to him. She didn't peep, not wanting to distract him, but after a couple of minutes, she lightly tapped his side with her shoe.

"Sir, give me the scoop," she said.

McFarland turned to her, shaking his head.

"The bad news is, the DNA analysis came back inconclusive, once again," he said, holding up the screen, where there was a bunch of small text that Madison could hardly read. "The good news is, we've got some close relatives, potentially. I'm sure if I had complete access to the registry, I'd be able to reverse-engineer this man's identity, but that would require me being on the ISH."

"Not again... Is this guy some kind of ghost, just like the assassin?"

"Hardly," McFarland said, pressing another tab at the top of the page. "You see, in the composition breakdown of his blood, you have the usual components. Around 55% plasma, the rest primary red blood cells, that's erythrocytes, and a very small sliver white blood cells, the leukocytes and platelets. But look at this. There are only trace amounts, but it's a hit with 93% certainty."

"Penyoxamine," Madison said, frowning. "What's that? I've taken two years of chemistry in college and that doesn't ring a bell."

"That's because it's information you wouldn't know, unless you worked in the government or had connections like me," McFarland said. "In the past couple of decades, the military has looked into better ways of improving morale and mental health, of granting courage and destroying cowardice."

"Okay... And that's relevant why?"

"Enter this super-stimulant. It's potent but safe. The only drawback is it is extremely expensive to manufacture, and some of the components are highly addictive. So, the soldiers take these boosters before a combat situation, and any cowardice or fear they might have experienced is suppressed. They are fearless. And in times of high pressure, when that gives them a jolt of energy, their will is unbreakable."

"That's insane," Madison said. "I've never heard any talk about this. Why? How?"

"There's a simple reason," McFarland explained. "It's treated like it's used as a simple drug ingredient. Its true effects are not highly publicized. It's a state secret. One of the American pharmaceutical giants, I forget its name now, has a patent and exclusively does business with the United States government when it comes to this drug."

"No way..." Cole whispered. "Bloody hell, are you saying what I think I'm saying? Because I don't like where this is heading."

"Yes," McFarland answered. "If we had any doubts before, then we should put them away. The people responsible for clearing out this ship, and scorching Earth... are American."

Chapter 21

"Hello, can you hear me? ISH, can you hear me?"

The question came over the radio comms at the front of the ship. Even though Lex usually worked in the back of the ship in the comms room, now they were out front with the rest of the flight crew, just for safety and openness.

"Yes, I can hear you," Lex answered. Right now, the only council member in the vicinity was Marcell, and Lex called them over saying someone was making contact.

Marcell hurried over, barely even using the cane. When he reached the destination, he realized he didn't even need the cane to maintain his balance anymore, and he let it clatter down onto the floor before asking.

"Who is this?" Marcell called over the radio.

"This is President Melero once again."

Marcell looked around, prayed someone else would assist him. But everyone was busy with their own business.

"I see a ship has docked onto the ISH from the Space Armament Station," he said. "May I ask what you were doing there?"

"Of course," Marcell replied. "Within the past couple of days, we've run out of food, as you know, and we came across this strange station. We sent out some ships to scout out the situation to ask for help."

"I understand. Did you find anything?"

Marcell couldn't hold himself back from a smug grin.

"Not yet," he lied. "There were several dead bodies. A little bit of food. You don't happen to know what could have happened to them, do you?"

"Of course not," President Melero, not an ounce of hesitation within his voice. "I'm assuming they got caught up with the wrong people when this all started. The Chinese. I am speaking of the culprits behind the destruction."

"By the way," Marcell said, ignoring President Melero, "I believe our leader has something to talk to you about in the next hour. About our deal."

***

Skye shook hands with Melero in the middle of the connector. Behind them, around ten or fifteen feet away, was a pair of soldiers on the S.S. Washington side, and, a similar distance away on the ISH side, a pair of security guards from the ISH (Ariel and Noah). Skye hoped nothing would go wrong, because although she didn't doubt the skills of the two security guards, she had no doubt their marksmanship training would be dwarfed by the thorough practice and routine from the American soldiers.

"It's good to see you," Melero said. "I'm assuming you've been deliberating over the last couple of hours?"

"Yes," Skye answered. "And we've come to a decision."

"What's that?"

"We have a counter-offer for you."

President Melero's face seemed to pucker up in discontent. But the President appeared to be open to some sort of negotiation, because he nodded. "No guarantees I'll accept it, but let's hear it."

"I accept the deal you have on the table, with the three weeks' meals for fifty women," Skye said. "However, we have a banquet first, tonight, in the ISH's cafeteria."

"I thought we agreed: it would take place on our ship."

"Yes," Skye responded. "But take this from our perspective. You showed us the crates of food you'd lend us, but we have no proof the food isn't poisoned, let alone that it was real food and not plastic."

"That's absurd," The President objected. "What could we possibly gai-"

"Then prove it," Skye interrupted. "We have a feast tonight, with our starving population, using your resources. You can invite everyone you have on board to feast. The ISH has plenty of room, but had a lot less people on board following Elliott's assassination."

"Okay," President Melero responded. "And what other stipulations do you have?"

"Glad you asked," Skye replied. "We'll help move our supplies from the S.S. Washington to the storage facilities on our ship over the next several hours, while verifying the integrity of the product. We can have a sort of quasi-open borders policy. You let everyone who wants to check out the S.S. Washington stroll around your ship, and in exchange your soldiers can do the same with the International Space Hotel."

"Why would we ever agree to that? So you can sneak about?"

"No. You can understand why I would be inclined to mistrust you... Especially considering the terms of the agreement. You allow this, and I am more likely to believe that you don't have such ill intentions."

"Perhaps," Melero managed. "That's it?"

"Yes."

"Very well," President Melero replied. "As you can imagine, there are certain areas on the ship that contain highly classified information, or dangerous weapons. Hence, all civilians will be strictly prohibited from entering these restricted areas. They can still walk around most of the ship, though."

Skye nodded. The entire time, she was thinking of ways that she could access those zones.

***

An hour later Graham was pacing around an office, distraught. Marcell was next to him.

"Oh shit, I can't do this, I can't do this," Graham repeated.

"Yes, you can," Marcell promised. "I would do it myself, if I wasn't still limp and slow as a snail. Besides, Melero is already aware that I'm on the council. He's never seen you in his life. You'll be fine."

"No, Marcell, I won't be fine," Graham said. "What if I'm caught, what then? The entire plan fails, I get killed, and the entire deal is off."

"Fine, I'll say it," Marcell responded. "It's Skye's plan. I thought that fact might influence your decision, so maybe you ought to reconsider."

"Skye?" Graham asked freezing. "Skye volunteered me to kill myself? Geez, and to think that I thought she liked me. Now that hurts."

"She likes you plenty," Marcell insisted. "As a matter of fact, she said that she trusted no one on board more than you. Which is why she thought you were the man for the job."

Graham paused for a moment. Surely this was some sort of manipulation to coax him into the plan. But he knew from experience, and from what Dr. Chetana said, that Skye *was* in charge. Which meant only one thing... that what Marcell was saying had to be true. Many people in relationships would stop at nothing to protect their special other, to keep them away from dangerous situations, but Marcell was claiming that in this case, it was the opposite, that Skye was personally using her boyfriend as cannon fodder. Did Graham buy that?

Knowing everything that had happened, the way that she had killed that one security guard without hesitation, whereas Graham had felt so much doubt rising inside of him before he had shot that one man, Graham believed it.

"All right," Graham sighed. "I'll do it."

"Thanks!" Marcell grinned. "I knew you'd come around to it."

"But I have so many questions about this. I'm not a sacrificial lamb. Practically, what recourse do I have if I get exposed? I don't think I have the skill, or the courage, to shoot my way out of it."

"I figured you would ask," Marcell said. He pulled out a black canister from his weapons belt and set it down carefully on a nearby table, and Graham stepped forward to observe it.

"What's this? Pepper spray? Seriously?" Graham asked, running his hands around the side, worried that it would explode at a moment's notice.

"This isn't any sort of ordinary pepper spray," Marcell said. "This pepper spray contains Noxium mixed in liquid form. These are usually kept in our armory. Fortunately, we a few spare canisters left from Operation Exodus to make this work."

"Sheesh," Graham replied. "Here we go again with chemical warfare again. That's good. So, I just spray them, and it knocks them out instantly?"

"No," Marcell said. "It'll burn them for a few seconds, and the victim will be in agonizing pain. After all, the normal components of Capsicum are present, but it's mixed with Noxium. The Noxium diffuses through the skin. I recommend the face for the fastest effect. They should be out in less than ten seconds at most, likely five seconds. Plus, they don't die, usually, and it's significantly quieter than a gunshot. Just steer clear of the clouds yourself, or you might pass out."

Graham nodded. "Okay…"

"You remember all the plans for tonight?"

"Yes," Graham replied. "Outfit, security room, check the footage, look for the registry, and then help you find Jacques Monreau, the chef. Sneak back to the ISH. Is that it all?"

"Well done," Marcell said. "To recap, this is what he looks like."

Marcell showed him a printed picture of Jacques Monreau that he'd evidently gotten from the hotel's security files.

"There's no guarantee the footage on their ship will be as high definition as this, you know," Graham said. "If it's not, then I don't know how you expect me to be able to make anything out. It'll be like searching for a needle in a darn haystack."

Marcell shrugged.

"I know," Marcell answered. "But we have to try."

***

"Is comms ready to go?" Skye asked Lex in the comms room. Lex sat in front of the familiar control panel where Skye had logged all of the fatalities on board.

"Indeed," Lex answered. "I think everything you said to me has been properly set up."

"Good," Skye said. She shook hands with them once again. Lex hesitated for a few moments.

"Can I ask... why? I'm really confused about what's going on tonight."

Skye thought for a few moments. On the one hand, she wanted to tell them everything that was going on. Lex could be trusted. On the other hand, the more secretive the plan was, the better.

"Don't worry about it," Skye said. "We've planned out everything, and one way or another, for tonight, and I'm sure you'll understand what this is about in the next several hours."

That incredibly vague reassurance did little to quell Lex's curiosity, but they nodded before handing over the microphone to Skye for the announcement she had come to make.

"Attention, everyone on board," Skye said. "As you all have known, the S.S. Washington has ported with the International Space Hotel's docking bay. Well, I'm pleased to announce that tonight, in our cafeteria, we will be having a joint banquet with the S.S. Washington's assistance. There will be plenty of food, courtesy of President Melero's generosity. This will take place at eight tonight. I know you are all starving, but I hope that this meal tonight will be to your satisfaction.

"As we speak, we are assembling a few teams from our warehouse crew and cafeteria to help move supplies from the S.S. Washington over to the storage warehouse here. As a part of this deal, the connector is now accessible. You can board the S.S. Washington right now if you so desire, and tour the unrestricted areas. I repeat, feel free to check out the S.S. Washington. However, also please listen to any of their rules and if they ask you to leave at any point, you must return to the ISH. I will also be breaking some major news tonight, about our future on this ship, so I know I will see you all there at eight. Be sure to vacate the S.S. Washington by then, if you choose to board. Thank you."

***

Skye's plan to mix the populations worked to their advantage.

Apparently, the S.S. Washington had a strict policy against drinking. Graham didn't know how a bunch of twenty-something men would possibly function with no family, alcohol, and few women without going completely insane, but they somehow must have. Because there were many soldiers on board the S.S. Washington who had survived to this point, and now flooded the corridors of the International Space Hotel looking for drinks. There must've been dozens and dozens crossing over in minutes, so many that the council ordered every service worker to help assist and ensure that no looting occurred and that men be limited to three drinks only, a rule which Marcell knew would not be able to be adequately enforced. While the ISH had completely run out of food, what they lacked in food they made up for with alcohol, gallons and gallons of alcohol. It was alcohol, however, that now ran the risk of draining out. Marcell imagined Fritz was deploying the whole security force that second around every bar area in the ship.

"They are drinking like they've never drank before," Nathan reported over the line to the other council members. He must've been at one of the other bars, which, Marcell imagined, was as hectic as this one.

"It can't be helped," Skye replied.

"There's going to be nothing left," Dr. Chetana complained. "Just so you know, since we thought our alcohol reserves were untouchable."

"That's a sacrifice I'm willing to make."

Now that the plan had been set into action, it made Marcell and Graham's job easier.

Marcell mournfully looked over at a bar, where, in the last couple of weeks, he had met Jordan. While many people had been drinking there at this time, now it was complete chaos. All of the taps were being drained, and some men held their mouths underneath each tap, the booze pouring into their mouths for seconds until the next man pushed his way in. All of the men cheered, cursed, and some of them even sang some sort of drinking song. Marcell didn't even know those existed anymore.

At one point, one of the men called out he was going to find the bathroom, and right on cue, Marcell grabbed Graham by his shoulder and escorted him in front of this man.

"Hey, sir," Marcell said, singling out the man. Sure enough, the height and size looked promising for an adequate fit, not too big, nor too small.

"What the fuck do you want?" the man asked.

"You looking for the bathroom?"

"Yes!"

"Well, if you help me out lifting something quick, I'll give you a free bottle of wine. If you can hold it for a second."

"I hate wine," the man said, shaking his head.

"A keg of beer, then," Marcell offered, and the man's eyes lit up.

Marcell led him straight into the same office he'd met with Graham earlier down the hallway a little bit, before opening the door and ushering him in.

"Hey," the man said. "What do I have to lift?"

"Just over here," Marcell said, waving him over, even though there was nothing conspicuous to lift up.

"Umm, excuse me?"

Marcell turned to look at Graham, and nodded. The next few seconds were a blur. Graham whipped out the pepper spray in his pocket, and sprayed it on the man's face. He screamed in pain, his face scrunching together and turning a shade of crimson red as Marcell wrapped his sleeved arm around to muffle his shouts, lest he alert any potential bystanders in the vicinity to the crime. The man wrestled in his grasp, sending Marcell toppling backwards onto the ground, and he groaned in pain, landing on the side with his wound, but not easing up, even as the man's hands grabbed at Marcell's face. Within a couple of seconds, the man's kicking slowed, and then seized, as his body loosened still. He was unconscious.

"Holy heck," Graham said. He set the pepper spray back down before helping Marcell up, who was wincing and gingerly touching his wound.

"You okay?" Graham asked. "Please tell me you didn't re-aggravate your wound."

"No, no, I'm fine," Marcell responded, but he had to lift up and check the wound on his torso, just to be sure, and it looked fine. There was no bleeding, his wound still recovering, and his stitches were still intact.

"What now?" Graham asked, looking down at this unconscious man.

"It looks like your assumed identity is going to be Sergeant Walton," Marcell said, pointing out the three lines on the man's sleeve. "You couldn't have been any luckier. If we'd have picked a private or private first class, it'd be much more likely that you'd get stopped for going places you aren't supposed to, or otherwise have a lower clearance level."

"Okay, so I put on his shirt and pants…"

Marcell grunted. "Yes, Graham. Do you need help doing that, or do you remember how to do that?"

"Stop it," Graham whined. "What about the unconscious body? We're going to have to make sure he doesn't get found over the next several hours."

"I'll take care of it," Marcell promised. "Trust me."

"And what about this?" Graham asked, shaking the glasses on his head. "I'm pretty sure the military doesn't accept people with vision deferments. Sorry to say my family wasn't rich enough to get me a procedure to fix my vision."

"Oh yeah," Marcell said, nodding. "You'll need contacts."

Graham gulped. This mission was getting more stressful by the second.

Chapter 22

There was no webcam that the others could watch Graham from, and in that sense, he was going to be all by himself.

Marcell did hand him an earpiece, which connected him with the members of the council. There was, however, the issue that the Sergeant Walton they knocked out actually did have an earpiece of his own.

"You can listen to it, muted," Marcell offered. "Put it on mute, and that way, if you get any interesting information, you can report back to us."

Graham listened to Marcell's advice, leading to him having an earpiece with the ISH in the left ear, and the S.S. Washington's on the right.

"Question," Graham said, frowning. "You said you made an extra effort when you sent that one guy out to the SAS to not transmit any radio broadcast. Yet you have us all communicate over radio to each other with these different earpieces. I don't understand the contradictory behavior."

"You're the engineering intern, not me," Marcell replied, shrugging.

Graham's eyes widened. "You're telling me you don't actually know?"

"No," Marcell answered. "Fritz would know the answer better than me. I think the short answer is that we can be much more confident these are on a secure line. This is top-of-the-line technology. This was developed by Ascendant Technologies, same people that helped design the SAS, and the S.S. Washington also worked with the International Space Hotel. They made sure we had secure lines for this system. It is, for all intents and purposes, invisible, completely encrypted in a way that, even if they listen in, renders all voices scrambled."

Graham figured he had too many things to worry about than to dwell on his own earpieces, so that he nodded, satisfied by the answer.

It was then that it was time for Graham to cross the connector. On the way, he passed some of the soldiers, still partying around the booze and raucously cheering. He hoped none of them would notice how he was out of place and stop him. But no one even batted an eye, and he continued on his way. Now that Graham wasn't wearing glasses, he at least was feeling slightly more confident.

"You can do this," Skye told him over the line, "I know you can."

The connector was the next phase, and he reached the doorway to see a clump of soldiers hanging around the entrance. He slowly approached, feeling like his cover was about to be blown before he could even leave the ship, but then they quickly dissipated, one of them jeering how they were going to hit the booze.

Then he slipped inside. The connector was, fortunately, several people wide, so that he felt like he could space out enough without being closely observed. A few soldiers passed him on the route, as Graham followed some of the other residents of the ISH back towards the S.S. Washington.

He wondered if the fact that he was the first soldier returning already would arouse suspicion, but found that there were no security checkpoints or even security guards to be spoken of.

Once he entered the hallways, he found that there were a few dozen of the guests and staff of the ISH who wandered around.

"I'm in," he mumbled into his earpiece, turning to the left. "I'm heading to the front."

Graham was extremely grateful for the cover provided by all of the guests. Skye's idea of somehow mixing up both ship's populations was completely ingenious, although he didn't know, still, that there were other components to the plan beyond his knowledge.

"Okay, good," Fritz spoke over the line. "This is the time where I take over. Do you see any rooms with security cameras?"

Graham looked at the rooms. He was glad that most of the doors appeared to be propped open, allowing him to glimpse through and see the inside contents of each room. Those that weren't had windows to look through, most of them with their curtains opened.

Storage room, nope. Janitor's closet. Some kind of war room.

It was oddly lax security for what he'd expect for a military warship, but then again, this plan had been so unexpected that he didn't doubt President Melero had been at complete ease, unprepared for an infiltration of this kind. Certainly, he couldn't have expected such a devious plan as theirs to be implemented with such speed.

Graham found the security office rather quickly, and with inexplicably good timing, too. He saw a man emerging from the room in uniform right as he was about to near the room.

The man nodded at him, and for a second, Graham panicked internally, not sure about what to do and for what rank it would be the proper etiquette to salute or be saluted.

"Good evening, Sarge," the other man said.

"Evening."

Graham also managed a friendly nod back, his heart in his throat as the soldier completed an about-face and started walking away. Graham hoped he hadn't messed up, but he hadn't gotten a second glance, so he thought he was in the clear.

A few people were in the hallways, although none so close now as the soldier who had just exited the room, and around half of them consisted of ISH guests. He cracked open the door, walked inside, and found that there was not a single soul in the room. Grinning, he ran up to the security footage.

His first impression was that the camera footage was perfectly normal. There were many different cameras showing many different angles and views spread throughout the ship, and Graham knew that there was no way in hell he would be able to find their target on the cameras, not without some sort of aid. There were simply too many screens. He dug through a couple of the drawers to look for papers.

Graham was lucky. Within only a minute of searching through two different rooms within the security room, he came across both a map of the entire spaceship, which identified each room number, as well as a printed registry of everyone on board the ship. Given that each camera showed a short abbreviation that also marked each room, that meant that he could easily identify which camera was showing which room, and also meant that he could cycle through some of the different cameras without being as lost as he would have been otherwise. Graham set the papers up, and also grabbed a pen, eager to start searching for the man responsible. However, before he could do anything, the door creaked open, and Graham turned to see a soldier, with his rank indicating either he was private first class or corporal (he didn't know which one), entering the room and stalling in the doorway. It was honestly a little shocking to call this man a soldier: he was a whelp, and while he was only an inch or two below Graham's height, his face looked like he was easily five years younger.

"Uh, sir?" the soldier asked. "I'm scheduled for the next shift."

"No," Graham replied. Graham swore he could hear a collective intake of breath from the other side of the line, from the council members who must've known that he was in trouble.

"No?" the man asked. "You can check the schedule board: I'm on shift in this security room. I double checked."

"Special orders from higher up," Graham bluffed. "As you can imagine, these are special times with all those guests scrambling about. I'm to look at the cameras for anything suspicious, and not you. That's an order."

"All right, sir," he said, about to step up. "Do I know you?"

Graham chuckled. "No, but I know you, runt. Go make yourself useful, and watch those visitors. *Now!*"

"Yes sir," the man assented meekly. Graham almost felt bad for the kid.

The soldier closed the door behind, and Graham sighed out in relief. A bullet was dodged yet, although Graham knew it wasn't at the end of the danger, not even close. Still, it was the best acting job he'd ever done. If he had impersonated a soldier like this, he had no doubt he'd have been an A+ actor.

***

"How do you know he's not in the International Space Hotel?" Graham asked. He received an answer almost immediately from Fritz.

"I'm looking at the cameras as we speak," Fritz assured him. "I've got some of my security team on the lookout, as well. There's nobody who fits the description, and we're analyzing the face of each person who passes through. Wherever that man is, he's certainly on the S.S. Washington, and not here."

"What if they got rid of them?" Graham asked. "He might have suspected we knew about him. Maybe he launched him off board, and we're looking for a man who's no longer alive."

"That's maybe possible," Skye admitted. "But if President Melero entrusted the Elliott assassination to that man, then I would doubt it. He's probably gifted in some way."

Graham opened up the registry. Whereas the registry at the ISH, which used to be continually updated before the Red Day, had been organized by role, with a list of interns, full-time staff, and clients, this registry was one giant alphabetical list. It did, fortunately, denote whether or not the individual on board was a Researcher (denoted by Res), a Politician (Pol), Civilian (Civ), or Soldier (Sol).

"There's no chefs here," Graham mumbled. "It organizes everyone by researcher, politician, civilian, or soldier. It doesn't say anything about whether they are chefs or not."

"Probably because the chefs are soldiers," Fritz offered.

"Are there any special markings on the page?" Dr. Chetana asked.

Now that Graham looked closely, there was. Some contained an asterisk by their name, others yet, a carat or a tilde. At the bottom of the document the indicators were listed out in the form of a key, explaining what the symbols represented. High-ranking officer. Special Forces. Not to mention...

"Chef," Graham said aloud. "Those with that squiggly line are chefs."

"It's called a tilde," Dr. Chetana said.

"Great, a tilde," Graham said, forcing a smile before remembering that he didn't have to act for the cameras. "It looks like there is a grand total of... Eight chefs on board. Damn, do I actually have to look for each of them on camera, one by one?"

"I don't know what to say," Skye said. "Can you do this?"

Graham looked to the wall, where, mounted on it was an analog clock. It read that it was about 4:06 p.m., which let Graham know that the ship, much like the International Space Hotel, followed Universal Standard Time. If the clock was accurate, then that meant only one thing.

"They must rotate shifts, every hour or two hours," Graham said. "Considering I dealt with someone around five minutes ago, that means I have time. All right, time to look."

Graham looked through the registry, before finding a spare post-it note, ripping it out, and writing down their individual names, as well as their listed residence on the registry. He also found a keycard sitting on the ground, and he pocketed it immediately, grinning.

"Good news. Got access to registry with their names, as well as a keycard that was left about, although I'm not sure what access that will have. Looking at the chefs, a couple of the names are Hispanic sounding," Graham said. "Another yet, clearly Chinese. I mean, it's safe to say our guy isn't one of them, right?"

"Unless it's a cover," Fritz offered.

"I think you do what is right," Nathan advised. "Just work."

"Wait a minute..." Graham said, voice trailing off.

Graham looked over at one of the other monitors, which contained numerous different buttons, including "past footage," "adjust settings," "monitor population," and "update registry," among a few others which he wasn't as interested in.

Graham clicked on the update registry button, which sent him to another page with a bunch of names, spelled out in alphabetical order. He clicked on the first one, and the computer loaded a high-quality headshot of a soldier on the screen.

"Jackpot!" He mumbled.

"What's going on?" Marcell asked. "As we speak, I'm preparing to help unload the ship. I'm making my way over to the S.S. Washington right now. Any updates?"

"I'm working on it," Graham stated. "I think I found what I need to identify his picture."

There were a few different dropdowns that appeared which Graham could select, such as "role" and "speciality." Graham selected a specialty, and from there chose chef among other options including interrogator, field medic, and technician, and was presented with the eight names. One by one, he touched the screen, going down the list until he was about halfway down, and stopped. The face was a perfect match to the one to the picture that Marcell had shown him, save for the fact he had no mustache.

"Jack Monterey," Graham said, reading the name off of the screen.

"Huh?" Skye asked. "Monterey Jack cheese? Are you pushing my buttons?"

"No," Graham said, smirking. "No, I'm not joking. The dude's name is Jack Monterey."

"Poor man." Fritz chuckled. "No wonder he adopted the pseudonym of Jacques Monreau. Not only so he could get away assassinating a high-profile politician, but to conceal the shame of his parents naming him after a delicious type of cheese. I bet his sister's called Brie."

Graham looked at the man's profile, too absorbed and nervous to laugh at Fritz's joke. It listed Sleeping Quarters 6 as his assigned residence. In addition to that, it listed information such as his date of birth (the man was aged 27), location of birth (contrary to what his accent had indicated to Skye long ago, he was born in Henrietta, New York), and his rank (he was a lieutenant).

Graham looked down at the cameras. Now it was time to find Jack.

Graham started by looking for the sleeping quarters. Of the twenty or so screens, it looked like a couple of them were focused on them, and, as he watched, they transitioned, from sleeping quarters 1 and 2 to sleeping quarters 3 and 4; now that he looked at it, it appeared that the cameras automatically transitioned to every minute or so. He was grateful to see that the quality of footage on the camera was excellent. From his past experiences on Earth, CCTV footage had hardly evolved in from its grainy view in the past half century, but the S.S. Washington was a clear exception.

Graham waited another minute until the screens switched to sleeping quarters 5 and 6. When he did, he tried messing with the cameras, but a lot of them, and by the time he figured out how to zoom on it, the camera flipped forwards to sleeping quarters 7 and 8.

"Grrr," he grumbled.

"What's going on?" someone asked from over the line, but by now he was blotting them out, intensely concentrated.

Within the next minute, Graham was able to navigate both to the right screen on one of the panels, as well as now zoom in throughout the room. Sleeping quarters 6 was almost empty, although a few people were lounging around. This camera was high quality, and enabled him to get a close look at all of their faces. A few troops were playing cards, and appeared to be gambling what looked like protein bars. Around five or so were fast asleep; he could zoom in to most of their faces, and, managing to skip to a camera on the opposite corner of the room, checked out all of them, except for one man whose face was buried in his pillow, and whose entire body was underneath the blankets.

"He's not in the sleeping quarters," Graham admitted. "I reviewed the footage. Let me check the kitchen next."

"It's been a few minutes," Marcell whispered. "I'm almost in their storage facility, with a bunch of these transportation carts... At this rate, I'm going to be doing manual labor waiting for you."

"I know, I know, I'm trying," Graham said.

Graham looked at the kitchen next, which was showing on one of the other screens. This time, he was able to figure out the button scheme more easily and use it to zoom in on a high-definition closeup of all the cooks. There were five in the kitchen currently. But Jack Monterey was not one of them.

"Ugh, no luck," Graham complained, and he started scanning as many monitors as possible.

By some miracle, in one of the corner cameras, he saw something catch his eyes. In the basement, a man, clad in his uniform, like most of the soldiers on the ship, was walking straight towards the camera. Graham zoomed in, saw the face, which was a perfect match to the face that appeared on the side monitor, and gasped.

"I got a visual! I got a visual!" Graham exclaimed. "Jack Monterey is in the basement!"

"On my way," Marcell said. Graham could see Marcell on one of the other cameras, somewhere in the storage facility area, limping, hopping behind the wheel of one of the transportation carts. He had no cane, but he, and a man next to him, who Graham recognized as another security guard from the ISH, wore backpacks.

"Just what are they doing," Graham mouthed silently. "What in the heck are they doing?"

As much as Graham wanted to wait and see, he didn't, because he had been told by Marcell what his task was, and that was leaving the ship. He first cleared up the evidence of his search on the one monitor, and then returned the screen to the default menu. Then, he checked the cameras once again to make sure that everything appeared all right. It looked fine. Although now that he looked at all of the different cameras, and quickly cross-referenced them with the map that he had taken, he found that there was a significant lack of camera coverage on the lower floor.

Interesting, he thought. *Why would this be the case?*

But it wasn't his job to evaluate camera blind spots, and he realized there was a real possibility that there simply were plenty of weapons and research facilities on the basement floor. Graham grabbed a clipboard, attaching the registry and map he'd taken to it, and then he walked back into the hallway, quietly whistling to himself to try to stop himself from hyperventilating.

Chapter 23

Marcell drove a transportation cart. In the side seat, one of the few remaining original security guards from his team, Noah, rode shotgun as they pulled into one of the large industrial elevators in the vicinity.

Noah had loaded a couple of crates onto the cart, which was crucial for their next phase, and Marcell was grateful that no one had been at the security checkpoint to check their bags. If they had, then they would have come across various ropes and a roll of duct tape, which probably would've led to their immediate detainment.

Marcell and Noah hurried out the elevator to emerge into an exceptionally long basement. It was by some miracle that they even managed to enter the hallway when he was still in it, walking away from them and towards an undisclosed exit somewhere.

"Hey, sir! Sir!" Marcell called, and the man turned around, looking at them. Marcell stepped on the gas, and they approached the man, waving for him to stop. The man frowned, evidently displeased by their arrival.

"What is it?" he asked, stopping in his tracks. "What are you doing here?"

No French accent, Marcell noted mentally. *Sounds like your average joe.*

"I was instructed to come down here, recover something from the secondary storage closet," Marcell said, stepping out of the cart and slowly approaching him. "You wouldn't happen to know where that was, would you?"

"No," Jack answered. "You must be mistaken. There's nothing down here. I'm going to have to ask you to leave these premises. Civilians aren't allowed on this floor."

Marcell stepped towards him, and it looked like Jack was reaching towards his gun defensively now. But Marcell casually pulled out his can of pepper spray, tossing it up into the air. Jack frowned, appalled and yet simultaneously transfixed by this man, who looked like he was about to spray paint something right in front of him.

"Don't mind me," Marcell managed, shaking up the can, and then aiming it at Jack. He squeezed the top to release the spray and Jack collapsed to the ground, writhing and shouting in pain.

"Ah! Oh *God*! *It burns*! Ahhh…"

The Noxium quickly went to work, the man's groans growing silent as he slipped unconscious.

"Let's move! Before anyone can witness this on camera!"

Marcell and Noah hurriedly loaded the unconscious body of Jack Monterey into one of the crates, tying up his hands, and using duct tape to cover up his mouth. When it was finished, they set the lid on top, careful not to completely seal it, since they didn't want to inadvertently kill the man with oxygen deprivation. The entire process took less than thirty seconds, but Marcell felt a giant cramp in his back when he was finished, and he leaned up against the wheel, wincing in pain.

"Are you okay?" Noah asked. Marcell nodded and slowly got behind the wheel once again. The process had been smooth, and Marcell hoped that there had been no witnesses. This was, of course, assuming that no one else apart from Graham had been manning the cameras, since he knew Graham had taken control. If there were other witnesses who had seen them through cameras, then he figured it would be a matter of less than a minute until the alarm was pulled and he was thrown into the brig.

There was no point waiting around to find out, however, and Marcell knew their chances were better the quicker that they had the move on. He pressed the button to the elevator before hobbling back in the vehicle.

Marcell was about to steer the vehicle back into the giant industrial elevator, but once the door opened, a few soldiers stood there. Their faces narrowed into frowns.

"Hey! What the hell are you doing here?" one of them asked, putting his hand on his holstered pistol.

"Sorry! I'm sorry, we got turned around!" Marcell asked. "We thought we had to get more stuff from storage down here. Right?"

"No!" The soldier said. Marcell expected any moment for them to pull out their guns or tell them to get the man out of the crate, but they didn't. It seemed like they had no idea what had happened a minute before at all.

"Did you see anything?" another of the soldiers asked, a private by the looks of things, and Marcell shook his head. He had no idea what that was supposed to mean.

"Uh, no," Marcell said. "Like what?"

"Get back in there!" one of the other soldiers said, and Marcell drove the vehicle back inside.

"All right," the soldier, the first one who had yelled at them, and the highest-ranking officer, said. "Private, you escort them back to the ISH, and make sure they don't go exploring places they aren't supposed to be going."

"Yes, sir," the man said. The other two exited the elevator, closing the door behind, while the private looked at both of them and shook his head.

"Idiots," the man muttered, shaking his head. "Fucking idiots."

"Sorry," Noah apologized. "We'll leave immediately."

Marcell wondered what they were hiding down there, but he didn't stick around to find out.

***

A few minutes later, Jack Monterey was bound up to a chair, and hurriedly woken up with a bucket of ice-cold water. His hands were bound, and his eyes were covered with a cloth. They had also already taken off his shoes and socks, so that the cold water splashed and settled around his feet.

Marcell never thought they'd have ever had a use for the interrogation room in the prison wing of the ISH, but for once, they did, as this was where they held the lieutenant captive.

"Gah!" Jack gasped as he woke up, his eyes flicking around the room from side to side in panic, only to realize he couldn't see through the cloth. "Where am I? Who are you?"

"Monterey," Marcell said glumly, "I hope, for your sake, that you cooperate with us."

"Look, this has got to be some kind of misunderstanding. I didn't damage the goods in the basement, that was Corporal Scanlon, I swear!"

"Huh? What goods?" Marcell asked, eyes widening. Fritz was shaking his head, not pleased with his blatant curiosity.

Jack Monterey fell silent for a few moments. "You mean you don't know? Wait, who is this? Can I get your name and rank please? If you're one of the interrogators… Valdez, Crest, is that you?"

"No, you cannot have my name and rank," Fritz replied. "You are subject to an official investigation."

All of a second, it looked like Jack had been jolted with a bolt of electricity from his seat, as his back straightened, and he struggled to open his arms. So, too, were his legs bound to the chair, and despite his best efforts, he couldn't move at all. This chair was nailed to the ground, after all. In the dim light of this particular room (which Fritz had set before they took him out of the box), and with the cloth covering his face, Lieutenant Monterey stood no chance of identifying his captors, but he was clearly trying.

"My brains must've been scrambled," he muttered aloud, his voice growing louder as he went on. "I remember now. I got pepper sprayed, and then, I passed out! It was you two! You from the Space Hotel! Do you realize how much shit you're going to be in when they find out what you've done!? You'll be in a world of pain!"

Fritz looked to Marcell.

"Looks like our cover is blown," he whispered. "What a shame."

"You're the one that's going to be in a world of pain," Marcell said in the most menacing voice that he could muster.

"I have nothing to say to you," Jack replied. "Do you know what I've been through in the military? I've trained my whole life for moments like this. I won't cave."

"You're awful vocal for someone about to face the most excruciating torture of his pitiful twenty-seven-year-old existence."

"Huh?"

"Furthermore, I was a military interrogator for five years," Fritz replied. He walked over to the toolbox on the nearby surface of a table, pulling out a small blade and looking at it glistening in the dim light. "It doesn't give me any pleasure to do this, but it sure as hell is going to hurt you a lot more than it will hurt me."

"I can't watch this," Marcell said quietly, turning away as Fritz approached, starting to cut the man's uniform away from his chest. Despite Marcell's reluctance, he forced himself to turn and watch as Fritz gashed the man's shoulder with a diagonal cut.

"Ah!" Lieutenant Monterey exclaimed. "Oh, the good old cutting method, huh? What is this, 18th century China? You really think this is going to make me break?"

"Oh, I'm just getting started," Fritz said. "First, I'll cut you up a little bit. I'll waterboard you. Then I'll break some of your fingers, rip off your fingernails. If that still hasn't worked, I'll castrate you. Is it really worth becoming nothing more than a broken husk of a man? Or, you could cooperate with us. Tell us the truth behind Grace Elliott's death."

Even though Marcell couldn't see Monterey's eyes, he was certain he would see fear flash in it if he had. It looked like he was sinking down into his own chair, too, as if realizing the gravity of the situation he was in had strengthened the artificial gravitational field that kept his feet to the ground.

Marcell stared. Fritz was terrifying when he was like this.

***

At around six, Skye came to knock on the door. Marcell told to hold it, cracked the door open a smidge, and saw Skye on the other side. Without exposing the scene inside, he opened the door, but that wasn't enough to stop the muffled screaming as he stepped out into the hallway with Skye.

"How's your progress?" Skye asked. "It's been an hour and a half, and I've heard no update from you guys."

"The man... he just isn't breaking. He said he wouldn't, and I can't help but think he might be right. Maybe it was a part of his training."

"Damn," Skye said. "Well, you know, we have to be done by eight. The banquet. Otherwise, I don't know, we'll be forced to take some drastic measures. And I don't think we'll win."

"Have our supplies been looked at?"

"Yes, they've all been moved to our warehouse area," Skye replied. "Our cooking crew is working with some of their chefs. I say some, because of course Monterey isn't with them."

"Has any alarm been raised? About Jack Monterey, or Sergeant Walton, missing?"

"Oh, of course not," Skye answered. "If it had, then we wouldn't be having this conversation. I'm assuming no one knows Walton is missing, and with Monterey's slip-up earlier today, I'm assuming he's pretty much being sequestered for the day, so no one would even check on him."

"That's a lot of assumptions."

"Maybe. Look, I need the confession, soon. It has to… it has to happen before or when the banquet is occurring, for obvious reasons, or we're all screwed."

"I know. We're working on it."

"Well, work harder. Has he really said nothing?"

"No, I wouldn't say that," Marcell said. "Now that I think about it, when we first woke him up, he was a bit confused, you know, so he was speaking a lot. He said it wasn't his fault that the goods in the basement were damaged."

"The basement?"

"It's where we took Monterey from. According to what Graham said after the mission, there was an apparent absence of cameras on the lowest floor."

"You think…" Skye was deep in thought. "There's something going on in the basement?"

"I mean, it's a military spaceship," Marcell said. "The ammo depot, and a lot of the weapons, are stored down there, right?"

"Yes," Skye said, pulling out a folded piece of paper from her pocket and unraveling the schematics for the ship that Graham had retrieved. "Yes, it is."

She looked through the diagram. "According to this, there's a large storage area for the weapons munitions, and an adjacent locker room. I wonder… The damaged goods he's talking about… No, it can't be."

"What?" Marcell asked.

"I don't know. Just keep on going. I have a sneaking suspicion the answer will clear up a lot of things for us."

***

Madison, in her boredom, had found a silvery bouncy ball, and was tossing it from one surface to another in the main quarters of Space Armament Station 2, the ball rhythmically bouncing once off the wall, once back onto the hard floor, and then into her hand, where the cycle would repeat. She felt she was getting into the flow of things quite well.

Thump thump clap! Thump thump clap! Thump thump clap!

Everyone else on board, seemed to be concentrating on their own respective tasks. But it appeared that their interests required a bit more peace and quiet than Madison was providing.

"Would you stop it?" Cole asked. "I'm trying to read here."

"I'm trying to bounce here," Madison retorted, resuming bouncing her ball. She was about to make a joke about how on his wheelchair he could roll, but probably shouldn't try to bounce, but she realized that her dark humor would probably garner a rightful slap to the face, and she bit her tongue.

"There's nothing else to do, anyway," Madison managed. "Unless someone steps up and cooks something for us. Then we all could satiate our appetites."

Cole sat his book down, and looked at Madison with a look of disgust. "Did you really just ask the man in the wheelchair, who'd been shot by your gun and almost killed yesterday, to go and make your lazy arse some supper? You, of all people, after you stole my ice cream sandwiches from underneath my nose? You twocker."

"I think almost getting killed is an exaggeration," Madison said, but her face matched his serious expression and she sighed. "Anyone here know how to cook? You get dibs on the first serving of food, of course."

One of the others nodded and verbally assented, but before they could arrange any plans for a possible dinner, Olivia opened the door from the control room, coming out holding something in the air.

"Hey guys," she said, walking over to the four of them that now sat in the living room. "Now that McFarland's left, I found this. It looks like he left us a letter before he got on his ride and left."

It was an envelope, and that caught Madison's attention. She stepped closer as Olivia ripped open the envelope, and set a piece of paper down on the table. Her eyes opened, wide, and Madison urgently read the letter.

Written in neat fine print with a ballpoint pen, was a single sentence. Madison couldn't tell whether or not it was a threat, a warning, or instruction, but the capital letters served only to stress her more. The words spelled out:

PREPARE TO SHOOT THE S.S. WASHINGTON IF PROMPTED.

Madison turned to Cole, whose jaw had dropped.

"Maybe… Maybe food can wait a few hours, after all," Madison offered.

Chapter 24

"Ah! Ah! Ah!"

Jack Monterey was gasping for air, shouting, as the water trickled down his covered face, but, somehow, he wasn't cracking. Fritz paused the water flow for a second, as Jack gasped to catch up his breath. His whole body was soaked, and he looked weak and horrified, so there was no reason that he could hold out any longer.

"You going to talk now?" Fritz asked.

"N-never," Jack sputtered. "You're going to have to kill me, because I'm never going to betray my country."

"Fucker," he mumbled, grabbing Marcell and pulling him to the corner of the room.

"It's been two hours," Fritz stated. "We only have an hour left until the banquet. We need to think of something, and fast. Otherwise, we'll be letting everyone down."

"I can hear you!" Monterey said from across the room, but it was clear that he was bluffing, because he started laughing to himself in a sort of frenzy.

"I know, Fritz," Marcell whispered back. "I'm not an expert on torture, like you. You're the interrogator here, think of something!"

"Oh, I was bluffing," Fritz said, and Marcell's face turned into one of genuine concern. "What? Did you honestly think I'd have experience as a military interrogator? Sure, I had a year in service before I broke my foot. Sure as hell didn't interrogate anybody."

"*Great*," Marcell said. "That's just great."

"Cuts don't do shit," Fritz said. "Waterboarding, which I'm pretty sure is what the Americans and FBI did in Guantanamo, and he still doesn't give in after an hour, despite all the screaming and agony. Maybe we should try the fingers next? That'll leave him with some real, lasting physical damage."

Marcell looked like he was deep in thought. "Maybe if... Maybe if we hit him where it really hurts, like you said, then he'll give in. The place a bit lower."

Fritz opened his eyes wide. "You can't be serious. Marcell!"

"Well, I hope he caves in. But I can't think of anything else that would compel a man to cooperate than that."

Fritz nodded. "You're absolutely right. A man prizes his family jewels."

Fritz opened up the toolbox, grabbing a hammer before approaching. At his command, Marcell helped lift him up from the sink basin he'd been held under and tied to, and, despite Monterey's flailing, he was no match for Marcell and Fritz's collective strength, who worked together to tie him back down to the chair.

"Come on," Lieutenant Monterey whined. "Just make this easier and release me. I'll tell you what. I'll even forget that this ever happened. I won't report you or escalate to my superior officers. If you just let me-"

He immediately stopped once Fritz ripped off the bag over his head. The lieutenant's mouth curled into a frown when he saw them. He wasn't surprised at all.

"You two!" Monterey exclaimed. "I was right... It was you two, playing stupid to kidnap me. I knew it."

Fritz and Marcell stood there, silent. Marcell folded his arms in front of himself, while Fritz casually held a hammer up in the air and slowly stepping forward towards him.

"What are you doing with that hammer? Guys!?"

Fritz stepped forward, raising his hammer.

"No! Don't hit me! *No!*"

Fritz swung the hammer down onto the man's bare foot. There was a snap of bone, and Marcell winced and turned away again, not wanting to look at the now mangled purple foot of the man, wanting to blot out the wails that reflected a deep pain so intense and visceral that Marcell could imagine what it felt like.

"Ow! Motherfucker! *Fuck*! You bastard! You broke my foot! You broke my-"

"Toughen up, buttercup," Fritz spat. "I've broken my foot before, and I didn't puss out like you."

"Ow! Oh, god! Please, let's just work this out. Let's-"

Fritz winded up his hammer again, smiling, and Marcell looked up at them, at Lieutenant Monterey's horrified expression.

"This time, how about I go for the crotch shot? Ever felt what it feels like to have 100 pounds of pressure on the most sensitive part of the body? No? Well, I guess you're about to find out! It's what I call busting your balls!"

"*No*! Oh *God*! *Anything* but that! Please! I beg you! Please don't!"

The lieutenant was trying to cover himself up, but it was impossible, his hands bound to the arms of the chair now. But his eyes were the most pleading Marcell had ever seen. It was jarring.

"Please! I'll tell you what you want! No! No!"

Fritz swung at him, but this time he purposefully swiped his hammer off course at the last second, slamming into the chair and knocking him over. Now Lieutenant Monterey was a sniveling mess, and practically moaning.

"Ugh... I'll tell you! I'll tell you whatever you want! Don't do that! Please! Waa..."

"Are you ready to cooperate?"

"Yes!"

Marcell lifted him up from the ground.

"Good," Fritz said, smirking. "Because if I suspect you are lying for one second, then your dick is ground meat. Got it?"

Lieutenant Monterey nodded, sniffling. "Okay. I get it. I get it."

"Why did you assassinate Grace Elliott?"

"I don't know. It was an order from my superior! I didn't question it."

"Who was your superior in that case?"

"General Amotu. But I think it came from higher up. President Melero."

"Why did they choose you to kill her?"

"I'm one of the top soldiers on the S.S. Washington. A Green Beret."

"Surely you had your moral objections to this."

"Melero promised me a promotion. Said she was conspiring against the country and planned to sell us out to the Chinese. I had to do it! Any refusal to follow orders would have me court-martialed."

The answer proved satisfactory to Fritz, who moved on to the next question.

"Over a month ago, the Space Armament Stations were cleared out, everyone on board was slaughtered. Did you do this?"

Monterey was silent for a few seconds, closing his eyes.

"Answer me, dammit!"

"We had to kill," he said through gritted teeth. "I... I was on one of the teams. We had to do it to try to prevent this global war."

"Those Space Armament Stations belonged to Ascendant Technologies. Not any particular military. You, in fact, triggered this global war the second you lied to get in and attack them."

"That's... not true."

"Goddamn right it was."

"No..."

"Don't try bullshitting me. Those stations opened fire on Earth, and scorched the surface with those beams. After you took them in operation. Why?"

"Because it was too late at that point. The Chinese had already launched their first nuclear missiles."

"You liar! Why would you do this to Earth? Why would you destroy Earth? Was it really just the money, your loyalty to the country, or the promotion? You were really willing to sell your soul, only for that?"

Monterey laughed out loud. Fritz looked at him, frowning at the sudden reaction. Lieutenant Monterey's eyes had a strange glint to them now, his expression looking like he'd finally snapped, and his muscles looked like they had swelled up, almost artificially.

"You want to know why? Because the world is fucked. President Melero promised me glory, and a position of leadership in the reconstruction of the planet. He lost everything, just like I did, and now, I have a second chance. You really want to know how everyone was hand-selected to be on board the S.S. Washington?"

"How?"

"By being broken," Lieutenant Monterey said. "By having nothing to lose."

All of a sudden, Monterey's right arm broke free unexpectedly from his restraints. Fritz stepped forward, but it was too late. He grabbed a cyanide pill in his pocket, and swallowed it before he could even get to him. For a few seconds, his body spazzed out, as he immediately went into cardiac arrest. Then, it went limp on the chair.

Marcell hit stop on the record button on the recording device, which cut off just before Fritz swore in frustration. He rushed over to him, trying to resuscitate him, but there was no hope, and he knew it. Fritz turned to Marcell.

"Did you get all of that?" Fritz asked. Marcell nodded.

"Good… That might be good enough. Let's get that recording to Nathan and Lex, compress the video, and air it for all to hear."

"You do that," Marcell said, nodding. "I'll handle security preparations for the banquet."

"You sure? I think you're a little bit less physically capable than I am."

"Yes," Marcell said, nodding. "I need this."

Fritz didn't fight him for it, but instead pondered the body for a brief moment.

"You have to wonder," Fritz said, "what would drive a man, to kill himself like that, when we had no intention of killing him immediately? The man was afraid of getting a hammer to the crotch but not death?"

"Beats me," Marcell replied. "Looks like he lost it all of a sudden. Like something snapped."

"Lost it, huh?" Fritz repeated. "Haven't we all? If you ask me, it was some kind of frenzy drug. It's done now, though, so there's no point getting worked up over it."

The two didn't stick around any longer. After a quick goodbye they ran out of the room, Fritz carrying the recording device, and neither of them even bothered with the disposal of the lieutenant's corpse. Doing so would risk them getting spotted in the hallways by the American soldiers, and then they would be doomed. All they did was take his body up and hide it behind some chairs and a table.

Chapter 25

When Skye heard the code phrase over the radio, *I think we're ready for the banquet*, she celebrated. She had to restrain herself from loudly whooping, because even though she was in the ISH for the time being, still, now less than an hour away from the commencement of the banquet, there were many soldiers roaming through the hallways, pillaging their alcohol reserves. She didn't want any of them to recognize her as the leader and report any suspicious behavior. The last thing she needed was President Melero, or especially President Melero's troops, backing out of this agreement.

"I trust you to handle the preparations," Skye said over the line. "With what has to be done."

"We got this covered," Fritz promised, and then he coordinated to ask to meet Dr. Chetana and Nathan in the comms room.

Skye knew that executing the remainder of the plan should be easy. The only significant wildcard was the potential consequences of the blowback from the soldiers, but she suspected the booze would help. But there was a little bit of unfinished business first, and she was ready to investigate it, no matter what it took her.

Marcell had told her about the basement, and now that she had her trump card, Graham, she was going to take advantage of him and get to the bottom of this. She returned to her room, which she'd been sharing with Graham the past couple of weeks, and opened the door to find Graham in the process of stripping out of Sergeant Walton's clothing, starting with his shirt.

"Nuh-uh," she chirped, shaking her head. "Put that back down."

"Why?" Graham asked. "Goddammit, Skye, I hate wearing this."

"We're not done yet," Skye said, and Graham threw his uniform top back on.

"Ugh…" Graham mumbled. "What is it now?"

"There's something going on in the S.S. Washington basement," Skye explained. "I suspect it's where they keep their women captive."

Graham fell silent. "Skye, I-"

"Don't."

"It's just, I walked around and the entire-"

"Did you hear me?"

"How about you let me talk? I walked around the entire ship on the upper floor, checked the interior of plenty of rooms on all the countless cameras, and there was nothing. I saw numerous female soldiers, and then yesterday there was a tour. There are civilians there. Families. You really think they could get away with this?"

"Just play along for a second," Skye requested. "Imagine that there are female slaves. I don't know if it's five, or ten, or thirty. We can't just leave them. We would have a moral obligation to save them."

"What is it with us, morality, and international intervention? You're acting like we're America and they're the Middle East, and we have some kind of duty to impose justice on them. Rather than leave them be. And they're *actually* America!"

"Graham!"

"Tell me I'm wrong."

Skye was growing more and more irritable. "Fine. You're wrong. They don't get a pass because they're America."

"It's not my responsibility," Graham said. He started taking the camouflage shirt off again, throwing it to the ground. "You want to, fine. Be my guest. But I'm done sacrificing my life for a plan I don't even get a say in."

"You're not going to back off. Don't be a coward. We've gone too far."

Graham turned red, shook his head. "I'm tired of you bossing me around. I'm tired of all of this shit. Leave me alone."

"You're tired? You think I'm *not* tired?" Skye spat. "Our entire life hangs in the balance, and you're ready to hang up the cleats! Real man. Real tough man. Grow a damn pair and be a man."

"You don't get to pull that card!" Graham shouted, spittle flying from his mouth. "You *damn* hypocrite."

"Oh, I'm a hypocrite?" Skye screamed back. "Who was it, back in that day that froze when Lusky tried to evict us in Operation Exodus? I saved your ass when they had their guns pointed at us, I stabbed that man, and you sat there like a baby when things got dirty!"

Sweat was running down Graham's face, and his fists were clenched tightly by his side. He stepped near her, looking about ready to lash out and strike her.

"Take that back!" he screamed. "I swear to God, I'll knock some sense into you!"

"What are you going to do!?" Skye grilled him. "Hit me, out yourself as an abusive piece of shit!? You do that, I never forgive you! You never talk to me again!"

Graham turned around, threw his hands into the air.

"You've changed! I get no say in nothing anymore!" he shouted, swiveling back to stare her down. "Dr. Chetana was right! You're unhinged!"

Skye laughed, a screeching sound that sounded more animal than human. "The only one who's losing it is you. I've worked my ass off these past couple of weeks, all day, every day. And I'm unhinged? *Please*."

"Stop pretending like you're somehow being so altruistic! It's all about you and you know it. You've *changed*."

"I haven't changed one bit! All I've done is step up to the plate! No more soft Skye! Now I'm the leader Skye! You don't have to like it but you *damn* well have to accept it!"

"Lies," Graham spat back. "Those are lies, and you know it!"

"There are women who are going to be raped if we let them take them! Do they get no say, too!?" Skye cried out.

Graham groaned. "I don't disagree with what you're saying! I just am extremely disrespected that you volunteered me like that. Without even talking to me! You went behind my back. I could've died. All the while, you sit back here, a general in this war, not doing any leg work, doing absolutely *nothing*. While Marcell and Fritz and I put our lives on the line, because of course we're able-bodied men, so our lives are completely expendable, right?"

Skye paused for a few moments. Part of her wanted to proclaim that he was a coward and berate him. But also, part of her realized he was right. Neither her, Dr. Chetana, or Nathan had done anything as far as risking themselves for this objective. And while Skye had concocted the plan in the first place, suddenly she understood.

"I... I don't... I..." she sputtered.

"*What*? What's your excuse, Skye?"

"Graham," she said this time, but it was full of compassion, her rage evaporated into the air like a wisp of smoke caught in the wind. "I'm sorry. I'm so sorry."

Skye leaned forward, hugged him. He didn't move, because he was indecisive and didn't know whether or not she'd actually changed her mind or whether she was kissing up to him to manipulate him into doing something else.

"I'm going to go do this. You're right. You have no reason to sacrifice yourself anymore," Skye said, nodding. "I'm going to do this. You don't have to do this, at all."

"It's okay," Graham said, although he sounded unconvinced. "It is."

Skye looked. "No. What I said... It was terrible. And not true. You saved me back in the prison cell, when you shot that man who could've killed me. I just, I was feeling the pressure to perform so much. I felt more pressure because I felt so insecure that you and Maddie stopped Operation Exodus. I was so worthless, and felt like with these plans, I could fix everything. Redeem myself for my failures and everyone who died. I now realize what you're saying is perfectly reasonable."

"I'm sorry for what I said, too," Graham said, sighing. "What I said. I didn't mean it, about you being unhinged. I just, I'm worried for you. It's like... like you don't even care how anyone else *feels*, and that matters. I mean, Skye, we're humans, not A.I."

"I love you," Skye blurted. It was the first time she'd ever told him those words.

"What?" Graham said, jaw dropping. Skye smiled.

"You heard me."

"I love you too," Graham said. He stopped in place, ready to kiss her again, but Skye started tying her hair into a ponytail, and he frowned.

"What are you doing?" Graham asked. After she tied her knot into a ponytail, she plucked the glasses from his face and slid them over hers.

"You have contacts, right?" Skye asked nonchalantly.

"Ummm, yes," Graham said. "I don't- I haven't used them at all since I've gone up here, apart from a couple of hours ago when I went on the ship."

"And you're nearsighted?"

"Yes."

"Good." Skye adjusted her glasses to make it more even when it rested on her face.

"What has gotten into you?" Graham asked. "Why did you take my glasses?"

"I'm going to explore the basement," Skye said.

"I'll go with you," Graham said. He reached into the pocket of his uniform, pulled out the keycard that he had lifted from the ship on his reconnaissance mission. "You'll need this."

"You could hand that over, and I'll be able to get around just fine," Skye replied. "I don't need your help."

"I know you don't," Graham responded. "But we're going to do this, together. We can do it. First things first, you need to change your outfit, especially since President Melero knows what you look like."

Skye nodded, moving over to the closet. It felt amazing to know he had her back in the end, even after the ugly fight only a few minutes before.

Chapter 26

Marcell, meanwhile, had a watchful eye over the cafeteria, which was gradually filling up with clients and soldiers alike. Some of the soldiers were quite intoxicated, and it appeared that whoever was behind regulating the alcohol supply had put a stop to the fountains, much to their chagrin. Despite there still being a great deal of time until food was served, the kitchens were being prepped, meaning that a great conflagration of various delicious scents wafted into the cafeteria, making many spectators' mouths water. A particularly rowdy segment of soldiers, now exiled from their drinking and riding the wave of intoxication that was impairing their judgments, had taken to pounding in the tables, repeatedly announcing their current feelings. There might've been a couple dozen of them, sitting in the middle of the cafeteria, away from any nearby ISH clientele, who gave them a wide berth.

"We want food! We want food! We want food!"

The cheering and slapping on the tables went on for a good five minutes until whoever was in charge of their little section of soldiers must've grown tired. Marcell and Jordan watched the whole time, surprised at how poorly behaved the American soldiers appeared.

Both of them carried weapons. It looked like President Melero, or General Amotu, whoever was in charge, had instructed them to leave their heavy weaponry behind before boarding the International Space Hotel. That bode well for their sake. Although Marcell didn't doubt that they carried pistols in their holsters, which would mean that they still significantly outgunned them.

"This must be the most poorly-disciplined, poor mannered group of soldiers I've ever seen in my life," Jordan observed from the side once the ruckus finally subsided.

"Never knew you were an expert on soldier behavior," Marcell responded, not without a bit of snark. "This is pretty much exactly on par for the course of what I'd expect. I'm assuming it's their day off."

"Well, good thing I'm here to keep them in line."

Marcell shifted uncomfortably from foot to foot. "Jordan, about that. I don't know how I should say this, but I think your talents might be better used, or rather, not wasted, defending this cafeteria."

"What's that supposed to mean?" Jordan questioned, eyes narrowing into a frown. "Marcell, what are you talking about?"

"It's going to be a bloodbath," Marcell warned, looking down at the ground. "I never was the biggest fan of Skye's plan, but I felt like we had no other options, to be honest. I feigned some of my enthusiasm."

"Skye? Your friend, right, the girl in charge? What about her plan? What are you even talking about?"

"I..." Marcell hesitated. "I can't say. Someone could be listening in on us."

"Like hell anyone is," Jordan said. He appeared concerned for a couple of minutes before his concern morphed into frustration. "Marcell, I love you. I told you that the other day, and I mean it. But you can't keep me from doing my job."

"Jordan..." Marcell said. He felt something rising in his throat, but he swallowed, and the feeling went away. "I told myself... I told myself I would never-"

"That you would never risk doing this again, I know," Jordan interrupted. "But better to have loved, and for it to end, than to have never loved at all. I'm not going to leave, even if my life is in danger."

"You don't have to tell anyone. There's a dozen of us, armed, and no doubt, we will get more on our side... I'll stay here. Just go away, hide."

"My mother didn't raise a coward," Jordan retorted. "I'm not a child. I'm going to fight here. I conscripted voluntarily a few days ago because I decided I wanted to make myself useful for the ISH and do whatever it took to defend it. Even at the expense of my life."

Marcell nodded. "I get it. But don't you get yourself killed."

Jordan smirked. "Or what? You'll kill me yourself? Think I've heard that one somewhere."

Marcell chuckled, and realized that this was all the extra motivation to carry this plan through to the end.

***

Back on board the SAS 2, Cole was telling the crew how to handle some of the controls.

"Well, we got to adjust the laser lance itself, as well as the electrostatic chamber. From there, you can fire the laser in a matter of seconds. It should be no issue destroying the S.S. Washington."

Olivia turned to Cole, who was in the control room with Jace and Madison as well. They looked through the front glass, which now was angled in the direction of a great black glowing rectangle, which they identified as the S.S. Washington, that blotted out some of the stars in the distance.

"Okay," Olivia said, about to reach towards the handle to begin the movement, but Madison was there to grab her hand.

"What are you doing?" Jace asked, confused, while Olivia just stared at her.

"No," Madison replied. "Remember what the letter said?"

"Ah, yes," Cole said. "Shoot if prompted. And we're getting ready to shoot."

"No," Madison replied. "I think there's a reasonable chance that they notice us, and that's *bad*. Very bad."

"The windows are tinted, specially designed so scout planes can't see through," Cole responded.

"Sure, but they certainly could detect movement from this ship, could they not?" Madison queried.

The question she posed resounded in the empty room for a few seconds as everyone processed what she had said. She did seem to make a fair point.

"Besides, who even knows if this letter is legit?" Olivia added.

"You're telling me that there isn't a stamp, a signature, or any proof on that paper?" Cole asked.

Jace and Olivia shook their head.

"No," Jace answered. "No name, nothing on the envelope, either."

"So, what are we doing here?" Cole chuckled. "We shouldn't even be doing anything, let alone blowing up the spaceship."

"No," Madison said, shaking her head. "I trust McFarland... The letter's authentic. Olivia, Jace, we listen to what the note

The Laser from Above

says. We just… we just need to be smart about this, and prepare everything before we move into position."

"I suppose you're right," Cole acknowledged. "We pre-set it, then. Just in case."

"Okay," Madison replied. "When we get the commands, we move. What about charging this thing up?"

"It's already charged," Cole replied, pointing from his wheelchair. Cole was extremely expressive with his gestures, so much so to the point that Madison questioned whether he was actually British, or secretly an Italian in disguise.

"Of course," Olivia affirmed.

"We can pre-set some coordinates to fire at the S.S. Washington before even setting this thing into motion," Cole explained. "That wouldn't draw anyone's detection, far as I could tell."

Madison nodded. Olivia mumbled something about how paranoid they were being, but Jace had no issues cooperating. Besides, Jace already been instructed by the council before: everyone had to listen to Madison's orders when it came to matters of the ship.

A couple of minutes passed as Cole pre-set the buttons, pressing a series of them and directing Olivia, Jace, and Madison, as needed when the buttons he wanted to push or pull were out of his reach. After a few minutes passed and they were finished, one of the buttons started blinking, and Madison realized they were receiving a signal from another ship.

"I wonder if this is it, our order," Olivia commented, before pressing the button to listen in.

"Hello, this is the S.S. Washington speaking. Hello? Is anyone there? Anyone? Over."

Olivia leaned forward to respond to press the response button, but this time, both Cole and Madison told her to leave it be.

"If anyone's here, we need to know," the voice on the radio said. "For your sake, I would evacuate this ship in the next twenty-four hours. I repeat, evacuate the Space Armament Station in the next twenty-four hours if you can hear me. The Station is not safe, and poses a threat to Earth in the event of an overheat. Over."

"What do you think the person meant?" Jace asked. "That sounds bad."

"It does," Cole replied. "Not to mention the overheating is a bunch of bollocks. This weapon isn't going to somehow randomly explode and harm Earth, and even if it blew up, half of the junk would just fly into space harmlessly. We don't pose a threat to Earth unless we want to."

It was clear, then, for Madison, that the impending destruction of the SAS 2 wasn't about the safety of Earth at all, but about the soldiers on the S.S. Washington saving their skins. Madison didn't doubt that President Melero would have some issues sleeping at night (or whatever their arbitrary version of night was) knowing that the people on the International Space Hotel were in control of a Space Armament Station and could blow him and his crew up at a moment's notice. He didn't like that, because it threatened his power.

Greedy bastard, Madison thought. *Politicians never fail to disappoint me, and I already have low expectations.*

Madison read the other people's facial expressions. Cole was determined, Jace anxious, and Olivia, jarred. Madison, meanwhile, felt like she was blind, like she didn't know what was going on.

Madison wished that Skye had a plan. But deep down, remembering how Graham, Marcell, and Skye had single-handedly saved everyone who was otherwise going to be evicted, she knew that Skye probably did. It was just a shame that they were a little bit too far out of range from the ISH, unlike when Madison first infiltrated the ship, to communicate with her via earpiece: but she knew it was time to lean into what she believed.

"Trust the process," Madison told them all. "If we're going to be blowing up their damn ship first, who cares if they plan to blow us up after the fact?"

***

Graham and Skye decided to wait until around fifteen minutes before the banquet to depart the room. They didn't want to get caught before then. If they did, and President Melero ascertained their identity, then the entire plan would be compromised. He would probably withdraw every single soldier, but maybe not before pillaging the hotel and killing everyone who stood in their way. She knew not to underestimate the brutality of the military. Fritz had hammered that point home in their emergency meeting that morning.

In the time that they had to wait, the two of them sat, Skye already having switched out into a different outfit. Graham's mind was certainly somewhere else, but Skye posed a question to him out of the blue.

"Can you tell me more about your home?"

"Huh?"

"Your home," Skye said. "We never did talk too much about it. Because it hurt. I mean, it still hurts. But I want to know about your home, more than I do. In case, you know…"

"Okay, sure," Graham answered. "Well, like I told you, I'm a small-town boy from South Carolina. Springfield, to be exact.

The media always seems to depict us Southerners as stupid backwoods hicks, and frankly, it's a bit offensive. Although the people I knew growing up weren't always the sharpest knives in the drawer."

Skye giggled.

"What?"

"I don't know, the way you said it, it's funny."

"Glad to hear that. Home was… home. My brother, Ty, he was like my dad. Way more outdoorsy like. I look like he did when he was young. But everyone always said I was much more like my mother. She would stay inside, read books. I'd do that too, on top of gaming and studying and whatnot. Robotics club."

"I can see that."

"They never understood why I couldn't seem to get along with everyone, you know? They didn't get it. That's just how many brain was wired, you know, always thinking and trying to do my own thing. They thought I was a recluse in my room, was depressed or something. Maybe I was. Although I always joined my uncle on his fishing trips, now those were fun."

"Small town life, huh? Not a lot to do."

"You want to know what I really miss about South Carolina, and the South in general? The food. Near my place, they used to always serve us boiled peanuts. There ain't nothing like that."

"Boiled peanuts? Ew."

"Ew? Now that's blasphemy!"

"Is it, though? Boiled peanuts taste like a mix between clay and a swimming pool. I tried them when I visited Georgia once."

"Well that's the charm, now, isn't it? Think of it as an acquired taste, kinda like bleu cheese. I miss that though. The soul food and the sea food, summers down in Myrtle Beach, although that city is overrated compared to the other gems around, let me tell you. But everyone's so kind and warmhearted. Even if the politics can be a bit backwards sometimes. Maybe a lot of the time."

"I see. That sounds so nice."

"My brother's the best. Looking at him you wouldn't have even thought he'd have been my brother, the guy's a player if you've ever seen one. He's-" Graham stopped halfway through his sentence, before his face fell. "He *was* a really cool guy."

Skye leaned over, kissed him. "Now don't you switch tenses mid-sentence. For all we know, they could all be fine."

"What about you?" Graham asked. "You never told me too much about home for you."

"I grew up in a cookie cutter suburb," Skye said. "In Minnesota. Called Roseville."

"That sounds… real rosy."

Skye snorted. "You couldn't help yourself, could you?"

"No, I couldn't."

"I had a younger brother and sister. My brother was always a good athlete, super sweet. My sister, she and I were best friends. We played together a ton when we were young, and hung out and watched stuff when we were older. She was much more the goth girl, tough, and always mouthed off my parents a lot, though, so they got into fights. I was a little bit of miss goody two-shoes, so I wasn't like that."

"Now that, I would've never guessed," Graham chirped, and Skye laughed and punched him in the shoulder.

"Minnesota was a great place, though. I do miss it. It sounds a bit boring, but you got everything. You got beautiful forests and lakes. You got the cool cities, the Mall of America, the calm suburbs and farms. The place is safe, educated, and very homey, for the most part. Y'know?"

"Yeah," Graham said. "It sounds great. Maybe if we get back to Earth, we can visit South Carolina, and then we can go to your home in Minnesota."

Skye knew such a proposition was absurd, and impossible, and that they stood pretty much as good of a chance growing wings and flying than they did ever somehow reconnecting with both of their families. Despite that, however, the words struck a special chord in her heart.

"Yes. I would get to introduce you to my family," Skye said. "My family would love you. Especially compared to the boyfriends and singular girlfriend my sister's been with. They were train wrecks, all of them."

Skye and Graham were silent for a couple of minutes as they reminisced. Then Graham leaned over and checked the clock, which read that it was 7:43 p.m.

"Look at that. Time to go already."

Skye smiled. "Looks like time flies when you're having fun."

They kissed. Then Graham took her hand for a few seconds, but Skye shook her head and told him, that President Melero and the others couldn't know, that they had to act as careful and undercover as they could when they were out in the public. Then the couple walked towards the door and left into the hallway, but not before Skye took out her earpiece and pocketed it, lest it draw any suspicion.

Even though neither Graham nor Skye knew whether or not they were ever going to spend another second in the room again, they knew that together, they had a good chance of making it work.

"We'll be okay," Graham told her. "We're going to win."

"I know."

The Laser from Above

Chapter 27

Skye and Graham hurried through the connector, taking the most isolated routes through the ISH. By the time they were crossing the connector, there were only a few stragglers around, and most of them seemed to be heading the same direction: towards the food, and away from the S.S. Washington. One of the soldiers, who fortunately didn't look closely at Graham (or otherwise didn't recognize him as an outsider) did stop them halfway to the other side, however.

"You do realize that you're heading the wrong direction, right?" he asked. "The food is thataway."

"That's correct," Skye said. "We'll be there soon."

The soldier shrugged. "Suit yourself."

They passed into the hallway and out of the connector. Along the way, they did pass a few women, of which a couple appeared pregnant, who escorted a few small children, who looked antsy the entire way.

See, Graham wanted to tell her. *There are women. Your theory of some sort of human trafficking ring is impossible.*

But Graham knew that the presence of a limited number of women didn't disprove Skye's hypothesis, not at all, and he was determined to make sure nothing happened to her. He knew that, otherwise, he would never forgive himself.

While the pair didn't have the map anymore to help them with their navigation, Graham had looked over the map thoroughly following his return from his first venture on board the ship and had a decent understanding of where most things were. He found a nearby stairwell, which he and Skye took down to the bottom floor. On the way, Fritz was asking them questions on the line.

"Just over five minutes until the official start of the banquet," Fritz said. "Any idea when we should uncover?"

"Fifteen minutes," Skye replied. Graham, who still had his earpiece with him, heard the entire conversation, so he didn't waste any time asking Skye about what was about to happen. Way he saw it, he figured he was going to find out, soon, anyway.

After entering through into the basement, they found the hallways completely vacant. He recalled the direction he'd seen Jack walking, and realized that their target destination was probably going to be either where he was heading, or where he'd come from, so potentially at either extreme of the hallway.

"Can't I at least have something to defend myself with?" Skye asked.

Graham ran his finger around his holster, pulled out the canister of pepper spray that Marcell had lent him earlier, and handed it to Skye, who raised her eyebrows.

"Don't trust me with the big guns?" Skye questioned, looking down where a pistol was clearly holstered, clearly the property of Sergeant Walton, who was still tied up in a closet back on the ISH.

"No, it's not that," Graham responded. "I don't want to kill anyone if I don't have to."

"Amen," Skye answered, "though if I learn these men have been keeping women captive, then I retract that stance."

"Let me take the lead here," Graham told Skye. "Because I'm the one in uniform."

Skye begrudgingly assented, and Graham tried the handle to the door at the furthest end of the basement, found it locked, and pressed his ear to it. He could hear nothing, and he opened the room with the keycard he'd taken from Sergeant Walton. The lights flickered on as soon as the door opened to reveal lines and lines of guns. This was probably one of many armories, but whatever else was in here, it certainly was not people, as there was not a single decibel of noise coming from the room.

Once they exited, Graham's earpiece—the military one he'd taken from Sergeant Walton, and not the one from the ISH—buzzed, and suddenly there was a voice in his ear. Graham motioned for Skye to stop and shush.

"Walton, come in," the voice said. "This is Private Lyles."

Graham didn't know exactly how to respond. His limited exposure to hearing Sergeant Walton was when he was bumbling around, intoxicated, so he figured he should try and emulate the voice.

"Private Lyles, ya fool, don't you have better etiquette than to not address me by my rank?"

"Apologies sir, just the whole squad is here in the Hotel at the banquet, waiting for you."

"Where am I?" Graham fake belched. "On the crapper."

There was laughing on the other side of the line, as the private recapitulated what he had said to the other soldiers who were presumedly near him.

"You're quite drunk, aren't you, Walt?"

"Got that right," Graham slurred, before taking the earpiece out, muting the roaring laughter coming from the other side, and stomping his foot on it, once, twice, three times, until there was nothing left but a couple of broken shards of the irreparably damaged earpiece.

The Laser from Above

"Hey!" Skye protested. "That could've been useful! We might've heard if they set the alarm."

"Nah," Graham responded. "I'm pretty sure it's a secure line for the squad, anyway. I definitely never heard any sort of announcements the entire time I had it in my ear. Besides, I probably look strange as hell with two earpieces anyway."

Indeed, now that the earpiece from the squadron was gone, all that was left was the line that connected with Dr. Chetana, Nathan, and Fritz.

Now that that business was resolved, Graham and Skye moved over to the next door over, some ten paces or so down the hallway. They found it to be locked; not only that, but, strangely enough, there was no keycard scanner at all, as if only manual keys, or perhaps fingerprints, unlocked the door. From Graham's recollections, this door led straight to a locker room. They tried the handle, and it was locked. There was next to nothing Graham could do but listen in to the room, to which he heard absolutely nothing.

Graham was about to move on to the next door, which in fact did contain a keycard scanner, when the door opened by happenstance, and a soldier emerged into the hallway. Tall, white, and with brown hair and a spattering of red acne covering his face, his voice, much like Graham's, was tinged with a Southern drawl, but the similarities ended there.

"Ooh, what do we have here?" he inquired in an oddly shrill voice. The surname Smith was stitched onto the left side of his chest, and the marking on his arms let him know that he was a Private First Class.

"Another guest," Graham said, smiling. "You likey?"

"Oh, yeah, yeah," the man answered, grinning. He licked his teeth, yellow, crooked teeth that made him look like he'd skipped the dentist's office the past few years. "I might have to come back to pay you a visit, babe."

What the hell does that mean? Skye thought. *Am I correct? No, it can't be.*

"Uh, Sergeant," Skye said, trying her best to play the part of an adequate actress, "Are you sure this is the right place? You told me the guns here were big, and there'd be a bunch of them."

"Oh, it is big, all right," the other man said. He laughed while he walked down the hallway, back towards the elevator, while Graham, who'd caught the door before it had closed, peered and opened the door, trying to suppress the pit of disgust and panic that had formed in his stomach following the encounter with the truly despicable human being that was Private First Class Smith.

Graham expected the worst now, and had more than a sneaking suspicion that Skye was right about everything. When he opened the door and pushed through, he found himself there was a small waiting room, with a giant green curtain of some kind separating a back area. In the front of the house, there was a little box that reminded him of the parking booth you'd see in cities. Waiting in the room was a man dressed in a plain white t-shirt and camouflage pants, who looked surprised at their arrival. In the background, it sounded like the sound of rushing water. Graham, as well as Skye, felt sick.

"Oh, hi," the man said, opening the door and stepping out. "I wasn't expecting any new arrivals."

"I've got a gift," Graham said. "Another one of the goods."

"Ooh," he said. "Dear, you don't know why you're here, do you?"

"What do you mean?" She asked, turning to Graham. "Where are the guns? Is this some kind of museum?"

Graham had to admit, Skye was acing the acting, so much so that he felt an outpouring of guilt for even allowing her to be in this dangerous of a situation in the first place.

"Don't you worry, honey," the man said, managing a smile so sinister that Skye could feel her whole body clench, "we'll take care of you."

The man turned to Graham, staring at Graham's face, and then the name that was stitched into his uniform. He frowned. "Sergeant Walton. Wait a second…"

"What? What is it?" Graham asked, heart thumping in his chest.

His face morphed into a snarl. "Who the hell are you!? What did you do with-"

"That's enough!" Skye shouted, pulling out her pepper spray and spraying the man in his face.

The man screamed, collapsing to his knees.

"Ah! Ah!"

The man who Skye had sprayed spread out onto the ground like Thunderbird on a totem pole, his eyes closing, his body calming as he slipped unconscious. And yet there were reinforcements. A singular shout hailed from behind the green curtain. Graham stepped closer to the threshold, and reached down towards his holster to pull out the pistol. But he was too slow. All of a sudden, another man, this one dressed in the full get-up of the Marines uniform, breached the curtain, sprinting at him and slamming him to the ground.

"You bastard!" The man growled, and Skye pried at him, as he punched Graham, once, twice, and Graham knew he was going to leave a mark. Graham learned what people meant when they said they could see stars: in a second his head was spinning and he felt like he was going to *lose* himself. His feeble attempts at knocking the man off failed to even slow down the man's assault:

and the man's knees bared down on his chest, delivering a sharp pain from the pressure that he prayed wouldn't result in severely damaged ribs. Graham could only look up and watch, see a globule of saliva hanging out the man's mouth, and think how much this man resembled a charging, rabid pitbull.

Graham managed to dodge one of his flurry of punches, and felt like a ninja for a brief moment until the attacking soldier followed his miss up with an uppercut to the side of the head, the blow somehow smacking his one remaining earpiece and unmuting it for the other line to hear.

Skye wasn't going to give up on Graham. After only a couple of seconds, and a few punches having been landed, Skye had readied her can of pepper spray. But the soldier was ready, turning his back towards Skye, so that the mist harmlessly soaked into the back of the man's jacket after she sprayed a blast. Meanwhile, the commotion must have been very audible to the other side of the line, because Marcell, Dr. Chetana, and Nathan all seemed to be asking, in different degrees of volume (for some of them must've been in public) what was happening. Graham was grunting and gasping for breath in a way that Fritz questioned out loud whether he was in an erotic or extremely dangerous situation.

The answer was, of course, that they were receiving a total beatdown, and this answer was received only a couple of seconds later by the soldier shouting at Skye.

"Get off me! You bitch!"

The man turned around and simply threw Skye: Skye was flying through the air, the canister of pepper spray catapulted out of her hands and clattering onto the floor several feet away. By some miracle, she managed to not land on her head. Instead, her left hand took the majority of the impact, and Skye could feel a deep ache and a pop when she landed on the floor, and could tell

The Laser from Above

that her wrist was going to swell up. Graham wasted no time at this diversion, standing up to his feet and reaching for his gun.

But Graham was not the quickest draw in the West; by the time the gun was out of the holster and in the air, the soldier had turned around already, and directed his attention towards Graham. Graham wasn't fast enough: the nozzle was pointed not at the soldier, but somewhere towards the ground and slightly to the side.

"Oh my God!" Dr. Chetana was gasping over the line. "What's going on? Graham? Graham?"

She, of all people, must have not been in public judging by her response. Either that, or she was seriously compromising their cover.

The man went for his gun, which Graham tried to angle the gun to the man's head. Graham grabbed on with all of his strength, as the man headbutted him, and he felt his grip loosening. He looked around wildly as his opponent kicked at his legs, praying for Skye to save him. At one point, he squeezed the trigger trying to graze the man's head, and the resulting gunshot made his ear ring, and the man winced in pain. Graham prayed the room was soundproofed. He followed the move up with a hard knee to the man's crotch, and he could feel the soldier's grip weakening, but despite Graham now getting both hands involved in trying to rip the gun away, he was unsuccessful.

During this short time, which could not have been longer than ten seconds, but felt like minutes for Graham, Skye had been recovering the pepper spray. Finally, she sprayed the pepper and Noxium spray as Graham closed his mouth and fell back onto the ground, hitting the ground with a thud and a jolt of pain. In the spur of the moment, his evasive maneuver to avoid the spray had paid off, because it had missed him for the most part.

The soldier was in the direct line of fire, the cloud enveloping his face. He won control of the firearm, but his hands, twitching, immediately dropped the gun, which fell like a heavy rock onto the floor. Then, the man fell onto his knees, his mouth a wide 'o,' and slumped forwards onto Graham, who still held his breath.

"Are you okay? Are you okay?"

Skye rushed forward, peeling the man off of him, holding her breath, although the menacing cloud of gas dispersed in a manner of seconds in the heavily ventilated air.

"Ow, ow," Skye winced, helping roll the man off of him before retreating to the corner of the room, still holding the can of pepper spray.

"You saved me," Graham said. He leaned over, hugged her, although with one injured wrist and the other hand occupied, Skye didn't reciprocate. Graham felt relieved, deeply grateful, and he explained over the line that they had just been attacked, but that their cover was still preserved.

"How's your wrist?" Graham asked.

"I think it's sprained," Skye theorized. "It's swelling up. We can have Maddie look at this when it's all over."

"Or me," Dr. Chetana countered over the line. Graham thought he was going to roll his eyes so much that the irises of his eye would leave his body.

"How's my face?" Graham asked.

"Nothing a touch of makeup wouldn't fix," Skye offered with a smirk.

"Good," Graham replied. "After this is over, you can be my makeup artist."

"Yes, I will," Skye said, before her face fell once again. "I didn't want to believe it. But here we are. I think I was right."

"Yes, I think so. I'm glad we made it, relatively unscathed."

But they weren't out in the clear. Not yet, and Skye reminded him of that fact. There was, chillingly, still the sound of running water in the background, and Skye knew that that likely spelled trouble. Graham muted the line on his earpiece to alleviate any distractions, and then he picked up the pistol from the ground and headed to the green curtain with Skye.

The two silently counted off to the count of three, and then they threw the curtains open.

Only a short distance away, there was yet another green curtain in the hallway, cordoning off a separate, darker section of the room on the other side. Before the following curtain, however, there were four separate shower stalls.

A couple had been recently used, but their white shower curtains were pulled open; there also was a third, appearing to be slightly drier, the shower curtains also open (it was now that Skye put together that the three had likely soldiers Marcell spotted had been there). But then, there was a fourth one still, behind which water rushed, and a person was humming to themselves. His clothes, a green uniform like the rest of the troops, looked to be sitting on some sort of outside shelf next to the shower.

"How in the hell did he not hear us?" Skye mouthed, and Graham shrugged.

The timing was perfect, and yet simultaneously tragic for the man responsible: all of a sudden, the shower stopped, and Skye looked to Graham, who nodded, his gun positioned up at the curtain.

In his free time, Graham practiced with some blanks with Marcell ever since they'd taken over the ship, and he had shot a gun a few times in his life, his family being the gun-toting type and all. He felt he knew his way around a gun, although he certainly felt he was no expert. So then when the curtains opened, and a nude man, whose muscular build indicated he too was a soldier, stepped out with some kind of shower-friendly, noise-canceling bulky waterproof headphones covering his ears, two things happened. One, the man stood up straight, reflexively putting his hands to cover up his exposed genitalia, and two, Graham squeezed the trigger.

Even though Graham felt zero mercy now for the soldiers after the fight he'd just been through, he didn't want to kill him. He aimed for the man's right shoulder, and the right shoulder he hit, punching a hole into the man's clavicle and sending his body careening back through the shower curtains onto his side.

He screamed in pain, pleading for mercy. Without making eye contact, Skye aimed her pepper spray and pressed down on it to blanket his face with the brownish cloud of chemicals. The man slipped unconscious in a matter of seconds. Although the shot man's long legs stretched outside the stall, Skye closed the curtains anyway, whether it was for decency's purpose, to cut off the Noxium, or to not have to look at the oozing red wound on the now-unconscious man's shoulder, she didn't know.

That was it. The two of them had single-handedly taken out three presumed soldiers, and now there was only one last threshold to cross.

The room was dim. So dim that they could hardly see beyond underneath the curtain, which looked like the plain white tile of any regular locker room.

Graham and Skye could've peeked inside and seen the interior of the room. But this thought never crossed their mind. Graham and Skye looked at each other, and counted down instead.

"Three," Skye started.

"Two," Graham counted.

"One."

The Laser from Above

    Graham and Skye pulled the curtain back, brandishing their weapons, and were presented with the worst sight of their entire life.

Chapter 28

There were times in Skye's life where she was proud to be right.

Even when things went poorly, there could be some glimmer of self-importance, an *I told you so*, that Skye would experience, and, despite tragedy, she would feel emotionally validated.

On one particular occasion when she was sixteen, Skye's sister Emily was invited to a party in the rough side of town with some friends who Skye didn't like. Although Emily was of the type to obviously not tell her parents, she told Skye, who told her no. Despite this, she went anyway. Sure enough, her drink was drugged. Although a friend whisked her away to safety before anything horrible could happen, it was a cautionary tale for Em, and for Skye, she had called it, and had known that her intuition was right. On yet another occasion, when Skye was eighteen, she had rejected going along with a cousin (the family troublemaker) to go spray painting in an industrial park in Minneapolis one summer. And yet again, her intuition had proven correct, as her cousin was arrested, and ultimately pleaded guilty to misdemeanor vandalism. Again, she felt a guilty pleasure after it all happened, not to mention she was relieved that he hadn't pulled Em into anything.

But in this case, there was nothing to celebrate. The soul-sucking sight was worse than she ever could have imagined, and both Graham and Skye dropped their weapons to the ground.

There were around eight various shower heads (and no stalls) located throughout the room. But it was the sight below them that tore her apart.

There were eight women in total. Five of them wore robes, three of them in the nude. All of them sat down in front of the drains. Two tubes led into their back, and plugged directly into the wall. All of them had blindfolds on, and muzzles. The fact that they had hair being grown out on most of their heads made Skye believe that they were not soldiers, but civilians, although she couldn't be sure. Although some of their hair wasn't intact. Some missed chunks of hair. Skye could guess why.

Graham had mentioned that morning how he wondered how hundreds of men could have survived on board the ship without their family, girlfriend, or mutiny. Here was his answer. President Melero's dirty secrets.

"Oh, fuck," Graham said. "This shit is *fucked. Fuck!*"

"No," Skye said, tears filling her eyes. "It wasn't supposed to be like this."

Skye pulled out her earpiece, which, miraculously, was still in her pocket (she was grateful for once that women's pockets were ridiculously small), putting it into her ear and tapping the unmute button on her earpiece. She felt like curling into a ball and wailing. Somehow, she was having more success remaining composed than Graham, who had fallen onto his knees by now.

"What is it?" Nathan asked.

"I was right. I was right," Skye repeated. "I said, I was right. They got sex slaves chained up to the walls. Tubes injecting some kind of drugs into them, I think. It's slavery. It's worse than slavery, it's…"

"Oh no," Marcell said quietly, in a way that let her know he was choking up.

"Oh *fuck*," Fritz grumbled. "Skye, we're playing the recording in two minutes. Can you handle this?"

"We need more than…" Graham started, but then he leaned over, vomiting all over the middle of the room, likely staining the white tiles an orange, although it was too dark inside the room to distinguish its color at that time.

"We need more time," Skye stated. "There are eight women in here, and we need to rescue all of them."

"I can make it five," Fritz said.

"More, please."

"Fine, ten. But that's it, and that's really pushing it. I don't want anyone finishing up their meals. I know you can do this."

Skye nodded, before remembering, once again, that there was no one to watch her, no one to hold her. The tears were blurring her face, but she knew she had to be strong. She had to. To save these women. And then, to make President Melero pay.

"Hey Fritz?"

"Yeah, Skye?"

"We're going through with the contingency plan. Blow up this entire fucking ship."

"I know. I'll have Lex broadcast to the SAS 2."

Dr. Chetana didn't raise any objections this time.

***

Despite their dangerous fights with the soldiers earlier, the alarm hadn't been raised. However, if at any point it was, Skye was ready to go down fighting. She would take out every person who stood in her way.

Skye now believed that the soldiers on board the S.S. Washington had no right to live. As a matter of fact, every impulse directed her to grab the pistol on the ground, and shoot the unconscious men on the ground in the skull, one by one, permanently ending their miserable existence.

No, that would be too merciful. A shot to the groin first, that would be far more fitting.

But Skye refused to sink to their level. Although every cell in her body was screaming for her to do so. They were going to get their deadly punishment, regardless, when the ship was blown into pieces in ten minutes.

Skye couldn't be one hundred percent sure, but she believed that the tubes pumped drugs to preserve the women in some sort of catatonic state. She was able to easily unplug them, and there was an easily accessible pile of towels to cover them up. Graham helped the entire time, although he was sobbing loudly.

The issue was that most of the women weren't responding at all. At least half were unconscious, and the ones that weren't, seemed to be in and out of consciousness, unable to speak, confirming to Graham and Skye that they had been drugged.

Skye tried picking up the closest one, but the pain in her wrist, which now was throbbing, flared up, so instead she and Graham worked together to move them. Graham channeled every ounce of rage and misery into helping carry the women. Most of them were thin, or even emaciated. The sick monsters had not only deprived them of any agency of their body, but had failed to properly feed them, as well.

Graham's familiarity with the map paid off. He knew exactly where the nearest escape pod was, a little way down from the elevator. Skye was grateful she hadn't gone alone, because it was Graham who was able to operate the escape pods, which seemed nearly identical to the ones on the International Space Hotel, only they were slightly larger.

"I looked at... at the manuals," he sniffled, pressing the button to unlock the door. The doors opened; the escape pods were active, which was great, because they would've been unable to rescue them otherwise.

One by one, they loaded the unconscious women into this escape pod, with Graham holstering the pistol by his side and ready to use it, no holds barred, at a moment's notice. No one came, however, so the gun wasn't going to be used.

"Ready now," Fritz said over the line while they worked.

It was sometime in the middle of this process, within the next few minutes after Fritz had said those words, that the alarm on the S.S. Washington went off: all hell had broken loose on board the International Space Hotel.

Chapter 29

Marcell was at the dinner when it all happened, and the final phase of his portion of the plan was put into place.

Dr. Chetana was sitting in the fringe tables of the room, ready to escape through the back door at a moment's notice. But Marcell was in the middle of the cafeteria, leaning up against a wall, ready to plunge himself into the fray. The confirmation from Skye gave him newfound courage and even more confidence to kill any soldier who stood in his way.

The meal had started out relatively normal. It started off with the cafeteria staff, as well as cooks, bringing out the food into the various serving containers in the empty restaurants, which led to many people in the room celebrating. Before the feasting could begin, however, President Melero yelled for attention and stood up to his feet.

"Attention everyone! I'd like to say a few words before our celebration."

The room fell silent quickly. All of the soldiers no doubt were accustomed to listening to his speeches, and everyone on board seemed to venerate President Melero, except for the council. Not that it was their fault. Next to nobody from the ISH had any suspicion on what was going on behind closed doors, and in their mind, they were in the room with the most important man in the world. The biggest leader of the free world, now ready to rebuild America from the ashes.

"This has been a glorious day," President Melero said. "The fact that we are all here today, about to receive great nourishment today, not as Americans, or as the Army or Marines, but as survivors, survivors who've made it over a month long after the most devastating day in the history of humanity, is nothing short of incredible. The International Space Hotel has proven to be an extraordinary safe haven. You are all very lucky."

President Melero folded his hands in front of him. Marcell could tell that some people were stunned, even starstruck, by his presence. Some of the women (and men, too) seemed wooed by his words, his dreamy voice and chiseled jawline that made him look like he could've been a model in an upscale clothing chain before it had all happened, and not an influential politician. Marcell did have to admit. If he knew Melero wasn't holding women captive on the S.S. Washington, as Skye had announced, and wasn't one of the leading figures responsible for the literal end of the world, he might've felt the same exact way.

The President resumed speaking after pausing for a few seconds.

"But I cannot emphasize it enough. Even though today we share a meal, and then we may go our separate ways, this is just the beginning of the hard work we have ahead. The beginning of a new America. The beginning of a new World. You all will be just as pivotal as me when it comes to rebuilding the Earth, and restoring order to the masses. We've all suffered so much. So much loss." He paused. "But now, we're on an equal playing field. The past might hold us back. But right now, we have to keep our chins up, and we can carve our own future. Thank you very much, residents of the International Space Hotel."

Marcell was unsatisfied. Somehow, he wanted him to say something else. To blow his cover about what he was going to do with fifty women, or about the space lasers from above that had scorched the Earth. But of course he wouldn't. President Melero was evidently not a moral man whatsoever, but he was a smart one. Although the more he thought about it, the more Marcell thought it strange: what he'd said about the equal playing field.

Dr. Chetana, meanwhile, stood up after President Melero had finished this short speech, starting to speak. They had limited options. Skye was on board the S.S. Washington, freeing their captives. Marcell was posted with the rest of the security guards. Fritz had just finished preparations with Lex in the comms room earlier, when it came to ensuring that the recording was functioning and ready to go. Now he was just outside the room, having stepped outside of the room, presumably to let Lex know to contact the SAS 2 briefly in order to destroy the S.S. Washington.

Meanwhile, Nathan was elsewhere, supervising the airlocks in the event that they needed to seal out any ruptured zones, and also managing the escape pods should they need to be activated. His help would be essential.

"I believe that I speak for all men, and *women*, on board, when I say, thank you," Dr. Chetana said aloud, placing an extra emphasis on women that Marcell hoped wasn't too on the nose. "For your generous gift of three weeks' food, we are grateful. We will be ready to offload some of our residents with the S.S. Washington with you, where they will be able to help usher in a new America."

Some people murmured at this. This was the first time they'd received notice of this supposed plan. Marcell was glad that at least none of them would be going with them in the end. By tomorrow, Marcell knew that the women on board would either be dead or rid of President Melero's envoy forever, and not tied up to a wall with tubes protruding from their body.

"Don't let me hold you," Dr. Chetana concluded. "Let's eat!"

A great crowd rushed towards the kitchen, where now the kitchen crew was ready to serve their portions. Some soldiers, too, were amidst the line, but it looked like a couple of the more senior officers were berating them to behave, because they stopped, lining up behind the guests of the hotel.

Fritz, meanwhile, spoke over the line.

"Ready now," he said. "I'm coming back for support."

Marcell turned to Jordan, nodded. Then, he turned to disseminate the message to the rest of his crew.

"Everyone get ready," Marcell told them. "Shit's going to hit the fan."

***

"Why did you assassinate Grace Elliott?"

The audio recording started exactly where Fritz and Marcell had wanted it, blasting over the speakers of the P.A. system and immediately snapping everyone's attention. Some people looked around the room, as if they weren't sure if someone was shouting, until it became clear that there was a recording being played aloud.

"I don't know. It was an order from my superior! I didn't question it."

Everyone had fallen silent now. Soldiers and civilians alike were stunned, but also confused, by who was speaking, by the contents of the message. Marcell hoped that they picked it up quickly. Their plan banked on that.

"Who was your superior in that case?"

"General Amotu. But I think it came from higher up. President Melero."

Marcell looked across the room. He saw President Melero staring blankly, some of the soldiers immediately rushing to his defense and clustering around him. A few of them were raising their guns up, ready to shoot whoever was responsible for this disturbance.

Some of the ISH residents were whispering nervously, a couple of people standing up and slowly walking out of the room.

"Why did they choose you to kill her?"

"I'm one of the top soldiers on the S.S. Washington. A Green Beret."

"Surely you had your moral objections to this."

"What the hell is this!?" A furious soldier asked. Even though he was halfway across the cafeteria, Marcell swore he could see veins popping out of his face as he yelled in President Melero's general direction.

Now a few soldiers joined in the uproar. They closed in like predators in the hunt, but their superiors were quick to react.

"Silence!" A dark-skinned general next to Melero, with various badges the color of the rainbow spectrum, yelled. This man, who Marcell assumed might have been Amotu, pulled out his pistol and fired into the air. Now the room was full of screams. Many of those in line started to scatter for the doorway, others still diving to the ground. Those at their tables dove for cover, while the soldiers gathered apprehensively.

"Melero promised me a promotion. Said she was conspiring against the country, and planned to sell us out to the Chinese. I had to do it! Any refusal to follow orders would have me court-martialed."

"Everyone, we're leaving right now!" Amotu yelled at the top of his lungs. "Any soldier who defies my order will be summarily executed for treason!"

"Oh no, you won't!"

The voice came from a megaphone, and almost everyone turned to see Fritz, who was in the back of the room, behind

Marcell and near the back entrance. "This is an interrogation of your own soldier, Lieutenant Monterey."

"What the hell did you do with Monterey Jack?" another soldier shouted. "Where is he?"

Despite the gravity of the situation, Marcell appreciated the man's nickname for a second as more of the recording continued. The noise was partially blotted out by the shouts now, but if you were listening close enough, you could still make out each word being played without significant difficulty. The P.A. system must've been on its maximum volume.

"This is your own doing!" Fritz ranted. "You, Bruno Melero, had Grace Elliot assassinated, so you would be next in line for the succession of the Presidency of the United States! You orchestrated the takeover of the space lasers under false pretense, and you brought the downfall of the entire planet! For nothing!"

"Follow me!" Amotu continued, as of the crowds of soldiers, several dozen turned to exit through the entrance. Many more, however, hesitated in place, despite the strict orders.

But there was one who acted differently.

Marcell saw the way this man, quite literally, stood out; the behemoth of a man towered over the nearby soldiers by at least several inches. He was drunk. That much was apparent by the way he swayed, and by the slurs of his words, and Marcell would've imagined taken a gallon of booze, to get someone of his size drunk. But he was.

Plying them with booze seems to have worked to our advantage, Marcell observed, as the tall man began to yell.

"Y-you lie! You ended the whole w-orld, and you lied to us all!"

Marcell could hardly see him from across the cafeteria, but he could hear the ensuing chaos as the man pulled out his gun, aimed it in the direction of President Melero. Someone else was

The Laser from Above

too fast to react, however, gunning the man down where he stood. He fell onto the ground with a thud, as others jumped back from the killing.

More screaming. More people diving to the ground. The entire serving station was abandoned for good, as the chefs from both ships scurried behind closed doors for safety, the doors to the kitchen slamming shut and locking. Marcell was glad that Fritz had brought the megaphone, because otherwise his voice probably wouldn't be heard over the screams that filled the room.

"You don't have to accept this!" Fritz continued. "You can join us! To make the world right. We can do it. Together."

Now, his speech was working. It started with only a couple, but the soldiers, one by one, listened, stepping backwards, away from the exit, and back towards the middle of the cafeteria. A standoff, of great size, was forming. And while Amotu and some of the other high-ranking officers were barking orders for them to listen, to not throw their lives away, it looked like a mutiny had splintered their ranks.

Meanwhile, Melero, still, was staring blankly at the sight, wordlessly. His eyes blinked rapidly. It appeared that a plan of this kind had never crossed his mind. If it had, then he came sorely unprepared. Still, from this distance Marcell could tell he couldn't get a potshot at President Melero if he tried. There were too many soldiers and generals huddled near him, no doubt willing to volunteer as his meat shield. But the President's eyes looked as empty as the chasm of space surrounding the ISH.

Bruno Melero, Marcell thought, *you're not as smart as I thought.*

Even though Amotu threatened to execute all of the traitors on the spot, it looked the tense situation was turning the tides against the U.S. Army and Marines, as soldier turned upon soldier, drawing their guns as their convictions solidified one way or another. Marcell ordered a few of their security guards to roll forwards, aim their guns at President Melero's detachment, and he could hear Fritz still pleading behind him. Fritz once again pleaded for them to join the cause, and promised that all of them would find their own redemption.

"You liar! Why would you do this to Earth? Why would you destroy Earth? Was it really just the money, your loyalty to the country, or the promotion? You were really willing to sell your soul, only for that?"

Monterey's chilling laugh played over the line, and now Marcell watched as the final words rattled many of the men to the core.

"You want to know why? Because the world is fucked. President Melero promised me glory, and a position of leadership in the reconstruction of the planet. He lost everything, just like I did, and now, I have a second chance. You really want to know how everyone was hand-selected to be on the board?"

"How?"

"By being broken. By having nothing to lose."

The audio recording stopped. The reception of those standing with him led Marcell to conclude that Jack Monterey was wrong. That some of these men did have something to lose, even if it was only their pride and dignity.

Many innocents were now crouching behind the tables, or behind the serving stations, next to the soldiers who positioned themselves opposite Marcell and their unit. Other civilians were caught in between the opposing sides and had simply crouched behind cover or lay on the ground. Others, braver or more stupid, fled for their exits, screaming, but both sides let them pass.

But this standoff wouldn't happen forever. Either President Melero and his remaining soldiers would peacefully retreat, or there was going to be an onslaught soon, much more than the single body on the ground. Because Marcell knew he wasn't going anywhere.

Marcell ordered for the security guards to help tip some of the lunch tables over to use as cover, and it looked like the idea had impressed the now-defected soldiers, because they followed suit. Marcell turned and saw Dr. Chetana, Dr. Silva and Dr. Wells filtered among their ranks, ready to tend to the wounded, not to mention a couple of EMTs. He also saw Mr. McFarland, having returned from the Space Armament Station, his face appearing calmer than pretty much anyone else in the room. He had a pistol. Even some other hotel guests and clients volunteered among their ranks, as Marcell recognized a couple that Madison had pointed out as Minnie and Drake, asking some of the adjacent soldiers for any weapons to let them assist as they hunkered several tables down, behind their makeshift barricade. Marcell was glad they'd all been proactive and holstered extra guns; it meant they could arm civilians as well.

Marcell didn't know who fired first. But one second, and the other soldiers who still remained loyal to Melero were taking cover behind the countertops of the empty restaurants where food was to be served, and then there was the loud gunshot, from somewhere to the left, and then another near his ear, and another one from across the room. The room erupted into gunfire, and the battle began.

Chapter 30

The gunfight lasted less than three minutes. But it felt like an eternity.

Marcell had killed before. He had shot Audrey the night that Skye and Graham had taken control of the International Space Hotel. But it was nothing like this. This was the first battle ever fought in space, if you count the clearing out of the Space Armament Stations as lopsided massacres, and that entailed a whole lot more danger.

First, the noise. The whole room was so loud, Marcell thought his eardrums would burst immediately. The noise blotted out the sound of anything, except for the loudest screams and the clanging of bullets ricocheting or chipping the floor. He stood, not without a bit of strain due to his prior injuries, peeked out, and saw the flashes of the muzzles from the other side. He added his gun to the fray and fired, before hurriedly pulling back behind cover. If he didn't, Marcell was certain that he would've been shredded within seconds.

Then there were the bodies. He looked to the side, saw a man clad in military uniform catch a bullet to the throat, toppling backwards like a chopped down tree, dead on impact with the ground. Another defected soldier was clutching his chest and rocking back and forth, blood running in between his fingers, and he saw Dr. Chetana, tending to the wounded man, a look of compassion on her face, and Marcell knew that his loyalties lay with the right side.

The Laser from Above

Every few moments, there would be a break in the fire, as everyone would load up their magazine. Jordan was beside him the whole way, shouting into his ear whenever there was a pause in the gunfight, and he and Marcell would point their gun out together, peek just their head out of if they had the bravery, and fire. Sometimes, they sporadically sprayed their weapons without even pointing their head out, when fire was particularly heavy in their areas, bullets clanging off the other side of their lunch table, which truly was a lifesaver.

At one glance, Marcell aimed behind the counter near the serving station on the other side of the room, saw a soldier lift his head out of cover, and fired. Although he pulled back within a second, he saw a mist of blood flying up, and knew he'd connected with his target.

"Fuck!" Jordan exclaimed after maybe two minutes of the gunfight. Marcell turned to him, horrified, and saw that Jordan's machine gun had clattered onto the ground. Then he saw Jordan, ducking behind the middle of the table, his back braced against the table for cover.

"I'm good, I'm good!" Jordan promised, although his wince seemed to state otherwise. Blood trickled out onto the floor, and Marcell felt his heart sink as he crouched down next to him.

"Oh no," Marcell murmured.

"Must've been a ricochet!" Jordan shouted. "I was in cover!"

"Bastards!" Marcell screamed, and he fired wildly, back to the enemy soldiers, his bullet striking an opposing soldier in the leg, who was dragged back out into the hallway and out of sight.

There was no conclusive end to the gunfight, but it tapered off over the course of a couple minutes. Footsteps retreated out of the hallway, and it became apparent when Marcell looked out five minutes later, that almost everyone was gone, apart from a couple of stragglers, who, at the advance of Marcell's fellow soldiers, dropped their guns in surrender before being handcuffed promptly by some of security with the help of the defectors.

And then it was over. Marcell could smell a slightly metallic smell, that mixed with the smell of the cooling food for a sickening combination. There was blood everywhere, so much you could smell it. And now that he poked his head out of cover, he saw a field of dead bodies on the opposite side, at least two dozen or so, spread out throughout the floor, some lying limply behind cover. Most were wearing uniforms, indicating they were from the S.S. Washington, but not all of them. There were also numerous wounded.

Among the wounded and dying lay Drake. Marcell could tell he was not in good shape, as blood pooled from underneath his body, and it looked like he was slipping away, although if it was to death or simply unconsciousness, his guess was as good as anyone's. Drake's girlfriend, Minnie, was crouching down next to him, sobbing.

Minnie leaned over to him, kissing his forehead over and over.

"Skye," Drake said quietly. "Skye."

"No! I'm not Skye! I'm Minnie! Minnie! I'm here for you."

"Skye," he wheezed. "Skye..."

"I'm going to have your baby...! It's me! Tell me you love me!"

Minnie broke out into sobs, and Marcell turned away from the scene, unsure of what to make of it.

But a moan, almost a sob, escaped from Marcell's mouth when he saw the civilians. There were at least ten or so of them dead. Most of them were in between the two fighting sides, and had been caught in the crossfire, but some had died evidently sprinting towards the exit. Not to mention that there were countless other civilians wounded, crying, moaning, and shouting. They had gone into the room thinking that they'd be getting a banquet, and instead they received a dose of heavy trauma, and there were no counselors in sight to save them.

Marcell saw Dr. Chetana run out of cover once the coast was clear. Dr. Wells, meanwhile, still tended to those behind the table. Dr. Silva was nowhere to be seen, and Marcell realized that he had caught a stray, and was lying unconscious a short distance away, his chest slowly rising with each breath.

"What have we done?" Marcell asked. "My God."

He looked to the side to view their own wounded and deceased. Their side had entered with the advantage of their assault rifles, and they had driven them back. Judging by the number of bodies, they had inflicted more casualties, with only perhaps nine or ten dead behind their barricades. They had won the battle, if only due to the number of those who had defected on their side.

But how could he even begin to call this a victory? A couple of the newly enlisted security guards had died, along with at least eight or nine of the defected soldiers. That wasn't even counting the wounded, who lay on the ground in various conditions, some groaning or crying in pain, others unconscious.

"They are retreating to the S.S. Washington!" Nathan called over the line, whooping.

"The alarms are going off!" Skye panicked from the other side. "What do we do?"

"The order's been sent out," Marcell said, "You guys need to move it. You probably have less than five minutes to escape until the laser is fired. Fritz already told them to go."

Marcell couldn't deal with Skye, not after dealing with this bloodshed himself. Nathan or Fritz would have to handle it. Marcell muted his side of the line on the earpiece, before he turned to Jordan, whose face was contorted in pain.

"Let me see it," Marcell said.

Jordan reluctantly showed his injury. A bullet had hit his ring finger. The wound was gruesome, the finger having been struck and almost cut in half. The end of his finger dangled by only a thread of ligament, and Marcell felt bile rising in his throat.

"Oh shit," Marcell said. "Oh no…"

"Oh, don't mind this ring finger," Jordan grimaced. "What do I need it for, anyway? A wedding ring? I always thought marriage was overrated as an institution, anyway."

"How are you joking? Your finger is *fucked*."

"Just trying to make a light comment," Jordan said. "There are people who have it worse…"

"Okay, okay," Marcell said, calming down.

"*No!*" Dr. Chetana exclaimed from behind him.

Marcell stood up, turned around, his heart racing, telling Jordan he'd be back. He'd had no idea how Dr. Chetana had already slipped behind him, but now that she had lost her wits, he knew something horrible had happened.

"Oh, no! *No!* Why?"

The source of her distress was Fritz. He was behind a back table, facing upwards. He was so still that Marcell at first thought he was dead. But then he approached. Marcell spotted at least two puncture wounds, one on his chest, another on his arm, and there were potentially more on his back. His megaphone was smashed on the ground, by the looks of things having taken at least an additional bullet as well.

"Did I do well, or what?" Fritz asked weakly. Despite what must've been excruciating pain, he was smirking.

"Don't talk," Dr. Chetana said. "Doctor's orders."

"I always liked you, doctor," Fritz said. "But I'm going to say no."

All of a sudden, there was a giant rumble, and Marcell stumbled forward, almost falling to his feet. Some of the bodies were jolted, and Fritz groaned in pain. It looked like several of the soldiers were eager to continue engaging the others; Marcell told them to go ahead, that he had no intention of following. In the meantime, Marcell briefly unmuted the other side of the line, as he and the security guards of the ISH regrouped and regained their wits.

"Our shields are taking heavy damage from the S.S. Washington, which is opening fire!" Nathan cried. "It's only a matter of time until we face irreparable damage and face breaches in our hull. I'll control the airlocks!"

Marcell tapped the line, muted it again.

"Huh," Fritz said. "Well, I trust Skye… to get the job done," Fritz said. "Now tell me, did I do well?"

"Yeah," Marcell said. Although his emotions had remained bottled up until now, tears welled from his eyes, as he stared mournfully at his boss, who had treated him so well. "You did great."

"That's good," Fritz said. Blood had stained half of his beard red, the other remaining a gray.

"You did great," Dr. Chetana agreed. "You saved us all."

"Yes," Fritz stated, his voice gurgling. "Finally, I've done something to be proud of, and carried it to the end."

Fritz exhaled loudly, slipping away from this life. Marcell wished he had the chance to thank him for everything.

***

"Fire now! The International Space Hotel is under attack!"

The voice belonged to Lex, and came over the radio of Space Armament Station two.

"So that's it, then," Jace commented.

"Yes," Madison said. "I guess we shoot them now."

Cole Caldwell didn't stick around and wait for anything else.

Within less than a minute after receiving the broadcast, Cole, with the help of Olivia and Jace, had angled the electrostatic chamber and lance in the direction of the S.S. Washington. The others were hunkering in the other rooms, and their weakness bothered Madison, who was eager now to finish what the others had started. She knew that if Skye and the others had ordered for them to blow up the S.S. Washington, then their theories about the destruction of Earth had been proven correct.

"What about the blowback?" Olivia asked.

"What? What blowback?" Madison asked frantically.

"The blowback of the ship into the hotel," Cole explained, as he ordered Olivia to press a button far up the panel, and he turned a couple of knobs clockwise. "When we blow the ship up, there's a chance that debris, chunks of the ship, will fly into the Hotel and cause irreparable damage."

"Damn," Madison said. "Is there any way that we can avoid that entirely? I don't think we went through everything with the hotel just for the hotel to blow up with them."

"Well, we can't just re-maneuver this ship," Cole said. "Of course, it would be better if we were in a better angle, and the ISH wasn't in it. But at least it isn't like the hotel is blocking our path. We should count our lucky stars that we have a direct shot. If we hadn't prepared for that, then this plan would've been impossible to begin with."

"So, we just hope it doesn't damage the ISH?" Olivia asked. Cole didn't answer.

Cole re-adjusted the monitor. On the screen, it looked like guns had now angled towards and were firing a few giant red laser beams at the hotel. At first, it didn't seem to be doing much, as if there were shields deflecting blasts from the S.S.

Washington, but soon it looked like there was a small explosion on board, and glass and debris spreading from the contact point. One thing was clear: the ISH wasn't designed to tank heavy damage, and if it took enough hits, then everyone would die. She would guess they only had a couple of minutes to spare.

"Oh my God," Madison gasped, jaw dropping. In that moment, she wished she still had her radio piece to contact Skye and the other council. But that had been one oversight in whatever plan they'd cooked up. They never anticipated needing her to be in contact with Skye and the others, because they had Lex to radio with.

"The hotel… was that an explosion?" Jace asked.

"It was," Cole admitted. "Looks like they were right."

Cole hit the unmute button to the radio.

"How bad is it, Lex?"

"It's bad," Lex said. "Hurry! There's been a battle on board and we need your help, *now*!"

Cole leaned over, as if to press a button and respond, but he didn't. Despite the intense pressure, he looked oddly calm. The only indicator that he was even remotely stressed was his scrunched-up eyebrows.

Cole pointed to a sliding button that was next to a series of notches, indicating some sort of scale, and then reached over with his hand, before hovering over the button.

"This determines the power of our charge," Cole explained at a hurried pace. "The higher it is, the higher the level of energy that is poured into this beam. If we turn this setting up too high, then the lance will pierce the ship, go through the S.S. Washington, and rip open the hotel, probably into two whole separate pieces. Everyone would die."

"We can't let that happen!" Madison cried.

"But if it's too little, it won't blow it up instantly, or might not even penetrate whatever shields they utilize. I guess we can always re-adjust the power back up, but we can't be certain there wouldn't be shields to deflect a low enough charge. The ideal amount is powerful enough to blow up the ship into as small of pieces as possible, without destroying the hotel in the process."

"Do you know how far up to put this then?" Madison questioned as he slid the button up.

"Nope," Cole replied. "I don't have time to calculate, and it looks like time is of the essence. I'm going to eyeball it."

Cole adjusted the slider up, pressing a sequence of a couple other buttons. On one of the screens that was looking at the S.S. Washington, a yellow crosshair appeared, and Cole grabbed the joystick and adjusted it until it was honed in on the center.

"Time to go," he said. Then he turned the key in the ignition, and hit the largest red button that was labeled the apt "FIRE." And the laser beam readied its blast.

It started with a rumble and a shaking that made Madison grab onto the control panel. She turned over to Cole, whose eyes were now closed, the movement probably unlocking a swath of memories that he never had wanted to revisit.

The sound of electrical whirring and crackling grew ever louder the next several seconds, intermingled with a deep bass that Madison could feel reverberate around her chest, making her entire body vibrate. The last time she'd felt this way, had been in a rave on Earth several months ago: but this was no upbeat electronic music, only a destructive dirge that preluded a giant beam.

"I should probably mention," Cole casually said. "It's super bright. Electricity has a blue tint in air, but this plasma beam will be pure white: I recommend-"

Before he could even finish, the laser discharged.

The Laser from Above

Madison found herself almost blinded by the light, and instantly closed her eyes. But for the brief seconds before she shut her eyes, she saw a giant beam, what must've been at least twenty meters wide, and equally tall, shooting out hundreds of feet per second. Everyone was almost thrown off their feet, although Cole harmlessly rolled a couple of feet backwards, and Madison ended up catching herself once again on the control panel.

She expected a giant explosion to wreck her ears, and she covered them in anticipation, but of course there was nothing: sound didn't travel through space, and Cole looked like he was about to lecture her on that, until he found himself too fascinated by the sight.

"Would you look at that," Cole said.

Madison looked up onto the monitor, and saw the International Space Hotel, a field of debris floating—no, shooting in all directions—in front of it, and at it. Madison was starstruck once again, too amazed to even reprimand Cole for his needlessly loquacious and tardy warning of the brightness.

Chapter 31

A few minutes prior, and Skye and Graham knew the clock was ticking.

"Lex has given the order to fire," Nathan said over the line. "Hurry up and escape! There's chaos on this ship! Bloodshed, bloodshed, bloodshed!"

That would explain the commotion. The alarms had been blaring for almost thirty seconds, but Skye and Graham were moving as fast as possible, now hefting the last unconscious woman to the escape pod.

Skye hoped Fritz and Marcell were okay; but the side of their lines had been completely silent, and the only acknowledgement from Dr. Chetana was that she was treating the wounded, and there were many of them.

"How many?" Graham wheezed as Skye pressed the door to open the door again and helped set the woman down into the escape pod.

"Too many," Dr. Chetana stated behind a backdrop of loud gunfire. "Too damn many."

It was then that they encountered the first squad of soldiers. No, it wasn't a squad; it could've been a whole division, there were so many of them, flooding through the various hallways, some of them bursting out of the stairwell which they had used to reach the floor. And they caught them red-handed, shouting and pointing at the intruders on their floor.

The Laser from Above

Graham closed the door behind them, as gunshots fired in their direction, throwing sparks off from the metallic walls nearby as they hurriedly slammed a button to seal the doors behind them. They were spared by the durability of the whole ship: the metal airlock sealed behind them, as well as the escape pods' thick titanium doors, and be it as they may, the American soldiers' attempts to shoot through the window of the S.S. Washington failed, the glass clearly designed to easily withstand assault rifles.

"Hurry!" Skye screeched. "Graham, they're coming!"

Graham slammed the start button, and jerked the joystick up. He slammed his feet onto the gas—he always thought it was funny that it was called gas, although gas vehicles had been almost completely rendered obsolete or outlawed years ago—and then they were off, detached from the S.S. Washington.

The ride wasn't smooth at all, and it seemed like Graham's movements had woken up one of the passengers, her head thumping into the ground among the jolting of the ship.

"Huh...?" one of the women, stirring, rasped. "Where am I?"

"Shhh, it's okay," Skye said, turning around.

"I'm... almost naked," the woman said, although a towel was wrapped around her. She slowly sat up, observed her surroundings. Skye was shaken. The woman couldn't have been much older than she was, if even that.

"Yes," Skye said. "Rest. Don't worry."

Skye's words seemed to have soothed the woman, because she leaned back up against the wall of the escape pod, silent.

Meanwhile, Graham focused on getting as far away from the S.S. Washington as possible. In the process, however, he looked back down at the hotel in curiosity: and he saw the S.S. Washington launched a few beams at the hotel.

"What's going on?" Skye asked, concerned.

"They're shooting at them," Graham said.

"Those cowards. When we don't even have any turrets to fight back," Skye replied. "Chickenshit cowards."

"We're safe," Graham said.

"We don't know that," Skye complained. "We can't just sit here…"

"There's nothing we can do," Graham said. "I'm putting as much distance between us and the S.S. Washington as possible. That's the best I can do."

"I just hope they hurry up and take care of this," Skye said. "I can't take this anymore."

And then, all of a sudden, she saw it. A giant white beam, like a giant lightning bolt, slamming into the center of the S.S. Washington, and rending its metal as if it was made out of paper mâché and not the sturdiest metals on the planet. Skye had to veer her eyes away, so bright was the beam, but she managed to glance back within only a couple of seconds to see the S.S. Washington blow up into disparate parts, fanning out from each other. A fiery inferno erupted, latching onto smaller pieces, which, despite now flying in all directions, were not extinguished by the vacuum of space, or at least not instantly. All of it was silent, which somehow contributed to the grandeur of all.

Graham turned to Skye, who was silent in shock. A great feeling of pride was bubbling up inside of her. Skye didn't believe in divine retribution much, but she figured there was nothing more fitting and poetic than a beam of light to send those perverted soldiers a one-way ticket to hell.

"Looks like your prayers have been answered," Graham said.

Skye smiled for a few moments, until she realized some of the smaller pieces were heading straight towards the hotel. Sure enough, some of the fragments crashed into the side, and she grimaced.

Some harmlessly bounced off the Space Hotel, and ricocheted off, but others seemed to collapse through the walls, a couple more resulting in small explosions, and she knew that might spell disaster. She reached her hand out at the window, before retracting away from the cold glass. She knew touching it was a bad idea.

"Relax," Graham said, putting his hand on her shoulder. "This is Nathan's job. He'll be on top of controlling the airlocks, and he'll save everyone. We did our job. It's time for us to trust him."

Skye met Graham's gaze. "Graham Scorsone... You are an interesting guy. And I don't mean that in the Minnesotan way."

"Skye Calvert," he countered, purposefully accentuating his accent, "You make me as happy as a pig in mud. And I can mean that in the South Carolina way."

Skye laughed. And she knew she had done her best: she hoped it was worth everything.

***

Madison and the others back on the Space Armament System, meanwhile, had nothing to do but sit for a long while.

Cole sent out several messages to Lex, but heard nothing back. Madison frequently checked the clock to see how much time had passed. With each passing minute, she was certain that the worst had happened. That they'd be trapped in this Space Armament System, with nothing but a single escape pod to return down to Earth. After all, they lacked the food supplies to live long in space anymore, not with several of them, and Madison's consumption of the ice cream bars were a testament to that.

It was an hour and thirteen minutes after the S.S. Washington blew up when they finally received a return broadcast.

"We're good," Lex stated over the line. "The International Space Hotel is okay."

"Oh, thank God!" Madison said, pushing Olivia out of the way and standing in front of Cole, who looked offended. "Tell me, do you know if Skye is okay?"

"They're out in space," Lex explained. "Her and Graham. We're about to bring them in."

"What about the dead? Any estimates?"

"We're still counting," Lex said seriously. "I knew you'd all want to talk about that. I would estimate at least a couple dozen."

"Oh shit," Madison mumbled under her breath.

"What about the damage?" Cole blurted out. "It looked bad, stray bits of debris were crashing into the International Space Hotel, and I feared the worst."

"It's not good," Lex admitted. "But we've sealed all the airlocks necessary. The ventilation systems remain intact: the hotel is, by all means, still functioning. No system failure is imminent, as far as all of our engineers can tell, but they are all at work and probably will be for the next couple of days. Nathan Xiong did a great job. If he hadn't acted as fast as he did, then there's a chance that many more people would've died."

"What was with the order?" Madison questioned. "You told us to destroy the ship. Was it true? That President Melero started it all?"

"Yes," Lex answered. "It's my understanding, that President Melero started the war and used it to take control of the country, even though everything is busted. Skye and Graham, however, confirmed our suspicions on board. They found enslaved women in... in... some sort of dungeon. Well, that was the final straw."

A couple of minutes passed, and Lex explained how yes, they could return to the hotel, but it would take a while to get ready, with all the dead, so they should wait until the next morning. They also delivered the news that Fritz Nussbaum had passed away: Olivia seemed to take the news particularly hard, and she walked out of the room to have a moment.

Cole and Jace asked some questions for a couple of minutes, until Lex had stopped. Madison figured this would be the end of the night, that they would all go to sleep victors, but it wasn't.

It was only when Jace was peering over the radar and evaluating the debris field that he saw something in the field. It was heading straight back down to the Earth. Cole was somehow able to replay a 3-D visual reconstruction of the feedback from the radar and cameras, and it showed an animation of the ship clearing some debris out of the way, indicating the presence of weapons, as it accelerated away from the explosion.

"That's a ship," Cole said, confused, when he looked at the radar. He decided to reposition the monitors to get a closer look at what it actually was.

The monitor was adjusted, and the scopes caught a sight of what it was: a large escape pod, with guns all along the sides. It was getting further, breaching down the atmosphere now, with streaks of fire tailing down from its end. The ship was much slower than the S.S. Washington had been, but its destination was obvious. Whoever it was inside, was they were trying to escape down to Earth.

"It can't be..." Jace said, as Olivia rejoined them back in the room, teary face and all. "Do you think it's from the S.S. Washington?"

"I don't know who else it'd be," Madison stated. "Unless they're from the ISH."

"Only one way to find out," Cole offered.

"Hello. This is the Space Armament Station Two reporting. Identify yourself immediately, or we will destroy you. Over."

Madison didn't know whether the President was there, but a quick look at the battery percentage on the console let her know that they'd only drained a few percentage points of the battery charge. In other words, they had enough energy to easily perform a follow-up strike.

After a few seconds, there was a response from the other side.

"Give me it." It sounded like someone was pushing someone else out of the way, and taking control. "This is President Melero of the United States. It's my understanding you destroyed our spacecraft. I caution you against doing the same to me."

Madison turned to Cole, who stared blankly. Jace and Olivia were comically surprised.

Why would he announce his existence like that? Especially after they destroyed the S.S. Washington? Madison didn't get it.

"When I found out you had recovered the remains of the SAS 2, I could've sent ships to blow your ship up. But I didn't. I gave you food, instead. To honor our deal. I could've slaughtered you."

It looked like Olivia wanted to do the negotiation. But once again, Madison barged in place. She knew her behavior could be characterized as rude or pushy, but it didn't matter. She was speaking on behalf of the leadership of the ISH, and Olivia, Jace, and, quickly enough, Cole, understood that.

"But you didn't," Madison said. "Instead, you tried to use fifty of our women."

"That... I'm not proud of that," President Melero said. "Sometimes, as a leader, you have to make the most difficult decisions. Soldier morale on board the ship was destroyed. I had to allow that and convince you by staging a tour. It was either that, or everything would've been lost. I made the right decision."

"Decision? You think those women could make any decision! You sicko."

"Is that it? You decided to kill hundreds of my men, brilliant researchers, civilians, all who could've helped rebuild Earth, because, hypothetically, we were going to take your women? Like any military in war?"

"No."

"What was that, then? Was it the fact that I orchestrated a takeover of the United States, and you felt like I was responsible for destroying the planet? Even though I never fired any nuclear missiles? I wasn't even the President at that time."

"No."

"No?"

"It was both."

"So, that makes it okay."

"Your mind games aren't working. I can sign off on your death, right now."

"No, listen to me. This is bigger than you, or me."

"There's nothing you can say that will convince me, unless you cooperate. Tell me. Tell me why would you do this?"

"Do what? I already told you about the women-"

"The takeover. Why? The planet. You can't be seriously sick enough in the head to think that billions dying, the mutually assured destruction of every industrialized country, that somehow you being the president makes it all right?"

There was nothing on the line for a few seconds, complete silence. There were the sounds of a struggle, and then President Melero seemed to grunt, a loud bang visible in the background.

Madison turned to the others, who were confused.

"Sorry about that," President Melero said. "I had some... loose ends to take care of."

"He shot them," Olivia mouthed, and Madison felt like she was going to throw up.

"You-"

"You wanted me to tell you why. General Amotu, were you with me from the beginning?"

"Yes, Mr. President," General Amotu said from over the line.

Madison frowned. There were multiple people on board their ship, after all.

"Were you with me, Richardson?"

"Yes, sir," another voice answered. "To the end."

"Sister? Were you with me?"

"In the end," came Amelia Melero's voice. "Even as everyone scoffed, I had my brother's back. Bruno knew what was right."

"I never wanted the world to be destroyed," President Melero argued. "I never thought any action I ordered would escalate to nuclear war. We were going to kill them, clean up the evidence, and call their demises a fateful accident. While Ascendant Technologies would claim to repossess and repair the stations, we'd have all of our men posted: essentially forcing a takeover of these space lasers.

"But it didn't go according to plan. When I took over SAS 4, with the U.S. Army and General Amotu's assistance, the Chinese told their government that the Americans had taken them, and the rest was history. You see, they'd had unauthorized additions in the form of a secret hidden warning signal they'd installed on board, without Ascendant Technology's approval. The Chinese never could help themselves, tampering with what was already perfect. We should've pulled our businesses out of their nation *decades* ago."

Madison didn't acknowledge the banter, although it disgusted her. President Melero was truly a callous person.

"But you knew the risk, capturing those stations. You knew it could easily start a nuclear war."

"Yes," President Melero answered. "It was a risk I had to take. You see, I lost everything. My family was taken away from me in a car accident. My pregnant wife, the love of my life. My son. Her future child. I couldn't earn my own happy life by God. I watched as my entire family, save for one sister, turned my back on me, as God spat on me and kicked me down. And I knew I wouldn't let Him take me down."

Madison trembled. She had thought President Melero would lie, trying to coax her into letting him live. But it was obvious that he was telling the pure, unadulterated truth.

"So I said what? *Fuck* you God, *fuck* you! No one thought I would've won my election in my district, but I did. I said, I'm going to be a God of this world, with my archangels—Amotu, Richardson, Kontos—and I'm going to step up, subvert you, and reclaim the world, piece by piece. I'm going to rule the world, and create a new one! I'll take out Grace Elliott, step up to the next in line for the Presidency. I'll leak the Space Armament Stations to all of the media, to weaken the current administration, breach the confidentiality of it all. If it takes rebuilding the world again from the ashes, then I'm going to do it. It wouldn't be pretty, but it would be fair, it would be just, and I knew it. Just like Noah and the Flood, except humanity won't sink down again.

Never again. I would rebuild it all if I had to. And you took that dream away from me..."

President Melero was unashamedly himself, and it was scary.

"So that's it then?" Madison asked, her voice cracking for a second before she cleared her throat and continued. "You have some kind of God complex, and you want to exercise your will over the masses?"

"I don't have a God complex," President Melero responded. "I am, however, God himself. I knew that when I emerged from that car wreck intact, and they were all dead."

"Great," Madison said, muting the line before turning to the others. "This man is *loco*."

"Yes," Olivia said. "To think... That's all that it took to destroy the world. One crazy person in a position of decent political power. *Shit*."

Operation Exodus. Addiction. Eva's betrayal. The world's destruction. Death and sex trafficking. What a terrible year. Shit, indeed, Madison thought.

Madison unmuted the line. "I'm not convinced. If you're God, do you think you will dodge this beam?"

"You kill me, the entire United States falls for good," President Melero said, his voice back to a more normal tone. "You want that blood on your hands?"

Madison turned to Cole, gave him the signal. She had held doubts earlier about the potential consequences what perhaps waited on the other side of death for blowing up this escape pod. But now, after hearing him speak she'd made up her mind.

Madison truly believed that President Melero was the Antichrist, and she clasped her crucifix necklace now, as if she was trying to repel demons from leaping out from the radio.

"I don't know if I'm worried about blood on my hands," Madison answered. "Way I'm seeing it, your hands are bloodstained. I don't think I'm going to lose any sleep over this."

The laser charged over the next minute. Perhaps it was cruel, but their side of the line was left unmuted, meaning President Melero and everyone else could hear the feedback as the laser charged. Madison could hear the ruckus from the other side as others clamored for the controls, as President Melero pushed them away.

"You're making a mistake!" His voice rose amongst the others. "You're not going to get away with it! I know you won't!"

"I have a family," a voice said, who Madison could identify as Amotu. "They got lost on the ground. Enough bloodshed! We've done nothing to deserve this. Nothing at all!"

President Melero was cackling now, as someone else called them murderers, said that they were going to get what was coming to them.

This time, when the laser fired, Madison made sure to look away. When she looked back at the monitor again, she saw the ship evaporate into a cloud of dust, snuffed out in space. There was probably nothing left of them, no trace to mark their existence apart from a cloud of scattered atoms sent drifting through space.

The crew of the SAS fell silent. There was no raucous applause, no cheers. There were no winners, only losers.

It was the last time a Space Armament Station was ever used.

After a few minutes of silence passed, Madison told Cole to try to get into contact with the International Space Hotel again. When they did so, there was a pleasant surprise waiting for Madison.

"Maddie!" Skye announced over the line. "You there?"

"Skye!" Madison grinned. "Yes!"

"You made it! I'm so happy."

"We did," Madison affirmed. "So much has happened."

"Yes. Yes, I agree. There's so much I need to tell you," Skye said. "I got Graham here with me."

"Mhm," Graham answered. "I can confirm, in fact, that I am here."

"Good to hear from you, too," Madison said. "Skye, what do you think we should do next?"

"What do you mean? You got a ride, we'll make sure you all can come back. I might have to confer with Nathan how to bring you back, since the docking bay might be a bit messed up."

"No, I mean, bigger than that. Lex told us to wait here for the night. What do we do, y'know, as an organization next? As a community?"

"Asking a real philosophical question," Graham quipped.

"What do we do?" Skye repeated. "We do whatever it takes to survive."

Epilogue

Three weeks passed since that moment where the S.S. Washington was destroyed. The month was riddled with fatalities: but all of them were ultimately gunshot victims who the doctors unsuccessfully tried to save. No one else died, as Nathan's maneuvering with the airlocks prevented a widespread technological failure or anyone from being sucked out into space.

It wasn't an easy month. Even as Madison and the crew on the SAS successfully made their way back to the International Space Hotel, and shuttered the doors behind them for the last time, people knew what lay ahead of them: the unknown.

There were clean-up efforts, and a great deal of funerals, including one for Fritz which was attended by the entire base of former clients and staff of the ISH, as well as the eight women who had been held captive in the basement of the S.S. Washington. There was no priest on board, so they couldn't conduct any formal funerals: but many prayed in their own religions, their own languages, and often times individuals related to the deceased would come forward and talk about them. In the soldiers' case, it was their fellow soldiers.

All of the soldiers on board the ISH who hadn't run into a deadly fate on the S.S. Washington, including the prisoners who had been captured, were welcomed to integrate into their community. And after, most of them did just that. Some of them helped lend a hand with security, although their presence was less needed following the battle.

There was only a limited food supply, and that food supply depleted faster than anticipated. They were out of food, despite their rationing efforts, just over two weeks later. But with the council in charge, they made the executive decision two days after running out of food to return to Earth using the escape pods.

There was, of course, a matter of determining the landing path, and in this case, there was a tie that had to be broken. With Fritz's death, there were only four council members, and they didn't take the time to elect anyone new, although they contemplated bringing in Mr. McFarland to the council once they'd returned back to Earth.

Both Dr. Chetana and Skye thought that for safety purposes, for all of the notes that they had dug up in the archives about where the previous regime had speculated where it was safest to land, that they should land in South America. Relatively untouched by nuclear strikes and the Space Armament Stations, they could make a new life there.

But most people on board were American, or otherwise from other countries outside of the continent, so that the option was not appealing to neither Marcell, nor Mr. Xiong. They wanted to go from where they came, and land back at the site where they had launched from, in North Florida, in the section still attached to the contiguous United States.

It was Skye who gave in and let them have their way. Even though she knew that they had a whole lot of guns, and if they stuck together—and she knew most of them would—with their guns in hand, they would be fine. No bandits would touch them, and by all accounts the radiation levels were at least manageable. People would rally to them. And she figured America could rise again. Not fueled by some ego trip by President Melero (Madison and Cole had explained the entire conversation to Skye), but by a desire to survive, to thrive.

Only two and a half weeks later after the destruction of the S.S. Washington, they made the stressful journey back down to Earth. Unlike Skye's trip up to space, there were no injections for everyone, and it was all around extremely stressful. Every single escape pod, except for one with some sort of unknown issue, was used in the process, programmed so that they would all space out and not land on top of each other, but rather land in the same field adjacent to the launch facilities. Almost everyone made the journey back down to Earth, including the wounded. Among them was Drake, who had survived a severe gunshot wound and, for whatever reason Skye didn't know, appeared to have broken up with Minnie.

Only two soldiers volunteered to stay back on the International Space Hotel. They knew they were going to die, by all accounts, but wanted to pass away in the solitude of space: Skye hardly blamed them, but made sure that Olivia taught them basic lessons of how to fly an escape pod, so that should they change their mind, they would be able to pilot the escape pod down to Earth.

In actuality, it was Dr. Chetana who made sure that happened. After all, Dr. Chetana assumed command of the council. Skye had taken note of what Graham had told her and realized that it had been going to her head a little bit. For that reason, she stepped down as overall leader, although she still maintained her position on the council.

The flight back down to Earth took several hours. For Skye, it wasn't so bad: not because of the experience, because it was stressful, and jarring, and intense, just like she had remembered from when the injections had failed during her takeoff to space. But it was tolerable because of who was with her.

Even though Dr. Chetana had instructed all council members to be in separate escape pods on their way down, Marcell had ignored the order, so that the ride back consisted of Skye,

Madison, Graham, Marcell, and Jordan. Jordan had had his finger amputated about halfway down following the combat: he called it his lucky stump, much to Marcell's chagrin.

While the ship jettisoned back down to Florida, they all chatted, drank the bottled water they had packed, and talked about what activities they wanted to do when they went to Earth.

None pretended like society was still what it used to be, and none of them mentioned their families. But, some of their desires were still impractical, and Skye knew that they probably could never happen in the glamorized version they hoped, or at least in the short term. Marcell said he wanted to golf, while Jordan said he wanted to bake a cake with real fresh eggs.

"You only need nine fingers, or so I'm told," he added.

"We'll bake a cake for Skye," Marcell said. "It's her birthday in three days, after all."

Graham, meanwhile, said he just wanted to cook some barbecue again, South Carolina style.

"What about you?" Madison, who had said she wanted to go for a swim in a nice chlorine, non-radioactively contaminated swimming pool, asked.

"Me?" Skye asked, aloud. "Oh, I don't know. I'll be happy just to be standing on solid ground again."

"Come on," Marcell urged. "Can't be that basic."

"Yeah," Madison said. "I think 'standing on Earth' hardly qualifies as a compelling activity, don't you think, Graham?"

"Nope," Graham said. "Come on, tell us."

"I think..." Skye said. "Camping."

Madison snorted, and most of the others grinned.

"We're going to be doing a lot of that," Graham responded, and Skye shrugged.

The Laser from Above

Finally, they neared the surface, and everyone looked down at the Earth. Skye was glad that they were landing out in the middle of day, and not night. They could make out how there were a couple of brown and level zones, decimated cities, and yet their landing zone, away from the facilities, looked relatively green, and as they neared the ground, it was clear that at least the buildings in the immediate vicinity hadn't been leveled. That was a plus, considering she'd almost considered the site to be a prime nuclear target.

They passed through a layer of clouds, and neared the Earth. And finally, after hours that were surprisingly enjoyable given the high levels of Gs, the escape pod gradually lowered down to softly land on a patch of grass. A couple of others had already landed, while others, still, slowly descended from higher up.

Graham read the display, reading off some of his findings for the rest of the passengers.

"Oxygen levels are normal," he said. "Radiation levels, category 2. That's a bit high but it's not too bad or dangerous in any way."

"Are we ready to go?" Madison asked. "I can't wait to sand on soft ground again! No more metal surfaces. I'm all natural from here on out, baby."

Skye stood up to her feet, nearing the door.

"I think she deserves to exit first," Jordan said. "After all, she's the queen who saved the ship, right?"

"That's right," Marcell agreed.

"Unless you think it's dangerous," Graham interjected. "If so, I volunteer Marcell."

"Hey!" Marcell exclaimed, but he was smirking.

"No, I got this," Skye said. She stepped forwards, and pressed the button to the left of the door. A gust of warm, Florida autumn air flooded in. Coming from Minnesota, Skye knew the weather would be completely manageable, but even this exceeded her expectations. It was a far cry from the chill, sterile air of the International Space Hotel, and was a welcome change.

Skye was finally back where she really belonged, Earth, and the realization was so powerful that she thought she could cry tears of joy.

Then the door hissed open, and Skye stepped out into the sunlight, home at last.

Printed in the USA
CPSIA information can be obtained
at www.ICGtesting.com
LVHW090550041123
763007LV00005B/15